THE WORKHOUSE GIRL

LYNETTE REES

Boldwood

First published in Great Britain in 2024 by Boldwood Books Ltd.

Copyright © Lynette Rees, 2024

Cover Design by Colin Thomas

Cover Photography: Colin Thomas

The moral right of Lynette Rees to be identified as the author of this work has been asserted in accordance with the Copyright, Designs and Patents Act 1988.

All rights reserved. No part of this book may be reproduced in any form or by any electronic or mechanical means, including information storage and retrieval systems, without written permission from the author, except for the use of brief quotations in a book review.

This book is a work of fiction and, except in the case of historical fact, any resemblance to actual persons, living or dead, is purely coincidental.

Every effort has been made to obtain the necessary permissions with reference to copyright material, both illustrative and quoted. We apologise for any omissions in this respect and will be pleased to make the appropriate acknowledgements in any future edition.

A CIP catalogue record for this book is available from the British Library.

Paperback ISBN 978-1-80549-007-4

Large Print ISBN 978-1-80549-006-7

Hardback ISBN 978-1-80549-005-0

Ebook ISBN 978-1-80549-008-1

Kindle ISBN 978-1-80549-009-8

Audio CD ISBN 978-1-80549-000-5

MP3 CD ISBN 978-1-80549-001-2

Digital audio download ISBN 978-1-80549-003-6

Boldwood Books Ltd
23 Bowerdean Street
London SW6 3TN
www.boldwoodbooks.com

This book is dedicated to my dear friend, Zoe, otherwise known as 'Sis'. We've had many ups and downs in our lives but have both emerged stronger as a result and still maintain a strong bond of friendship after fifty fabulous years!

1

MERTHYR TYDFIL, 1885

Fourteen-year-old Enid Hardcastle straightened her shoulders, jutting her chin in a determined fashion. She was used to the catcalling about her vibrant red hair by now. If it wasn't "carrot top" it was "ginger nut" after the popular biscuits of the same name. It wasn't only her hair colour that caught people's attention either, because she had a smattering of freckles across her face, so "freckle face" was another common one. Most of her friends had ditched the nicknames long since, and besides, as she aged her hair wasn't as red as it once was. As a young child, the mention of it had caused her to lower her head and draw into herself. These days though, she'd accepted the colour as some people told her how beautiful her hair was, describing it as "Titian coloured". She was fast becoming a young lady who attracted attention but now in a different manner altogether. The freckles, although still there, had faded with time.

The young lad calling out wasn't being mean though. It was Daniel Owen. She knew he liked her and that's why he was trailing behind, following her home. She'd been to the marketplace to fetch some provisions for her mam. The wicker basket over the crook of her arm was full to the brim with a loaf of bread that the baker sold off cheaply this time of the day, a pat of butter, a wedge of cheese and three slices of bacon and some eggs. Mam would be serving it all up for the family this evening before Dad left for his night shift at the Cyfarthfa Ironworks.

There were three other ironworks in the area beside Cyfarthfa: Dowlais, Penydarren and Plymouth. Iron was key, being essential to build engines, ships, and railway lines, and the area had the natural resources to produce it. Mines and quarries were plundered and horse-drawn canals and railways built to transport it. Merthyr was a general hive of activity as it drew in people to work in heavy industry.

Dad wasn't himself of late, though. There seemed to be some sort of trouble brewing at Cyfarthfa and it was taking his toll on him. Often, the family was late with the rent payment to the landlord and had been threatened with eviction on more than one occasion. This evening's meagre meal wasn't the best but it would do for now. It was no use grumbling as many had it worse; they had a lot to be thankful for.

'Hey, carrot top!' Daniel shouted after her, causing her to spin around and face him, but she wasn't angry, she was giggling.

'What do you want?'

He grinned at her. 'Got your attention, didn't I?'

'You might have. I need to get this lot back home,' she said, glancing at her basket.

'Here, give it to me,' he said, standing beside her.

Gratefully, she released the basket into his care, and they walked together in an amiable fashion towards her house in the China area of Merthyr. This was a place where many feared to tread, but Enid had got to know its courts and alleys like the back of her hand and who to trust and who not to. Any stranger stood out a mile.

'I was just wondering if you'd like to come for a walk with me after chapel on Sunday,' Daniel said, his eyes shining. She didn't like to disappoint the lad but he'd gone from being a friend to someone who was showing an interest in her in another way, and she wasn't too sure whether she liked the attention or not. Lads were starting to notice her as she'd developed womanly curves of late, and to her horror, even older men turned their heads in the street.

Mam had warned her to take care last year when her monthly courses had begun. 'Always keep your hand on your penny at all costs!' she'd said as she'd wagged a warning finger.

Enid had known full well what she meant: that her virginity was something to hang on to at all costs until the day she wed. Well, she had no reason to do anything like that out of wedlock, but her mother had persisted that some lads would try it on nevertheless and it was her job to say "No!" to them.

She drew in a composing breath and released it before replying. 'I'm sorry, Daniel. I can't make it this Sunday,' she said with the fingers of one hand crossed behind her back. It seemed easier to tell a white lie than say she'd rather not go for a walk with him in case he had wandering hands. Enid knew of one girl her age living a few doors away who had got herself pregnant and no one knew who the father was as she refused to tell anyone. The rumour was that it was a much older married man. She had no idea whether that was true or not, but she knew all too well the consequences of having a sinful relationship out of wedlock.

As they reached the front step of Enid's house, Daniel looked at her in expectation as though she might offer to invite him inside for carrying her basket, but she simply smiled at him as she took the basket and thanked him.

Even once inside where she'd closed the door, she realised he'd be waiting outside for a while before choosing to leave. That was the effect she now had on him and she didn't know whether she liked it or not. Being a young woman wasn't all it was cracked up to be. Sometimes she yearned for the days when she'd been a carefree child, even though she'd felt like an ugly duckling sometimes. Now, she was being considered a beautiful swan and she didn't know how to handle it.

* * *

Maggie and Elgan, neighbours to the Hardcastle family, had started giving bed and board to parish orphans, those lads who otherwise would have to go to the workhouse. At one time, there were three lads boarding with them. Maggie, according to her mother, was paid two shillings a week for their upkeep. They were right tearaways and all. Two of them were renowned pickpockets and it took some time to stamp out that habit in them. But with love and attention, the boys thrived. They were all at an age where they were too old to be thought of as children and too young to be considered men. The truth was, staying with Maggie and Elgan was like a stepping stone in their young lives until they could work and live independently.

Then one day, Enid heard that a new boy had moved in with them, replacing another lad who had left to work for the local blacksmith. The new lad had been staying at the Hughes' house for a few days when she encountered him while fetching water from the pump. The pump area was considered a communal meeting place in the same way the washing lines were.

The boy studied her curiously behind dark lashes. then his lips curved into a big smile. His blue eyes shone with familiarity, but still Enid was baffled. Who was this lad who was looking at her as if he knew her?

'Enid! It's me!' he said softly, but she didn't recognise his voice.

'Sorry.' She frowned. 'You seem familiar but I can't quite place you?'

'I'm Jimmy, Jimmy Corcoran. I used to live here a few years back!'

'Oh, Jimmy!' she cried. 'I didn't recognise you as you've grown so tall!' Memories flooded back to the young lad she used to play with in the street until his widowed mother passed away and he ended up at the workhouse. There had been suspicion at the time that his mother may have been murdered as her body was found floating in the River Taff, but nothing could be proven. Enid was seven years old back then and Jimmy not much older. Her ma hadn't spoken much about the matter at the time, but in the intervening years had explained that Jimmy's mother, Ginny, had been one of the unfortunates who'd sold her body to men. That had horrified Enid. Poor Mrs Corcoran had obviously resorted to desperate measures when her husband had died, badly burnt in the ironworks by all accounts. Her heart went out to the lad.

It wasn't just his appearance that had changed, Jimmy's voice was now a little croaky as though it was breaking.

'But how come you're staying with Mags and Elgan?'

'Quite simple really.' He dug his hands in his trouser pockets as he answered. 'Elgan has been visiting me regularly at the workhouse over the years and he put in a request so I might board with him and his missus.'

'I see,' said Enid. She was never really sure if Elgan had married Mags or not but Mam had said she thought they were "living over the brush", whatever that meant.

'It was sad news to hear that Thelma passed away,' added Jimmy. 'She was so kind to me. Elgan said if she hadn't had a dodgy ticker they'd have taken me on when my mam died.'

Enid recalled a time when she and some friends had tried to get Jimmy out of the workhouse and back to China but their plan had been scuppered by Sergeant Cranbourne when he and another policeman had come checking around the houses to find Jimmy hidden away in one of them.

'Yes, that's true.' Enid remembered Elgan's wife well. She'd been a kindly soul but she'd been unwell before her untimely death. 'She told my mother that. But tell me, what happened to you after you were carted off by the cops that day? I'm sorry, we shouldn't have snatched you from the spike like that. And then our parents wouldn't allow us to go near the place ever again, so we didn't know what had happened to you,' she said, shaking her head.

'It's all right, gal.' He shrugged. 'Afterwards I was taken back there but I wasn't punished as I feared I'd be, as that nice policeman told them I was taken against my will. Which as you know wasn't true but it saved me from a beating from the birch, at least on that occasion.'

'Oh, Jimmy,' Enid said softly, feeling sorry for the lad. 'Were you punished often in there?'

'No, not really, it only happened a couple of times. Once when I was caught sneaking some food from the kitchen when Cook's back was turned, and the other when I caused a bit of a riot in the boys' dorm. After that, I was boarded out to a greengrocer in Georgetown. I hated it there. He was a brute who used a leather belt to keep me in order. But once Elgan found out about that, he applied to take me in at his gaff.'

'I'm so sorry for what you've been through, Jimmy...' Now tears were streaming down her cheeks.

'It's all right, love,' he said, giving her hand a gentle squeeze, then glancing at the bucket of water, he added, 'Here, let me carry that for you.'

She nodded gratefully and looked at him as they walked together. In the intervening years, he'd turned into a handsome lad.

When he paused outside her house, he laid down the bucket and dipped his head to plant a kiss on her cheek. As he walked away, she touched her face where he'd kissed her and she smiled to herself. Danny hadn't had the courage to kiss her without asking like that. It seemed that Jimmy was different – he made a play for what he wanted in life. It seemed as though those workhouse days had made him grow up fast.

* * *

By the time Enid reached the age of fifteen, her family, which now consisted of two more offspring and a young baby, had been slung out onto the streets for late payment of rent, far more times than she cared to remember. It was usually the same old story: Dad not getting paid on time, then Richards the landlord taking possession of the house key, and then they had to pay a fee for its return. They'd either have to wait a few days for her dad to make payment or else the key was returned immediately but with a hike to the rent. The family just couldn't win and it was wearing her parents down.

A time that came to Enid's mind was the night she had encountered a young girl called Betsan. The family had taken her in for the night as they huddled outside the house in a snowstorm, waiting for the house key to be returned from Richards, the landlord, again for a fee.

Betsan had approached them, asking for help, as she was distressed about not being able to find her aunt, who turned out to be Maggie who lived with Elgan.

Enid hadn't seen Betsan since that night, but she hoped she was well. She often wondered if their paths might cross again.

* * *

'Enid!' a voice cried out. A pair of hands playfully covered her eyes. Thankfully, she recognised the voice. It was Jimmy and she didn't mind at all. He dropped his hands and spun her around to face him.

'Guess what!' he said excitedly. He was so close she could feel his warm breath on her face as her heart hammered beneath her blouse.

'I don't know. Please tell me?'

'Baxter the cobbler says he can give me some work to take home with me.'

Enid wrinkled her nose. 'How'd you mean?'

'Repairing boots and shoes from home. He's been teaching me the tricks of the trade these past few weeks. It'll mean I can now contribute something towards my upkeep. I think I'll call around later and put a proposal to him.'

Enid blinked. 'A proposal? What sort of proposal?'

He paused for a moment as he glanced at the ceiling as though deep in thought before his gaze landed upon her. His eyes were shining as though he was excited about something or another.

'I've had this idea, you see.'

'Idea?'

'Yes, that I offer to help Mr Baxter in another way. I had the idea that maybe we could offer to do a collection and delivery service around the big houses in the area. It will drum up some more business for him, and as he's teaching me the tricks of the trade, as it were, I can help with a lot of the easier repairs. Of course, I'll get to learn from the master himself! What do you think? Might it work, Enid?'

Enid smiled at him. 'I think it's a great idea. Strike while the iron's hot. Go and ask him today.'

Jimmy nodded eagerly.

One thing she'd noticed about the lad was that he was proud. Not proud in such a way as to be mindful of his appearance or anything like that, more in the way of not wishing to be a burden to his benefactors.

'I haven't said anything to them yet about working for Mr Baxter as they've not come back – they both went out earlier. Elgan told me he had some deliveries to make to some market traders and Mags went along with him...' He frowned for a moment. 'But...'

'But what?' She angled her head to one side, curiously.

'But I can't help thinking something has happened. They both said they weren't going to be long and would be back within the hour but that was three hours ago.'

'Maybe they've gone Christmas shopping or something?'

He shrugged. 'Anyhow, would you like to come inside for a cup of tea? It's perishing talking out here.'

She hesitated for a moment. It wasn't the done thing to be alone with a young lad indoors but Mam wouldn't know that Mags wasn't home. In any case, Enid trusted Jimmy implicitly. Her lips curved into a smile as she nodded.

'Yes, I'd like that. Thank you,' she said.

She'd never been inside the house before, only ever stood on the doorstep when Mam had asked her to run an errand. Mags often borrowed things like a cup of milk or sugar, but equally, she insisted on returning what she'd borrowed and often gave back extra in return as she realised how hard up the family was.

The size of the house was similar to theirs but equally shabby, though it was obvious that Mags had done her best to brighten up the place by adorning the walls with paintings of familiar Merthyr scenes.

The table at the centre of the room was covered in old newspapers and piled high with shoes and boots, to the side of which were some work tools along with a duster and a couple of tins of polish.

'I don't expect Mags will be keen on seeing that mountain of footwear on her table.' Enid chuckled.

Jimmy grinned. 'I'll have to sweeten her up a bit, I suppose. Maybe I'll offer to wash the dishes later or I'll fetch her a bowl of faggots and peas from Ma Swindley's shop.' His smile vanished as solemnly he added, 'But surely she'll be pleased there'll be extra money coming into the house?'

'Oh yes, of course she will, Jimmy. I'm just kidding with you. She'll be delighted, I'm sure. I don't remember any of the other parish lads who boarded with her ever bringing in any income.'

'That's true enough. They did help Elgan with his round but none of them got a job until after they left here and could fend for themselves. Aye, they're good sorts are Mags and Elgan. Can't understand why they've never had any kids of their own, mind.'

'But they did!' Enid blurted out suddenly, then slapped her hands over her mouth. She'd once been told a secret by her mother and had sworn not to tell another living soul but now it was too late to retract her admission.

'Huh?' Jimmy furrowed his forehead. 'I've never been told any of that.'

Enid dropped her hands to her sides as she felt her face flush beet red. 'I'm sorry, I shouldn't have said anything, but it's just Mam told me that about three or four years ago, Mags was pregnant but she thought she'd miscarried at first and had gone away for a while to get over it. But it turned out she'd given birth to twins, a boy and a girl, apparently.'

'Aw, that's sad,' said Jimmy, slumping down into the armchair closest to the hearth as he tried to make sense of it all. 'That's maybe why she's been taking on us parish lads then as boarders. We're like adopted sons to her.'

'I would think so.'

Jimmy drew in a deep, composing breath and let it go again, then he rose from the armchair and looked at her. 'Where are my manners, Enid? I offered you a cup of tea and a cup of tea you shall have.'

It was obvious though, he'd been thrown off course. This was big news to him and now Enid wished she hadn't mentioned it at all in case it should cause trouble.

He knelt in front of the fire and threw on a log, then stoking it up solidly with a poker, he said, 'I want to keep it nice and warm for Mags and Elgan for when they return.'

By the time they'd finished their teas, Jimmy was frantic with concern for the pair.

'I think I'd best go out and search for them,' he said.

But as Enid made to leave and he opened the door for her. It was blowing a blizzard again. 'You'd better stay put,' she advised. 'It's too dangerous to go out in this weather.'

'Let me walk you back home then,' he suggested.

'No need, it's just across the way – but thanks for the offer.'

He stooped to kiss her cheek and she just knew he'd be watching every step she took until she was safely indoors.

* * *

The following day, Jimmy called to inform Enid that Mags and Elgan still hadn't returned home and now, as it had stopped snowing, he was going to see if he could find out what had happened to them.

'Come in, lad.' Enid's mam beckoned to him as they stood on the doorstep. 'It's far too cold to be stood out there on ceremony!'

Enid felt herself blush. She'd never have asked her mother could he come inside their home, but as it was her mother herself who suggested it, that was fine.

Martha held Baby Jonathan snuggled in a woollen shawl, Welsh fashion, in her arms – it was a way of wrapping both mother and child in the shawl, which left one free hand to carry on with household tasks. The rest of the children were amusing themselves playing some sort of game in front of the fire.

Jimmy did as he was told, stepping tentatively over the threshold and stamping his snow-covered feet on the doormat. Enid smiled shyly at him and when her mother wasn't watching, he tipped her a wink, which made her blush even more. Despite trying to remain cheery though, it was obvious how concerned he was.

'Sit yourself down, Jimmy,' Martha said firmly, pointing to the armchair. 'Now let's get this right – you're saying Mags and Elgan have still not returned home, are you?'

He nodded. 'Yes, I am. The last time I set eyes on either of them was this time yesterday.'

Martha frowned, her lips pursing in puzzlement. 'Well,' she said finally, 'the only thing I can think of is that maybe they've both gone off on a bender somewhere as it's the Christmas season. Maybe a landlord at some pub or another offered them a lock-in overnight or something and they woke up this morning and started all over again! You know how fond Mags is of the gin bottle and Elgan likes a drink too.'

'I'm well aware, Mrs Hardcastle,' Jimmy said with a solemn expression on his face as he looked at his flat cap, now in his hands, as if it somehow held the answer to the pair's mysterious disappearance. 'It was my first thought, to be honest with you, but Elgan had the horse and cart with him and Mags has been abstaining from the hard stuff lately. In any case, Elgan did have business in the town to attend to.'

'I see,' said Martha gently, 'so unlikely to be some sort of drinking spree then. Not unless the person they were doing business with wanted to celebrate the deal maybe and has them stopping over along with the horse and cart? Maybe he's got a stable or something or they've paid to stable him at an inn somewhere?'

Jimmy appeared deep in thought for a moment and then he slowly shook his head. 'Unlikely as they were looking forward to us spending time together last night as it was Elgan's last drop-off before Christmas. Besides... they'd never let me down purposely. I just know they wouldn't – they'd be here if they were able to be.'

There was a tone of desperation in Jimmy's voice and, for a moment, Enid feared he'd break down in tears, but instead he swallowed and sniffed to compose himself.

'So, what do you do now?' Martha stared at him.

'Now that it's stopped snowing, I'll head off to the marketplace to see if anyone knows anything.'

'If you wait a while, my Arthur will be home soon to go with you,' Martha said.

Jimmy held up his hand as if to decline the offer. 'It's very kind of you but it's all right, Mrs Hardcastle – honestly it is. I'll go soon before it gets dark.'

'At least have a bowl of lamb cawl before you leave.'

The aroma of cooked meat and onions wafted towards him.

He nodded. 'Thank you. I haven't eaten since yesterday and it smells delicious.' He rubbed his stomach.

'Wasn't there any food in the house for you?' Enid asked.

'Not much. Mags was supposed to be bringing some back home with her but of course she never arrived. There's still half a loaf of bread there and a piece of cheese, but to be honest with you, I didn't have no appetite for it.'

Enid exchanged a concerned glance with her mother. 'May I go with Jimmy?'

Martha looked at her and, for a second, Enid feared she'd say no, but then she smiled, handed the baby to Enid to sort Jimmy out with a hot meal, and said, 'Yes, as long as you wrap up well and if it snows heavily, you return home immediately, you hear, my girl?' Enid nodded. 'You too, Jimmy!'

Then Martha made off to the scullery to ladle the cawl into a bowl for Jimmy. A loaf of bread lay on a wooden board in the centre of the table, so Martha sawed off a slice for him. Jimmy sat to eat, grateful for the impromptu but satisfying meal.

* * *

The ice-cold air stung Enid's face as they left the house. Snow hung from low-lying rooftops and the white, pristine, formerly virgin snow had now changed to a grey sludgy mess underfoot. Most sensible folk had remained indoors, not venturing out unless necessary.

Enid glanced at Jimmy who had both hands tucked into his trouser pockets. He appeared to be wearing one of Elgan's old thick jackets as it swamped him. Around his neck, he wore a woollen muffler and his flat cap kept his head warm. Enid had borrowed a second shawl and some mittens from her mam. Her bonnet kept the cold wind from getting into her ears, but the icy cold slush seeped into the soles of her leather boots and even though she was wearing woollen stockings on her feet, nothing kept the wetness from seeping in and chilling her to the bone.

'I do hope you find them, Jimmy,' Enid said, blowing out puffs of steam as her breath hit the freezing afternoon air.

'I don't know what I'll do if I can't.' He let out a little sigh, no doubt he couldn't imagine life without either of them.

'You could ask at the police station, I suppose?'

'Oh no, never!' He suddenly stopped in his tracks at the mention of the police. 'I'd better not.'

'But why ever not?' She paused too now.

'Because Elgan has been in trouble a time or two. Nothing serious but the police have got an eye on him.'

'Better not then. So what do you plan on doing?'

'Asking around the market traders – they know Elgan well.'

'But maybe they won't have set up their stalls in this weather?' She frowned.

'Believe me, most will have as most can't afford to lose the trade. They might not be at their pitches all day though. They'll more than likely pack up early due to the bad weather; that's why I want to set off now, so as not to miss them.'

She nodded. 'Mam told me to tell you before we left home that you're welcome to come to ours for meals until Mags and Elgan return home.'

'That's very kind of your mother, thanks, but I have got a little bit of money in my pockets.' He jangled the coins as if to prove that really was the case.

'Oh? How'd you come by it?'

'Mr Baxter paid me.'

'Before you did any work for him?' Enid asked in amazement.

'Yes, he trusts me. Half now and half when I've finished off that stack of footwear for him. So if Mags and Elgan don't return, I'll buy some provisions off the market. I put that proposal to him as well, about the home delivery and repair service. I can use Elgan's horse and cart when he doesn't need it.'

'And?'

'And, he and his wife mulled it over and they said they'd give it a go.'

'That's wonderful, Jimmy. I'm so pleased for you.' She hugged him warmly, before breaking away. She bit her lower lip.

Enid worried in case Jimmy was left to fend for himself. He was only a year or so older than her. He could end up being evicted if he couldn't keep up with the rent and, who knew, he might well end up back at the spike. She prayed a silent prayer of hope for him.

As they neared the marketplace, Enid realised that Jimmy was right: apart from one or two empty stalls, most traders kept working despite the harsh weather conditions. There was Mrs O'Connell's bloomer stall as her mother referred to it – it wasn't just a bloomer stall though, it sold petticoats, nightdresses, men's long combinations, blouses, even breeches for young boys. The bakery stall nearby had all but sold out of their goods going by how empty the counter was. She guessed people were panicking in case there was another heavy fall of snow that might block everyone in their homes. Even the toy stall was trading today but then they'd be foolish not to when customers were still shopping for Christmas gifts.

The leaden sky threatened more snow to come, and Enid looked at Jimmy anxiously, hoping everything would be sorted out soon for him.

'I think I'll ask Mrs O'Connell if she's seen Mags and Elgan,' Jimmy said decisively as if she was the best bet out of all the people he knew. 'She knows Elgan quite well.'

Enid nodded. It seemed a good prospect. The woman and her late husband had arrived in Merthyr from Southern Ireland several years ago and she was well respected in the town.

Mrs O'Connell had just finished serving a customer. She handed over some coins in change to an elderly lady. The woman immediately dropped them into her purse, which she then hid in the bottom of her laden basket. It wasn't worth risking the work of pickpockets even if the marketplace was quiet.

When Mrs O'Connell noticed Jimmy approaching, her face broke out into a smile. 'Hello, lad!' She nodded at him. 'What are ye doing out now in this sort of weather? To be sure, the only reason I'm stood here is not to let my customers down, otherwise I'd be in front of my fireplace, toasting my trotters!' She threw back her head and laughed.

Jimmy sighed. 'Hello, Mrs O'Connell. It's Elgan and Mags – they've gone missing! They went out yesterday afternoon and haven't returned home as yet.'

Mrs O'Connell furrowed her weather-beaten brow. 'Oh, now then, that is very troubling indeed. Where did they say they were off to when they left?'

'I thought they were going to the marketplace for Elgan to trade some goods. They were supposed to be gone for only an hour or so.'

'Don't worry, Jimmy. I'll see what I can find out for you. And tell me now, who is this fine-looking young lass beside you?' she said, appraising Enid with her rheumy eyes.

'This here is Miss Enid Hardcastle!' Jimmy proudly announced. 'She lives near me.'

'Ah, and would your ma be Martha Hardcastle, then?' She quirked a curious eyebrow.

'Yes, she would.' Enid nodded, feeling slightly embarrassed that the woman had drawn attention to her.

'I know her quite well as she often stops for a chat here on my stall, can rarely afford anything, mind you...' Then as if realising maybe she shouldn't have said so, she gazed intently at Enid as she added, 'Well, haven't you got beautiful flame-red hair, young lassie?'

Enid hoped her face hadn't flamed as red as her hair. As if realising Enid felt uncomfortable with the attention shone on her, Jimmy said, 'So, who will you ask about Mags and Elgan?'

'Er? Oh, Mr Evans. He has dealings with him from time to time. He's just nipped to the pub on a call of nature. He won't be long.'

Jimmy nodded, then in the distance he noticed a large middle-aged man striding towards them. He wore a long black coat with an astrakhan collar that looked as if it had seen better days. Enid guessed maybe it had once belonged to a toff who had sold it second-hand.

As he approached, he looked at Mrs O'Connell and, nodding, said, 'Thanks for keeping an eye on my stall, Bridget.'

'Sure, it's not a problem, John. Have you a moment to spare?'

'Yes.' He drew closer.

'This is Jimmy Corcoran who lives with Mags and Elgan. He's been looking for them since yesterday. They went out and so far haven't returned home. Have you heard anything about their whereabouts?'

The man hesitated for a moment as if he knew something but then he answered, 'No, not really.'

'Come on now, John,' Bridget said, not taking any messing from him, 'would you happen to know something or not? The lad is worried about them. 'Twill be a bad doings if you know something but won't say what it is.'

He let out a groan. 'All right. I'll let you in on what I do know...' John's voice had an edge of reluctance to it. He glanced sideways as if to ensure there were no eavesdroppers. 'There's something going down...'

Jimmy and Enid drew nearer as he lowered his voice, the whites of his eyes now on show.

'Huh?' Jimmy frowned as if it was the first time he'd heard such a notion.

'When I said, "Something's going down," I mean dodgy dealings, if you get my drift.' He tapped the side of his nose with his index finger. 'Elgan's been dealing goods that are hot to handle, as it were. Not his fault but he's been conducting business with some right sorts lately, those that are up to nefarious matters. Now, I haven't told you any of this, are you understanding me?'

Jimmy nodded. 'But did you see either him or Mags yesterday at all?'

'Yes. Yes, I did, but it weren't for long. He sold me some pots and pans for my stall and then said he and his missus were off to meet a couple of business associates. She'd had a few, that wife of his, mind. She can drink like a fish when she wants to!'

Jimmy smacked his own forehead with the palm of his hand as if in desperation. 'Oh no! She must have hit the bottle again. She'd been doing so well lately too!'

The man nodded. 'The pair seemed to be celebrating something or other. At least that's the impression I got.'

As Jimmy frowned, Enid wondered what on earth they had been celebrating.

* * *

Sergeant Cranbourne observed Elgan through the cell bars. The man had his head down and appeared to be mumbling to himself. He had no real beef with him but he did sail a little close to the wind at times and, on this particular occasion, the wind had blown him all the way to the police station where he was now under lock and key. The trouble was, if it hadn't been for that overzealous young constable, who just happened to be the inspector's nephew who arrested him, then maybe he'd just have been sent on his way with a serious ticking-off not to handle anything "hot" again. Instead, though, he now faced a court case for handling stolen goods.

And that wife of his, Maggie, she hadn't helped. Drunk off her face she'd been, shouting and swearing like a fishwife, which had resulted in her being locked up too. No court case for her though; she was just being made an example of. Left to sleep the alcohol out of her system and given plenty of fluids to drink.

Sergeant Cranbourne had even had someone to take care of the horse for them at the back of the station. He'd been stabled and fed for the night.

Nice horse he was and all. But then again, Cranbourne had a soft spot for Elgan as he was a kind man really – despite his shenanigans. He remembered that time he'd saved a donkey from a severe beating, paying the fella to take it off his hands and then kept it as a pet. Then there was young Jimmy whose mother had been drowned in the Taff. It was treated as a murder inquiry at the time but as no one was put in the frame for it, even though there were suspects, it was written off as a tragic accident. That poor lad. Cranbourne had always suspected it was one of the China bullies. Maybe she'd set up business on her own instead of allowing one of them to conduct it for her. Who could blame her though if she had – he knew they'd have taken a lot of her earnings and beaten her from time to time.

Maggie, though, the sergeant was concerned about. The woman had hit the bottle yet again and now it was entirely possible that her husband might end up with a gaol sentence at Cardiff Prison.

Oh no, there she went again. He could hear her rattling the cell bars. She was being held in a separate cell to her husband and now she was singing some lurid song, which he'd never heard before.

> *A maiden from the valley*
> *Whose name was Sally O'Malley,*
> *Attracted men near and far*
> *As they stood at the bar*
> *As they all loved Sally's alley*

'Stop that racket, Mags!' Cranbourne yelled, causing her laughter to cease. He walked over to the cell and, holding on to the bars, he peered inside. 'Now, your Elgan is going up before the judge tomorrow afternoon so you need to sober up. I'm sending someone in with a jug of water and something for you to eat. Then if you sleep it all off, I'll be happy to release you in the morning, no charge!'

Mags hiccupped loudly.

Cranbourne realised if he released her right now she might well turn to the drink again and that wouldn't do Elgan any good whatsoever.

'All right, Sarge!' she said suddenly. Then she hiccupped again. 'I *promish* to behave *myshelf!* Hic!'

2

It wasn't until the following afternoon Jimmy discovered what had happened to Mags and Elgan. Enid found out for herself when she next spoke to the lad. The sad thing was, although Elgan wasn't the principal guilty party with regards to the handling of stolen goods, it was he who bore the brunt of the blame, while the other two "business associates" got away with it. It became obvious that they'd set him up as a scapegoat.

'Mags is devastated,' Jimmy told Enid. 'It's just as well I've got this new job working for Mr Baxter. I've a good idea an' all how I might help increase his business prospects. Mags is going to need every extra penny she can get with Elgan stuck in the slammer.'

'It's good that she's got you though.' Enid smiled, lightly touching his shoulder.

They were both chatting in Enid's living room as Jimmy didn't want to discuss such matters in front of Mags and he didn't intend leaving her too long on her own either. It was bad enough that Elgan had gone to prison but now the pair was left to fend for themselves. The only bright spot was that Mags had since been reunited with Betsan, the young girl who Enid had shared her bed with that night of dreadful snow conditions.

'What upset me was,' said Jimmy, 'the fact Mags had been drinking during that time. She's sober again now.'

'Do you think she'll stay that way though?' Enid angled her head to one side.

Jimmy puffed out his cheeks and let out a long, slow breath. 'Dunno, to be honest. It was nice Mags got to see her niece again but her sister – the girl's mother – has since passed away. That's dreadful for her to come to terms with. She fell out with her and her brother-in-law about three years ago due to her drinking habit. Now she realises she'll never see Gwennie ever again. Elgan going to prison has put the tin lid on things for her. It's a bit like a double death for her to deal with.'

'At least she'll see him again and he'll be back home to stay,' Enid said hopefully.

The front door flew open and Dad emerged in his work clothing, grubby from his toil at the ironworks. Enid could tell from the expression on his face that something was dreadfully wrong.

'Where's your mother?' he demanded without even greeting either of them.

'She's upstairs with the little ones,' Enid said as she exchanged worried glances with Jimmy.

Not stopping to explain the situation, her father climbed the stairs and then she could hear muffled voices from above, after which her mother emerged at the foot of the stairs with a wide-eyed expression on her face.

'Here, take the baby,' she said, handing him over to Enid. 'Something awful has occurred.'

'What's going on, Mam?' Enid raised her eyebrows.

Her mother looked heavenward for a moment. 'There's a possibility of a strike at the ironworks,' she said. 'Quickly, go and fetch Tom Davies and Jack Griffin. They're in bed after a night shift right now but your father said the striking men need the both of them to help out at the picket line.' Her mother huffed out an exasperated breath. 'Things have broken down between the ironmasters and the workers. They're talking about slashing the men's wages. We can hardly survive as it is. If your father's wage is cut any further, we'll end up back on the street or even worse.'

Enid realised that her mother was speaking about the workhouse. There were many families who might go hungry.

'Your father's concerned there'll be rioting like what's occurred in the past. Troops were even brought in to deal with the crowd when it happened. The Crawshay family won't want to see the likes of that. Now, run over and summon Tom and Jack immediately – most of the men are going to protest. They may be gone for hours on end.'

She sighed as if this was the last thing she could do with right now. They needed to avoid a strike breaking out at all costs.

* * *

It was the following day when Dad returned home with a worried expression on his face.

Enid looked up from where she'd been laying the table for their evening meal as Mam came rushing out from the scullery.

'Arthur, what's happened?'

Enid swallowed as she waited for her father to respond to Mam's question.

'It's all over, Martha. I've been sacked along with a few others. We were deemed "troublemakers" as a lot of the men didn't agree with taking strike action. Cowards, the lot of them!'

'You should not have got involved in that protest!' Martha complained as she slammed the wooden breadboard down with force on the table. 'Things were hard enough; we were living hand to mouth as it was.'

'Quieten down, woman!' Arthur yelled. 'You were all for the protest when I told you about it!'

That was true. Hadn't it been her mam who had sent her off to fetch Tom and Jack? Who'd immediately risen from their beds to join forces with her father and a few other militant sorts? The truth of it was, there was no messing with the Crawshays. They were hard taskmasters who over the years had learned how to deal with their workforce. Robert Thompson Crawshay, the head of the family, had passed away in 1879 and since then his sons were running the works.

Enid's mother grabbed the remainder of their last loaf of bread and took it over to the breadboard. She began sawing away at it with a murderous look on her face.

'Be careful with that bloody knife, woman!'

Martha stopped what she was doing, and to Enid's horror, burst into tears.

'Oh, love,' said Arthur, rushing to cradle her in his arms. 'I didn't mean to sound so sharp with you...'

'It's not that,' said Martha, looking at him through glazed eyes, 'it's just that I fear now for all of us. The kids don't deserve any of this.'

If Enid was being honest with herself, she feared for their future too.

* * *

It was another month of living hand to mouth and dodging Richards that the family finally found themselves thrown out on to the street. It had happened previously, but those times were only shows of power from Richards who knew full well he'd return the key eventually, allowing the family access to their home after a short period of time. Previous times, it was only as if to keep them on their toes.

This time it was different.

Word had got around that several men had been laid off from the ironworks, and now, learning that Arthur was one of those men, Richards realised he'd be waiting for his rent payment forever and a day. So out the family went while he moved another family in.

And so it was to the workhouse for the Hardcastle family.

3

The worst thing was being separated from the rest of her family. Enid had to be admitted to the girls' dorm where girls aged between seven and fifteen years old resided. Thankfully, Mam was allowed to keep Baby Jonathan with her in the women's wing as he was less than two years old. Dad was admitted to the men's wing. Wasn't it bad enough that he should lose his job and home without him being distanced from the rest of them, too?

A surprise though was that Betsan and her father were interned there, so it was good to see a friendly, familiar face in her dorm.

On initially entering, Enid bore the humiliation of being bathed in a communal area, having to be stripped naked and scrubbed with a bar of Lysol soap using a stiff bristle brush by one of the staff; then having her hair cropped to the scalp and checked over for head lice as a large-bosomed nurse in a pinafore washed it in a solution of soap and vinegar, which made Enid's eyes sting and her nostrils sore from the smell. A fine-toothed comb was raked through her hair to check for any unwelcome visitors. She winced as the woman combed through it with a heavy hand. Thankfully, despite the thorough examination, there was no sign of any head lice. Mam did a good job keeping all her children's hair clean and well inspected.

***

Enid had been in the workhouse for a few weeks when she was called into Master and Matron Aldridge's quarters. Fearing she was going to have a ticking-off she looked nervously at Betsan.

'It can't be all that bad,' Betsan reassured her. 'I can't see that you've done anything wrong, Enid.'

'But what if it's because I accidentally smashed a plate when I was helping in the kitchen the other day?'

Betsan smiled. 'I doubt if it's that. You didn't do it on purpose and they must be accidentally smashing crockery from time to time.'

Enid nodded, realising Betsan spoke sense. Whatever it was the Aldridges wanted to speak to her about, it was most certainly not a dropped plate.

Tentatively, she knocked on the door.

'Enter!' boomed out the master's loud voice.

As Enid entered she was pleased to see the master and matron were smiling at her. Both were seated in armchairs like a pair of bookends near a roaring fire. It was always comfortable in their quarters, not like the draughty corridors and cold dormitories the inmates had to endure.

She wasn't invited to sit so Enid stood with her hands behind her back.

'It's come to our attention,' began Matron, 'that you've been doing very well helping out at the workhouse. Cook speaks highly of you...'

Enid's face flushed and she hoped she hadn't gone as red as her hair. 'Thank you, Mrs Aldridge.'

'And as a result,' said the master, 'we both think you are ready to be boarded out. A vacancy for a maid of all work has just come up. Would you be amenable to it?'

For a moment, she wasn't sure what he meant by amenable but then she guessed it meant would she like the position offered. She hadn't been expecting this so it was some time until she found her voice. 'I would, Mr Aldridge. Where would the position be?'

'The Clarkson family house. Mr and Mrs Clarkson are friends and great benefactors to this workhouse,' he said, exchanging glances with his wife who was nodding in his direction.

Enid had never heard the family name nor of the house before, but she thought she'd better agree as it didn't seem as though opportunities to escape the workhouse arose all that often.

Finding her voice, she said, 'Yes, I would be pleased to accept the position and thank you both for thinking of me.' This might be just the opportunity she needed to help her family. Maybe if she earned enough they might be able to afford to leave the workhouse and rent another property. Oh, wouldn't it be wonderful?

* * *

Later, Enid was to discover that the Clarkson family was wealthy and well known in the area. Their vast house stood loud and proud on a hill overlooking the other smaller mineworkers' and ironworkers' houses and cottages. She was floating on air at being given the opportunity to better herself.

Most of the girls in the dorm were envious of Enid having the chance to leave the workhouse, even though it was only on a trial basis to see if she was suitable.

Enid had been allowed to see both her mother and father for a visit at the same time, but only on a Sunday afternoon once a week up until now, and she wondered would this continue when she left. Mam seemed to be faring very well in the workhouse. Baby Jonathan was her prime concern. The other children were being fed and had a roof over their heads along with daily education in the schoolroom. Dad, though, she was concerned about. The light in his eyes had long diminished, and although he'd been given the daily task of tending to the workhouse allotment, which some inmates would have loved instead of oakum picking or bone crushing, he seemed to see himself as a failure for losing his livelihood and, consequently, the roof over all their heads.

It was Enid's final visit with both of her parents before she was to leave to work at Hillside House.

'Now be sure to mind your P's and Q's,' Mam warned with a twinkle in her eyes.

Enid had to smile at that remark, as she only ever used bad language if she was in a temper. Mam was far more likely to explode with expletives than she was.

'We're very proud of you, Enid,' said her father as he took his wife's hand beside him. 'It hasn't been ideal here by any means, but one day we'll all be together again.'

Her mam nodded with tears in her eyes.

'I'm going to have to leave soon as one of their coaches will be picking me up at the main gate at four o'clock.'

'I bet you'll look lovely in your maid's uniform,' Dad said, smiling.

'Pity about my hair though,' said Enid, removing her cap and running a hand through the tufts that were left of her once lovely, lustrous locks.

'It'll grow again,' her mother said, reassuringly. 'You haven't had it cut properly since you were six years old. I just used to trim the ends for you. Just a half-inch every couple of months.'

Enid shook her head as she remembered how her hair had extended to as long as her waist. She'd learned to come to terms with her hair colour as Jimmy had told her how eye-catching it was, saying he thought she was really pretty.

Jimmy! How she missed him. It was ironic that once upon a time he'd been here too.

* * *

The idea was for Enid to spend a full month in service at Hillside House and then return to the workhouse where it would be decided whether the Clarkson family would employ her, or failing that – if they were unsatisfied with her work – whether another workhouse girl would be given the opportunity to prove herself instead.

When Enid alighted from the black coach, she stood for a while gazing at the house in absolute awe – it was even bigger than she had imagined.

A long, gravelled drive led to the imposing building and then there was a flight of stone steps to the house itself, with a concrete lion's head majestically mounted either side of the steps. Flanking the wide black-panelled front door were two large columns, giving the house a very grand impression indeed.

Surrounding it were beautiful grounds with a stone fountain spraying water; luscious green manicured lawns dotted with attractive, colourful flower beds. The house's privacy was maintained as it was surrounded by large oaks and silver birch trees.

Enid could hardly believe this was happening to her. She began to ascend the flight of steps when a footman appeared. The man was dressed in a smart dark green tailed jacket, embellished with gold buttons at the front and cuffs, and over the knee breeches and cream stockings. In all her born days, she had not seen anyone dressed like that before and was quite taken aback by his appearance. His dark hair was slicked down with what might have been pomade – he looked a right dandy!

'Er, not that way, Miss Hardcastle,' he advised. 'It's the back entrance for servants.'

So he'd obviously been expecting her, then. Enid felt mortified. No one had warned her of this and her cheeks blazed with humiliation.

'It's all right, miss. You're not the first to make that mistake and you certainly won't be the last, I'm sure.'

She smiled. 'Please call me Enid. And you are?'

'Jenks, I'm known as here. Phillip Jenkins, miss. I'd better keep up formalities in case Mr Dunbar, the butler, or Mrs Webster, the house-keeper, overhears me speaking to you.' He raised a white-gloved hand as if to hide his mouth by cupping it, but then added, 'But if you and I are alone, then we can use more informal names for one another.'

She nodded and smiled tentatively, looking at him in a curious fashion. He wasn't that much older than herself by the look of it but he seemed far more worldly-wise in such matters.

'How long have you worked here for, Mr Jenkins?'

'About two years – well, in May that will be. But something I'd better warn you about...' he whispered surreptitiously. 'Take care when you're around the master's son. Watch you're never left alone with him if you possibly can. Or if you have to be in the same room, try to stay in close proximity to the door.'

Enid's eyes widened. It sounded as if he was warning her off. What on earth did he mean by that?

'Pardon?'

'He has wandering hands, miss. He tries it on with most of the young female staff here and always takes particular interest in any new ones that arrive.'

Oh no. Now she understood perfectly well. She gazed up at one of the windows and thought she saw, as if on cue, a male figure staring down on her. Was it just her imagination? She glanced again but whoever it was had gone.

Swallowing hard, she looked at Jenks and said, 'I appreciate your warning. Thank you.'

Jenks nodded solemnly. 'Come on,' he said. 'Let's get you into the kitchen for a cuppa with Cook and some of the other staff. They're looking forward to meeting you. Meanwhile, I'll take your luggage to your room.'

Room? Did she have a room all to herself?

'You'll be sharing with another maid called Maria. She's Spanish.'

'Oh?' said Enid. 'I haven't met anyone from Spain before.'

'Believe me, you haven't met anyone like Maria either!' He chuckled.

* * *

'Well, now then, this is the new young lady,' said Cook as she surveyed Enid who stood with Jenks at the entrance to the kitchen. Enid smiled and nodded shyly. 'Come in, dearie, and take your jacket and bonnet off!' Cook commanded. 'Go take them from her, Alice...'

Alice, who looked around twelve years old to Enid, immediately appeared at her side. She appeared to be some sort of kitchen maid. Enid wriggled out of her jacket, neatly folded it and handed it to the girl. Then Enid undid the ribbons of her bonnet and placed it on top of the jacket in Alice's outstretched arms. The girl then turned and walked towards the far end of the large kitchen where she hung the jacket and bonnet on a peg.

'Enid's your name?' Cook asked.

'Yes, that's correct, ma'am.'

'You don't need no airs and graces with me.' Cook chuckled. 'You can call me Mrs Shrimpton or Sal, if we're on a break, and no formalities are necessary.'

Enid nodded. Then she noticed the other staff seated at a pine table at the far end of the room.

'We're just about to have tea,' Cook continued. 'I held back our break as I knew you were due to arrive soon. I've baked some scones. Do you like those?'

Enid smiled. 'Yes, I do, thank you. Haven't tasted one for ages.'

Poor Mam didn't go in for much baking. The only things she ever baked were apple pies or the occasional Welsh cake but they weren't the best – she often burned those.

'Come and sit down then and I'll introduce you to everyone. Phillip will join us soon.'

As she followed Cook to the table, she noticed three young women seated one side of it. Two of them smiled at her and nodded but the third dark-haired one did not. She guessed she was Maria, the Spanish girl, as she had an exotic beauty about her.

Opposite them were two well-dressed men. One wore the same outfit as Phillip so she guessed he was another footman, but the other wore a black jacket, white shirt and black cravat. She wondered who he was.

Alice appeared behind Cook.

'See that wooden stool in the corner?' Cook said to her.

Alice nodded. 'Yes, Mrs Shrimpton.'

'Go and get it – there's a good girl. You'll have to make do with that at the end of the table as we have an extra one for tea this afternoon.'

Thankfully, Alice didn't seem to mind that she was usurped by a stranger at the table and was more than happy to perch on the stool. Meanwhile, Maria appraised her with hard eyes as dark as coal.

'This is Mr Dunbar, the butler,' Cook said, introducing him with a wave of her hand. So that's who the man in black was.

'Hello, Mr Dunbar,' Enid greeted.

'Miss Hardcastle.' Mr Dunbar nodded. He seemed a very stiff, formal sort.

'This is Geoffery Acaster,' Cook then said, gesticulating in the footman's direction.

He grinned broadly.

'The ladies are all maids here: Jen, she's a parlour maid, Doris is a kitchen maid along with Alice here, and finally Maria Garcia. Maria's family are from San Sebastián in Spain.'

Maria did not smile, which unnerved Enid. What was the matter with her? Instead, she regarded her coolly, eventually nodding in her direction. Maybe she didn't speak either English or Welsh? But then as they sat around the table and Cook poured tea from the large silver pot into all the awaiting teacups, she heard Maria chatting happily away to Doris and Jen beside her. She didn't include Enid at all.

In front of them was a china cake stand piled high with delicious-looking plump scones and two pots of jam and cream. Enid's mouth watered at the prospect of devouring one – a rare treat indeed. She was flabbergasted when she not only got to eat one but was offered another. As most were taking a second scone, she gratefully accepted. If no one had, she would have declined out of politeness.

Phillip eventually joined them at the table and kept the conversation going, trying to include Enid in matters. Some things she felt part of, others she did not, especially when they spoke of Mrs Webster, the housekeeper. The woman sounded like someone to be feared and Enid wondered why. Even Mr Dunbar rolled his eyes when she was mentioned.

Whilst the others were chatting, Enid whispered in Phillip's ear. 'Why didn't Mrs Webster join us for tea this afternoon?'

'She never does,' he whispered back. 'She prefers to take her meals in her quarters. She has a bedroom to herself with a small living room and office.'

Enid thought it sad that the woman wasn't included by the rest of the staff. Surely it must be dreadful for her to be confined all alone in her quarters when not working? Being brought up in the China district, Enid herself had never sought solitude as it just wasn't possible. Their house had been so small and she'd had to share a curtained-off bedroom with her siblings while her parents slept the other side of it – that's when Dad wasn't working a night shift.

* * *

Finally, as they were still seated at the table, a tall, reedy-looking woman with sharp features and dark hair scraped back appeared in the kitchen doorway and stared at them all. She wore a long black dress with a white frilled collar and cuffs and at her waist dangled a chatelaine of keys.

'Isn't it time you were all at your stations?' she asked gruffly.

Enid watched Phillip exchange glances with the maids and she thought she heard Geoffery mutter "old dragon" beneath his breath. Enid was amazed how quickly everyone shot up from their seats to return to work, apart from Cook; Mrs Webster was on her territory now and didn't have much sway there. Cook remained seated and poured herself and Mr Dunbar another cup of tea from the pot. He didn't seem concerned either, though Enid guessed it was because he was a higher-ranking servant than the others and maybe on a par with the housekeeper herself.

Mrs Webster's eyes fell on Enid. 'Enid Hardcastle?' she questioned.

'Yes, ma'am.'

'On your feet when I address you, girl!' she bellowed, which caused Enid to tremble and Cook to purse her lips in disapproval, though she didn't intervene.

Enid quickly rose, scraping the legs of her chair on the flagstone floor in her hurry. 'Sorry, ma'am.'

'That's better. You have some rough edges – I can tell. They all do when they start here, but we'll soon knock them off you and polish them up!' she said in a softer tone. 'I'll just show you to your room, so collect any belongings you have.'

Enid nodded her thanks to Cook who whispered "good luck" to her and then she retrieved her jacket and bonnet from Alice's outstretched arms. Smiling, she whispered a "thank you" to the girl.

She trailed behind the housekeeper out of the kitchen and down a long corridor, the woman keeping her head held high as she strode briskly along, the keys around her waist jangling as she swept across the parquet floor. On the walls were several photographs of the staff, either taken as single portraits or else in groups outside the house. Enid had never had her photograph taken in her life, though her mother had pencil sketches an artist had made of Enid and her siblings when they were young.

Finally, they arrived at what appeared to be a set of backstairs behind a narrow door.

'These are the staff stairs,' Mrs Webster said curtly. 'You are only permitted to use these. I must stress, you're never to use the main staircase. That is for the family only and any visitors they might have such as Doctor Jarman or sometimes Mr Clarkson, senior, might take his accountant or bank manager to the small office he has.' She paused with her hand on the brass doorknob. 'Now these stairs lead to the staff quarters on the upper floor and also to the attic bedroom where you are to sleep.'

'Thank you, ma'am.'

'You'll be allowed one half-day a week off following the church service that you are expected to attend every Sunday morning. Should you be fortunate enough to secure a permanent position at the house, then you will receive a full day off as well as another once a month. Come along with me.'

Enid shadowed the woman as she opened the small door, leading her up a narrow stone staircase. She paused at the first floor and opened the door slightly.

'The Clarkson quarters,' she said quietly. 'If summoned, you are to enter this way. Even when transporting food from the kitchen, you carry it up the backstairs way and not up the main staircase. Understood?'

'Perfectly, ma'am.' Enid nodded.

They climbed another flight of stairs where Mrs Webster opened another door. 'Most of the servants sleep here. It's a floor separated into male and female sections. I, myself, have my own rooms. So does Mr Dunbar. All the rest of the males – footmen, hall boys, grooms, coach drivers, gardeners, et cetera – sleep one side of this floor and the females – Cook, maids, governess, et cetera – sleep the other. There are two attic rooms. You shall share yours with Maria Garcia. The adjacent room is shared by Alice and another you've yet to meet, Jess, who is a maid-of-all-work. Both she and Alice tend to do the more subservient jobs around here.' Enid didn't realise that so many of the staff lived in at the house. 'Just another floor to go,' the housekeeper said, smiling.

Enid wondered why the woman didn't smile more often as her face lit up and it made her features look quite attractive, no longer sharp – but she would never dream of saying this.

Finally, they ascended another set of steps through yet another door, which led to the attic. The housekeeper pushed a door to reveal a small room with a window situated high up but it reflected plenty of light. The room was painted white and although quite stark, it was far better than anything she was used to.

Either side of a plain wooden set of drawers were two single beds neatly made up. In the far corner was a walnut wardrobe and a matching stand that had an oval free-standing mirror on it as well as a floral porcelain washbowl and matching jug. There was even a small bookcase packed with books.

Noticing Enid's interest, Mrs Webster said, 'So, you read then, do you?'

'Yes, ma'am.'

The woman nodded approvingly. 'Well, apart from reading the Bible – there's a copy there – I suggest you read *The Daily Prayer Book for Servants* and *The Servants Rule Book*. Apart from those, if you have the time, there are several books by Charles Dickens for you to peruse. Now about Maria...' Enid tilted her head to one side to listen. 'She's a Catholic so you'll find she might wish to return to the room to pray the rosary from time to time. She's dreadfully homesick and most of her family have returned to Spain, apart from her father and uncle who both work at the Dowlais Ironworks. She doesn't attend church with the rest of us once a week but instead is given dispensation to attend daily Mass at the Catholic church.'

Enid nodded, wondering if it affected the girl's working day at all. But realised it must be difficult for her with most of her family back home in Spain.

* * *

Enid was given some time to settle in to her room, where she hung her few pieces of clothing in the wardrobe beside Maria's and placed some of her possessions, like her hairbrush and a rose brooch Betsan had given her to bring her good fortune before she left the workhouse, in an empty drawer in the chest of drawers. Mrs Webster then escorted her to the sewing room where she was to be fitted out for her new uniform. Mrs March, the seamstress, was already there in waiting for her, a rosy-cheeked woman with sparkling eyes.

When Enid had been kitted out with the new uniform, the housekeeper wanted her to help serve dinner for the Clarkson family later that same night.

When the housekeeper had departed, Mrs March smiled pleasantly at her. 'Don't worry, you'll soon get used to your surroundings,' she reassured her. 'Most people working here are friendly enough. Now,' she said as she appraised Enid's physique, 'I can tell your approximate size by looking at you. Although you're quite slight in the frame, you do have a well-rounded bosom, young lady. I have just the right dress for you though I think I might have to pin up the hem and alter it for you.'

It wasn't long before she was stood on a wooden box as Mrs March hemmed the dress. The woman had been correct in her assumption about the fit of it too as it skimmed her bosom nicely. Afterwards, Mrs March sewed the hem with a treadle sewing machine as she removed the pins.

Soon, Enid was wearing her new maid's dress as Mrs March stood back, hands clasped together, apparently pleased with her handiwork.

'This should complete the look,' she said, handing Enid a white starched pinafore and cap. 'Now I know your size for sure, I'll sort out another dress for you. You'll need to have two. One to wash and one to wear. You do look lovely, dear. Now you'd better go and find Mrs Webster. She doesn't like to be kept waiting – that much I do know.'

'Oh! I'm not sure where to go?' Enid's hands flew to her face.

Mrs March escorted her to the door. 'That way, along the corridor there on the left and down the staff staircase. I expect you'll find Mrs Webster in the drawing room or in the kitchen. Someone will tell you where she is if you can't find her.'

'Thank you, Mrs March. Do you live in here too?'

'Oh no, dear. I live in a little cottage just down the road with my husband, Mick. He's a gardener here. There are other gardeners who live in here, but my husband is the head gardener; he makes all the decisions,' she said proudly.

Enid smiled. 'Thank you for sorting out my uniform,' she said, and made her way from the sewing room feeling quite pleased with herself.

* * *

As Enid walked along the corridor, she noticed the door at the far end leading to the staff staircase. Now if she went down there, as Mrs March said, she'd get her bearings at the bottom of it. There'd be another corridor to follow, which should lead past the drawing room and if the housekeeper wasn't there, she decided she'd call to the kitchen to ask where she might be. Someone would help her.

She had just begun to descend the stairs when the hairs on the back of her neck bristled. It was such an odd sensation, as though someone was behind her, following, watching. The stairs were winding so every time she glanced behind, she could see no one there. Maybe she'd imagined it.

Then she heard it, a door opening and closing from above and echoing footsteps – there *was* someone behind her. Her heart began to hammer beneath her dress and her breaths became ragged. As she remembered Phillip's earlier warning, she began to burn up and perspire, but then she heard a voice.

'Enid! You forgot this!'

Turning, she was relieved to see Mrs March, a couple of steps above her, thrusting a bundle into her hands. She took the clothing she'd been wearing before being fitted for the dress.

'Oh, thank you so much!' Enid gasped, her breathing now steady.

'Leave the bundle in the kitchen with Cook. She has a walk-in cupboard there. If you return to your room right now, you may be late for Mrs Webster and that just wouldn't do!' She laughed.

Enid nodded and smiled. She was becoming scared of her own shadow at this rate.

4

Mrs Webster wasn't to be found in the drawing room so Enid went in search of Cook with her bundle of clothing beneath her arm. As she entered the kitchen, she noticed how the atmosphere seemed so different now that work was in progress. Cook was wiping her forehead with the back of one hand and stirring something bubbling in a large pot on the range with another.

Alice was clearing the decks, hefting heavy metal pans over to the large sink to wash, and Daisy was checking the oven where a delicious aroma of roast meat drifted towards her.

Cook turned when she noticed Enid's presence. 'It's a roast beef dinner tonight and apple pie with custard.' She rolled her eyes. 'Asparagus soup to start with.' She pointed to the ceiling. 'That lot never have less than three courses at dinner, sometimes five when they have dinner guests!'

Enid smiled. 'May I leave my clothing in your cupboard, please? I've just been fitted for my uniform and I don't want to keep Mrs Webster waiting.'

'Oh, I can see.' Cook smiled. 'That uniform looks real smart on you. Yes, take your bundle to the cupboard and put it on one of the shelves. It'll be safe in there.'

'Thank you.' Enid did as told and then returned to Cook's side. 'Would you happen to know where Mrs Webster is right now?'

'I think you'll find her either in the laundry room or the storage room next door to it.' Realising Enid had no clue where they were, she added, 'You're needing to go back out the door and turn left, and it's the far end of that corridor on the right.'

Enid nodded and smiled, but before she could turn to leave Cook had spoken again.

'You can stay for a cuppa if you like?' she said.

'I'd better not as I need to see Mrs Webster right away.'

'Do you know what she's got planned for you this evening?'

'Yes, she wants me to help in the dining room.'

Cook smiled broadly. 'Well, you will be back here then to take the dishes up and down the stairs like a yo-yo all evening – that'll keep you fit. When you've finished the girls here will wash the dishes and you and I can have a natter and a cup of cocoa before you set off for your bed. A slice or two of toasted bread would go down a treat, too. Then you'll be up nice and early Monday morning to start all over again!' She chuckled.

Enid was no stranger to hard work by any means as she'd risen early at the workhouse and had to engage in particular duties there too, like scrubbing the floors, but what did she know about the cleaning and tidying of a large house like this with all its fancy finery and fripperies? It was a far cry from life at the spike.

Finally, she located Mrs Webster in the laundry room where she was in the middle of instructing a couple of maids who were looking at the woman as if they were fed up to the back teeth of her telling them what to do.

'Ah, Miss Hardcastle,' the housekeeper said, appraising her over her gold-rimmed glasses. 'This is Tilly Cooper.' She pointed to a well-built girl with blonde hair. 'And this is Jess.'

The girl beside Tilly was much shorter and appeared younger too. Enid was surprised just how young some of the maids were at the house.

Tilly, who had a full, round face and big blue eyes, smiled welcomingly, which was in stark contrast to Maria's earlier hard stare.

'Hello, Enid,' she greeted.

'Hello.' Enid returned the smile.

'The girls are about to iron and fold the weekend's laundry,' said Mrs Webster. 'I prefer it all put away in the store cupboard by midnight on a Sunday night ready for a Monday morning, as that's always our busiest day – all the beds are stripped and changed on Monday mornings. Usually, the girls have finished the laundry by ten o'clock and can get to their beds though.'

Enid glanced around at the piles of clean laundry, which appeared to be mostly white sheets, pillowcases and tablecloths. She wondered how the maids would manage to get through that lot by midnight, never mind ten o'clock!

'I'd like you to pitch in here for the next hour and then report to the kitchen at six thirty sharp. The family dines later on a Sunday as they attend an evening service at church.'

'Yes, ma'am,' said Enid.

'Tilly will show you what to do.' Then she turned on her heel and left the room.

For a few seconds, Enid felt unable to utter a word until Tilly burst out laughing. 'Don't take no notice of her; she's not as hard as she seems. She just likes lording it up over us all. The only one she can't do that to is Mrs Shrimpton who, as well as being her senior, she has absolutely no authority over, and Mr Dunbar, the butler, of course. The kitchen is Cook's domain and Old Frosty Drawers knows nothing whatsoever about cooking!'

Jess began to giggle at Tilly's description of the housekeeper.

Feeling as though she didn't want to get caught out laughing and joking on the first day, which would have meant instant dismissal, Enid just smiled and asked, 'What would you like me to do?'

* * *

Helping in the dining room certainly kept Enid on her toes. She hardly had a moment to herself what with rushing up and down the narrow staircase while carrying various laden trays assisted by Phillip. Mr Dunbar oversaw the dining service as Maria dished up the food from a side table.

It was the first time for Enid to set eyes on the Clarkson family. Not one of them spoke to her or acknowledged her presence, but then again, she rightly guessed it was probably not the done thing. But surely at least one of them would have noticed a new member of staff in the dining room?

Seated at the head of the table was the master of the house.

'That'll be Mr Donald Clarkson,' said Cook when Enid had rushed back downstairs between courses with a tray of dirty crockery. 'He's a fair-minded sort. The mistress is Mrs Dorothea Clarkson. Comes from very good stock, has fancy ideas, but to be fair to her, does a lot for local charities.'

'And the two young men and the young woman?'

'The dashing-looking one is Anthony, he's the eldest son. He works in his father's business, hopes to take it over some day...' Cook paused for breath. 'He's a healthy young man... how shall I put it... with a young man's needs. He tends to get a bit fruity with the maids. Take care with him. He wouldn't harm Alice nor Jess as they look even younger than their actual ages. But someone like yourself who is fast becoming a young woman will attract the likes of him.'

Cook's remark reminded Enid of Mrs March's comment about her bosom earlier.

'B... but, I don't want to do that anyhow!' said Enid, feeling quite affronted at what Cook was suggesting.

'No, I know you don't but you're an attractive young lady nevertheless. Keep well away from his roving hands!'

Enid nodded. 'Someone else warned me about him.'

'Oh?' Cook quirked a silvery brow beneath her mob cap. 'And who was that?'

'One of the footmen.'

'I see. Well, we all know the likes of Anthony Clarkson but we tend to keep our traps shut if we wish to keep our jobs here. His mother thinks he can do no wrong, mind you.' She shook her head and pursed her lips in a show of disapproval.

'And the other two, who are they?'

'The brother and sister?' Cook sniffed. 'Sebastian and Bella. Sebastian is nice to the staff, courteous and polite. A dreamy, artistic sort. Now, Bella, she's another sort altogether!' Cook rolled her eyes. 'A wilful young madam who thinks most highly of herself. Stands up to her mother, she does, but is the apple of her father's eye.'

'So, Sebastian is the black sheep of the family?' Enid blinked.

'Aye. You might say that. But how did you work that one out?'

'Easy, really. You made it sound as if Anthony is a mother's boy and Bella is a daddy's girl! When it came to mention of Sebastian there was no talk of either parent favouring him.'

'You'll go far you will, my girl!' said Cook in an incredulous fashion. 'Speaking of going far, the beef course is now ready for upstairs. Take that silver salver up and return for the vegetables with both footmen as there's a lot for one person to transport. Now be careful carrying the big salver as it's tricky to navigate those narrow stairs. There's a fine art to it.'

Enid gulped and then nodded, half wishing Cook would've asked Phillip or Geoffery to carry the *pièce de résistance*. But she had to learn quick and there was no better way than to learn the hard way – on the job.

When she returned to the dining room, Mr Dunbar was already at the double doors awaiting arrival of the silver salver of beef, which he took over to a side table to neatly carve up.

Maria approached Enid and said in a quiet but harsh tone, 'There are more dirty dishes to remove before we serve the next course. You should have returned from the kitchen sooner!'

Enid gritted her teeth. How was she to know? Was it her fault Cook kept her nattering in the kitchen? But instead, she smiled sweetly before replying, 'I shall take more care in the future.'

Then she listened as the family spoke with one another. It was almost as though she was invisible to them.

If there was one word that could describe the Clarkson family, then that word was "flawed".

'Oh, Father, please may I have a pony?' Bella was pleading as she held the palms of her hands together as if in prayer. Her father, who had a mischievous twinkle in his eye, was a handsome man despite having a receding hairline and grey temples; his azure-blue eyes and the chiselled cut of his jaw made him attractive.

Enid estimated that Bella was a couple of years younger than herself and she had her long, ringleted dark glossy hair loose on her shoulders. Enid thought the gown she wore, in a deep iridescent plum colour that shimmered and shone beneath the candlelight, was beautiful.

Donald Clarkson appeared to be teasing his daughter until Dorothea suddenly butted in and snapped, 'For heaven's sake, put Isabella out of her misery so we can eat our food in peace!'

The master suddenly stopped what he was doing, the light and laughter now dissipating from his eyes. 'Yes, dearest Bella, you shall have your much-coveted pony sooner than you think!'

Now Bella was up on her feet and making her way to her dearest papa. She wrapped her arms around his neck, much to her mother's disapproval.

'Do sit back down, Isabella.'

Dorothea fixed her daughter with a hard, cold stare, reminding Enid of the disapproving look Maria had given her when she first arrived at the house. It was then Enid noticed that the rest of the family addressed the girl as Bella, but her mother did not. She was Isabella to her, the formal version of her name. It spoke volumes about the gulf between mother and daughter.

As Enid stood sandwiched between Mr Dunbar and Maria, waiting for any commands, she noticed Anthony laughing at his sister. Sebastian, meanwhile, seemed to be in deep thought and not mentally present.

Enid's legs began to tire and ache from standing so still for such a long period as the family took their time over each course consumed. Towards the end of the meal, Maria went to offer the family a second cup of coffee from the pot and as she approached Anthony, Enid noticed her flinch. It was almost as though she were expecting some sort of unwanted physical contact from him, and then, when she backed away with the empty coffee pot in her hand, she looked positively relieved.

Eventually, the family tossed their linen napkins onto their empty plates and rose from the table, Dorothea and Donald rising one after the other as the butler drew their chairs back from them. This was followed by Anthony, Sebastian and Bella – in the respective pecking order of their ages.

When the family had left the dining room, Mr Dunbar summoned Enid, wiggling a white-gloved index finger.

Oh dear! Had she done something wrong?

'Well done, young lady,' he complimented. 'You did well there for your first time in service.'

Enid nodded and smiled but then she caught Maria's eyes, which were fiery and full of rage.

When Mr Dunbar was out of earshot taking a tray of various wines back to the cellar, Maria came to stand before her.

'Quickly. Collect all *zee* crockery on *zee* tray, *por favor*!' she commanded with a sharp edge to her voice.

Enid wasn't sure if she was supposed to take any orders from her but decided that maybe it was better not to rock the boat so she did as instructed. Several trips were necessary, carrying loaded trays of crockery, wine glasses, cutlery and table linen, to clear the table and, when she had done all that, the room had to be cleaned and polished. Enid watched as Maria just flicked a feather duster over a few ornaments on the mantelpiece. She was well aware that the girl was not pulling her weight and taking advantage of her; to Maria, Enid was just a "workhouse skivvy" sent from the spike as an extra pair of hands.

When the room had been cleared and cleaned, Enid rubbed the back of her neck, feeling ready for her bed, but then she remembered how Cook had told her to call to the kitchen for a cup of cocoa. In any case, she had to go there to retrieve her bundle of clothing.

When she arrived, it was good to see the kitchen was now peaceful and all tidied up. Nothing was out of place and all the tops had been wiped down. Cook was seated by the fireside with her boots off, feet up on a small wooden stool. There was a hole in one of her stockings and her big toe was comically poking through, but she made no attempt to hide it as Enid approached.

'Oh, there you are!' She smiled broadly. The woman's cheeks looked fiery and flushed. At first Enid thought it was due to cooking in a hot kitchen but then she noticed the bottle in her hand.

'What's that you're drinking, Mrs Shrimpton?' She half expected it to be lemonade.

Cook threw back her head and laughed. 'It's my regular bottle of stout. Fair play, it's one of the perks of my job. A bottle a night I'm allowed. It's because I'm on my feet in this place all day and it gets so ruddy hot, plus Mr Clarkson reckons it's full of iron, which is good for the body.'

Enid nodded. It sounded as though Mr Clarkson was a kind and understanding master.

'Would you like one too, *cariad*?'

Enid shook her head. 'Er, no thanks.' She held up her palm. 'I'd prefer a cup of cocoa.'

Cook made to heave herself up from the armchair but Enid said firmly, 'No, please stay where you are, Mrs Shrimpton. I'll make it if you tell me where I can find things. Would you like one too?'

'No, not for me. I prefer my stout. You'll find the cocoa powder and sugar on the counter ready for you, and a jug of milk in the pantry. There's a small pan in the bottom cupboard beside the stove and the cups are in the cupboard above.'

Enid did as told. Cook seemed to have forgotten her promise of a slice of toast and now Enid's stomach began to growl with hunger. On cue, and as if she could read Enid's mind, she said, 'The staff usually have a light supper of an evening, but you were busy so I kept some for you. It's on the counter covered with a cloth.'

Enid nodded her thanks and went to take a look where she found two slices of buttered bread and a thin slice of beef, sandwiched together beneath a muslin cloth.

'There's a jar of mustard in the pantry,' Cook added.

Enid enjoyed her unexpected and impromptu meal and her cup of milky cocoa. As she tucked in with relish, she listened to Cook regale her with tales of what it was like when she was in service as a young girl at the house.

Glancing at the wall clock, she was surprised to see it was eleven o'clock. Where had the day gone? Gasping at how late it was, she said, 'I'd best be off to my bed. Thank you for the meal, Mrs Shrimpton. Shall I wash up for you?'

'No need, dear. Alice can do that first thing in the morning. She'll be up at five.'

By the time Enid got to her bed, Maria was already fast asleep, which she was thankful for. She couldn't stand the thought of any antagonistic behaviour at this time of the night.

Enid undressed in the darkened room, the only light shining in from a bright full moon outside. It had been an eventful first day and she wondered what tomorrow might bring.

* * *

'Up out of your bed in there!' someone shouted.

In the middle of her slumber, Enid was dreaming that Richards, the landlord, was rapping at the door but his voice had become decidedly female. Then she sat bolt upright with a start as she realised this was no dream, it was now morning.

It took her a moment to get her bearings. Of course, she'd spent the night at the big house and had been so exhausted she'd slept through from just after eleven to... What time was it? Maria was missing from her bed. It was neatly made up as if she hadn't slept there at all, yet Enid knew she had. Where was she? And why hadn't she woken her up?

'Come along now, Miss Hardcastle!' It was the housekeeper's voice.

Enid shot out of bed and ran barefooted to open the door. Blinking, she stared at Mrs Webster who thrust some sort of garment into her hands.

'This is a grey pinafore,' she said in a brusque manner. 'You need it as your first task is to clear the grates and light the fires in the drawing and dining rooms, then you are to sweep the floors. After you've done that, you get cleaned up and then you change into your white pinafore before attending breakfast in the kitchen with the rest of the staff. Your white pinafore is for the rest of your daily tasks.'

Enid nodded, feeling like curtsying to the woman, though she did not.

When she'd washed, dressed and donned the grey pinafore, she went to the drawing room.

'Oh, there you are!' Jen beamed. At least someone was pleased to see her. 'Now then, I'll show you how to rake out the ashes, which you'll need to sweep into the metal bucket and take to the pile out at the end of the garden. The gardeners use them, see, for some sort of fertiliser for their produce. Then when you've done that, I'll show you how to set a fire with balls of newspaper, sticks and coal. There's a knack to it.'

Enid didn't have the heart to tell the maid that she already knew how to do so as she'd watched her mam do it often enough. Her mother's hands had been roughened and calloused and at times black from coal dust, not the hands of a lady by any means. Enid doubted either Dorothea or Bella would ever have to set a fire in their lives. Instead, she just nodded her thanks and allowed the girl to run her through the protocols of the big house.

When the fires were lit and blazing away heartily, the floors had to be swept. Enid was looking forward to her breakfast. Her stomach was growling – all this hard work was giving her a serious appetite.

And what a breakfast it turned out to be. Thick rashers of bacon, fluffy fried eggs, slices of crusty white bread slathered in farmhouse butter, and all washed down with two cups of tea.

Cook smiled in her direction as she poured tea for herself from the pot. 'It's good to see a healthy appetite,' she enthused.

'Where's Maria?' Enid asked. She had noticed an empty chair at the table.

The others exchanged glances as if they were in on something she wasn't privy to.

'Maria attends Mass first thing of a morning at the Catholic church. She has returned and gone for a little lie-down as she doesn't feel so good this morning,' Cook said in a quiet manner.

That appeared odd to Enid as she seemed fine last night, not ill or anything, but she said nothing of it and carried on eating her breakfast. As Maria wasn't around, Jen and Doris included her in the conversation, which would hardly have been the case had Maria been present. Thinking back to the previous evening though, something had definitely been off with Maria's behaviour in the dining room. She'd seemed on edge and snappy for some reason. But Enid didn't know the girl properly as yet, so might she be like that anyhow?

When breakfast was over and almost everyone had departed, Cook handed Enid a small tray containing a piece of dry toasted bread and a weak-looking cup of tea.

'Take this up to Maria,' she instructed.

Enid frowned. What was going on here? Something wasn't right.

As the final servant out the door was Enid, Cook looked at her and in a whisper said, 'You might as well know, as you're sharing a room with her and most of the staff already suspect... Maria's pregnant...'

Enid drew in a sharp breath and let it out again. 'Oh no!' She paused. 'Is it Anthony Clarkson's baby?'

Cook shook her head vigorously, 'Shh! Don't say things like that. You might lose your position here if someone overhears! What makes you think that anyhow?'

'Sorry,' Enid whispered, remembering where she was. 'It was just the way Maria behaved around the master's son during dinner last night. I caught her flinching and backing away from him.'

Cook raised her silver eyebrows. 'Aye, she would be but so would most of the maids here. Like I said, he has difficulty keeping his hands to himself. I've no doubt he wouldn't do anything under his parents' watchful eyes, but Maria obviously feels intimidated by his presence.'

'But if it's not Anthony's baby then whose baby is it?'

'Not for me to say,' said Cook curtly. 'I know who the father is but I don't think the others here do. If Maria wants you to know, I dare say she'll tell you herself given time.'

Enid thought it hardly likely the girl would choose to confide in her, but everything that was going on for her might be the reason she'd been so snappy. Most of Maria's family were in Spain and surely the only people who were in Merthyr – her father and her uncle – would be none too pleased to hear this news.

'Run along now, Enid. Take those to Maria. They will help keep her morning sickness at bay.'

Nodding, Enid left the room, now feeling a great deal of sympathy for the girl and the plight she now found herself in.

Tentatively, Enid knocked on the bedroom door but there was no answer. Then she heard muffled cries coming from inside. She turned the doorknob and slowly pushed the door open to see Maria sprawled out, face down on the bed, sobbing her heart out.

'Cook said to give you these.' Enid was quite prepared to lay the tray down on top of the cabinet and leave, but Maria turned herself over, sat up and dabbing at her watery, swollen eyes with a handkerchief, sniffed loudly. '*Gracias.* Thank you.'

It was the first polite comment Enid had ever received from the girl.

'Is there anything else I can get for you? I have a few minutes before I'm due to help back downstairs...'

The girl shook her head. 'No, no one can help me now. I suppose you have heard about *theez* pregnancy?'

Feeling honesty was the best policy, Enid nodded. 'It must be very difficult for you?'

'It is. Believe me.' It was Maria's turn to nod. 'It will bring shame on my family.'

This was the first time Enid had not felt any frostiness being emitted from the girl. Then she said something in her native tongue that Enid didn't understand.

'Please, if Mrs Webster asks about me, tell her that I have... how you say?' She patted her stomach.

'A stomach upset?' Enid suggested.

'Yes, that is it. Thank you.'

If Maria had morning sickness, it was hardly a lie to suggest such a thing but the girl wouldn't be able to keep it a secret from the housekeeper for much longer, nor anyone else for that matter. It was beginning to make sense why Maria had been so hostile towards her, having been forced to share a room when she wanted to hide her pregnancy. Whoever the father of the child was, could she rely on him to do the decent thing and stand by her? Jimmy would never leave her in a position like that if they'd have got carried away – she was sure of it. But then again, Jimmy never overstepped the mark and was content to just have a little kiss and cuddle. As her thoughts turned towards him, she wondered what he was doing right now.

* * *

Jimmy hadn't had much time to himself of late now he was working for Mr Baxter, going around the big houses in the area seeking customers for the man. His idea to provide a home delivery service had turned out to be a profitable one, because the larger houses in the town often gave piles of boots and shoes for repair. It was rare to employ a cobbler at one of those grand houses. A seamstress or a handyman, yes. A cobbler, no. Though he was aware that some handymen might be able to turn their hands to many things and be able to glue a leather upper worked loose or tap a seg into the sole of a boot, but most wouldn't be all that skilled.

So today, he'd had a good idea how he might kill two birds with one stone. He'd heard Enid had been sent into service at the Clarkson House for a couple of weeks, so he intended chancing his arm as he missed her so much.

Whistling good-humouredly to himself, he knocked back the peak of his cap with his hand as his eyes drank in the beauty of the house and its copious grounds. Even the black double wrought-iron gates at the entrance were magnificent. There was a small lodge house just past its entrance on the right.

Noticing Jimmy on the cart, a man dressed in a tweed waistcoat and matching trousers came bounding forwards to check him out. He looked middle-aged and he also wore a flannel shirt and a muffler around his neck.

'What are you wanting here, lad?' the man barked.

Jimmy smiled as he often got that sort of response from these sorts of houses. People were suspicious of his motives but today, he'd made a special effort. He was well turned out in his new jacket and shirt and his boots were highly polished. Clothes might not maketh the man but they surely helped to maketh a good image, he thought.

'Pardon me, sir,' said Jimmy politely. 'I'm the chief assistant to Mr Baxter the cobbler on the high street in Merthyr. Do you know of him?'

'Aye, I do.' The man narrowed his eyes with suspicion. 'You haven't come here to try flogging something, 'ave you? The master doesn't like peddlers turning up at the door!'

'Oh no, sir. Well, not in a manner of speaking. Mr Baxter has now started a home delivery service for the best houses in the area. Those families that have a good reputation...'

'What kind of a service?' The man sniffed, his interest now piqued.

'I deliver the shoes and boots to the shop and we repair them then I bring them back here, fixed and nicely polished. For a fee, of course.'

The man looked dubious as he rubbed his chin in contemplation. 'You mean you'd come all the way here, take away the shoes, repair them and bring them back again? What's the catch? Usually one of the maids takes them to a cobbler shop for repair and goes back after a few days to fetch them.'

'There's no catch, mister. For a limited time there's no extra fee for the delivery service either. The first-time delivery will be free of charge.'

The man removed his flat cap and scratched his head. 'I have to admit it does sound too good to be true to me, sonny. How can we be sure you're not going to do a runner with a load of shoes and flog them on the marketplace?'

Jimmy cocked him a cheeky smile and handed him a letter through the gates' railings that Mrs Baxter had written on behalf of her husband. The letter was on special headed notepaper, with fine penmanship, and it spoke of how trusted Jimmy Corcoran was and how he was of fine moral standing, honourable and loyal. At the bottom, it was signed by the pair.

The man replaced his cap on his head before reading the letter with interest.

'You'd best come with me then, lad. We'll have a word with Mrs Webster the housekeeper. I'm not promising anything, mind you. But you'll have to run it past her before you get anywhere with this.'

'I understand.' An idea occurred of how he might set eyes on Enid again and validate himself in front of the housekeeper. Deciding to take his chance, he added, 'I've just thought of something...'

'Aye, go on then...'

'There's a young lady I know called Enid Hardcastle. She's just started work here as a maid on a trial basis. She'll vouch for me too as I was a neighbour of hers and she knows Mr Baxter.'

'Very well,' said the man, now smiling. 'I'm Mr Ives. Clarence Ives. I'll hop on board the cart with you to ride up to the house. My legs aren't what they once were. I'll just open the gates.'

Jimmy nodded eagerly and watched as the man unbolted the gates, drawing them wide open for him to drive the horse and cart through before closing them behind him. Then Clarence hopped on board as they headed towards the house.

All the while, Jimmy took in the magnificent grounds. He hadn't been on a property of this standing, ever. It was breathtakingly beautiful with its magnificent lawns, fountains and flower beds.

Jimmy pulled the cart up at the back of the house as instructed.

'I'll just see if I can find Mrs Webster,' Clarence said as he clambered down from the cart.

Jimmy guessed he might have arthritis or something, going by his slow, stiff movements. He watched the man take a small flight of steps and then he knocked on the back door.

A rotund woman aged about fifty answered. Was she the housekeeper? But no, a housekeeper wouldn't wear a mob cap like that, he was sure; she'd be more formally dressed. Going by the wooden spoon in the woman's hand and her flushed appearance, he guessed she was some kind of cook.

Clarence must have asked about Enid as the woman descended the steps and asked, 'Looking for Enid, are you, dearie?'

Jimmy nodded. 'Yes. She's an old pal of mine. Thought I might kill two birds with one stone if I can see her as I'm here on a bit of business.'

The woman chuckled. 'Hopefully, the housekeeper will bring Enid out to you soon.'

She winked, and to his embarrassment, he found himself blushing profusely.

5

Mrs Webster arrived in the laundry room as Enid was about to carry a pile of neatly folded towels into the storage area.

'Leave those a moment, Miss Hardcastle,' the housekeeper said, peering over her glasses. 'A young man has just turned up here at the house. He's here on business apparently and he claims to know you?'

Enid furrowed her brow. 'What young man, Mrs Webster?'

'His name is Jimmy Corcoran. Do you know him? He has a letter of recommendation from Mr Baxter, the cobbler on Merthyr high street. What do you know of him?'

Enid beamed at the mention of Jimmy's name. But how did he know where she was? 'I used to be a neighbour of his before being admitted into the workhouse, ma'am. He's a good sort. I can vouch for him. Honest and hard-working, he is. He had mentioned he was going to start up some sort of delivery business on Mr Baxter's behalf.'

The housekeeper smiled and nodded her approval. 'Very well, then. I want you to tell him to call back here tomorrow at around the same time when I shall have all the shoes ready for repair. Meanwhile, I'll allow you a few minutes to speak to him. He's waiting in the kitchen. Cook's just made him a cup of tea.'

Enid laid down her pile of towels on one of the wooden counters, then turning to the woman said, 'Thank you, Mrs Webster.'

Jimmy's face lit up as Enid entered the kitchen.

'Your young man is here,' Cook teased as she tipped a wink at Enid. Jimmy rose from his seat at the table as she approached and he pecked her on the cheek, before reseating himself.

'How are you doing, my darlin'?' he asked, his eyes shiny and bright.

'She's settling in here very well!' Cook called across the kitchen, answering for her.

'Is that so?' Jimmy said, gazing deep into Enid's eyes as if to gauge a reaction.

'Yes.' Enid nodded breathlessly.

'Oh, I have missed you so.' Jimmy took both of her hands in his own across the table. 'How was it for you in the workhouse?'

Enid shrugged. 'Not as bad as I feared, though I prefer being here.'

'I did try to get to see you a couple of times but wasn't allowed in there. The porter on the door said I needed special permission to get in.'

'Aw, that's such a shame. I would have loved a visit from you.'

'I'm waiting for the housekeeper to put me out of my misery!'

'Oh?'

'Mr Ives, the lodgekeeper at the gate, went to speak to her earlier on my behalf about that delivery service for Mr Baxter I was telling you about.'

Enid smiled. 'It was she who sent me to you to give you the message that if you return the same time tomorrow, there'll be a pile of shoes waiting for you to take away for repair.'

Jimmy heaved out a sigh. 'That's a relief. It was hard to get past Mr Ives on the gate as it was and even though I won him over so that he trusted me, I had no idea if anyone else would!'

'I've only a few minutes to speak with you as I have to return to the laundry room soon.'

Overhearing them, Cook said, 'Why don't you ask *Old Frosty Drawers* if you can change your morning break time tomorrow to coincide with Jimmy's visit? Then you can both have a cup of tea and some breakfast together undisturbed.'

'That's a splendid idea!' Jimmy beamed.

Enid nodded enthusiastically. As long as Mrs Webster agreed then that was that.

* * *

The housekeeper gave permission that Enid be allowed a late breakfast with Jimmy, especially as they were both under the watchful eyes of Cook and couldn't get up to any shenanigans. After what had happened to Maria, Enid guessed the staff were more watchful though she had no idea if the housekeeper knew about that or not, and she didn't like to ask Maria about it either.

As Mrs Webster presented Jimmy with ten pairs of staff boots and shoes for minor repairs and four pairs of shoes belonging to family members, his face broke out into a pleased grin. She also advised him that she had no doubt there'd be more to repair in a few weeks as the staff were on their feet all day long, so their footwear took a pounding. He scribbled out a receipt and signed it, before handing it to the woman, who seemed impressed.

'What do you say to that then, Miss Hardcastle?' Jimmy winked at Enid across the table after he'd returned from loading up the shoes on the cart.

Cook had prepared a light breakfast of scrambled eggs and toast for the pair and a pot of coffee.

'You two are so lovey-dovey that I doubt you'd both manage a fully cooked breakfast!' Cook jested.

And she was correct. Enid could barely eat a thing with Jimmy's eyes on her, but she loved listening to his tales of back home in China and how everyone was getting on there.

By the time he was ready to depart, a sad, hollow sensation gnawed the pit of her stomach as if she was already missing him.

'Things won't always be like this,' he assured her in a whisper so Cook and the other staff wouldn't overhear. 'One day we'll be together and I'll marry you, Miss Enid Hardcastle! I'll have my own cobbler shop by then too. How does Mrs Corcoran sound to you?'

Enid melted when he said that because those were the words of her heart too, though she'd never voiced them to him. Her cheeks blazed red-hot as breathlessly she said, 'It sounds very good to me, Jimmy.' Her mouth was dry and then when no one was paying attention, he swept her up in his arms and kissed her tenderly on the mouth. Thankfully, Cook, Doris and Alice were too busy at the other end of the kitchen to pay them any attention.

As they broke away from one another, Jimmy said, 'Let's write to each other while we're parted like this, shall we?'

Enid nodded. She knew the staff were allowed letters and thought it a marvellous way to correspond with him as she'd be able to read his words over and over and even sleep with the pages under her pillow.

* * *

There wasn't much time to dwell on anything in the house as Enid was kept busy: lighting fires at the crack of dawn, cleaning and polishing both furniture and ornaments, spells with her sleeves rolled up as she worked in the laundry and kitchen – the list was endless but she was never shy of hard work and it all stood her in good stead. Cook had said her position at the house was as "maid-of-all-work" but she had no doubt that if she continued to work hard and did not get into any trouble, then she'd be taken on permanently. Possibly then she'd be assigned as a parlour or kitchen maid. Either way, it didn't much matter as she enjoyed her work.

She'd been at the house for a full week and was sorting out books in Mr Clarkson's private library, which was a part of his study, when the door suddenly burst open.

Enid startled, her eyes large. She was relieved to see it was Donald Clarkson and not Anthony.

'Good afternoon, young lady,' he greeted. She bobbed a curtsy and smiled shyly. He had a rolled-up newspaper tucked beneath his arm as he made to sit in a comfy fireside chair. Enid thought it ironic she'd seen Mr Dunbar ironing that newspaper earlier and now it was rolled up.

Mr Clarkson glanced at her curiously before opening it. 'And how are you getting on here? Don't think I haven't noticed you!' He smiled broadly.

'Very well, thank you, sir. I'm enjoying working here.'

'That's good. And what are you doing there?' He quirked a silver brow.

'Oh sorry, sir. I had thought it a good idea to reorganise the bookshelves into alphabetical order of the authors' surnames.'

'What a marvellous idea!' he enthused, his eyes lighting up. 'Please carry on er... what's your name?'

'Enid, sir. Enid Hardcastle.'

'Before you make another start could you please summon someone in the kitchen to arrange a pot of coffee for me, Enid?'

She nodded enthusiastically. 'Yes, sir. Of course,' she said, bobbing another curtsy. She'd noticed whenever the master was around, his presence seemed to bring a warmth to the house, but the same could definitely not be said of his wife – it could feel decidedly chilly in her presence. She'd witnessed first-hand how the woman constantly fussed around Anthony as the eldest child but constantly bickered with Bella and hardly bothered with Sebastian. Anthony was the golden child to her, her precious firstborn and first served.

Enid laid down her feather duster on the bookshelf, then went in search of one of the kitchen maids to ask her to prepare a tray of coffee for Mr Clarkson.

'He can have some of my shortbread biscuits to go with it,' said Cook as she went rummaging on her hands and knees in a low cupboard in search of the biscuit tin. Meanwhile, Doris was already watching a kettle boiling on the range. No doubt she and Cook had been just about to sneak a crafty cuppa before they got on with their tasks, one of the perks of working in the kitchen. They were both entitled to it though, thought Enid. Doris had a pile of dishes ready to be washed and Cook would be preparing another meal for the family soon enough.

'What's the master up to this afternoon?' Cook asked as she pulled herself up onto the counter top with one hand while clutching the tin of biscuits in the other, her face looking decidedly flushed.

'He's just reading the newspaper in his study at the moment.'

'Oh?' said Cook, furrowing her brow as she placed the tin on the counter and arranged the shortbread biscuits onto a pretty china plate. 'Hurry up with that coffee, Doris!' she yelled across the kitchen. Then turning back towards Enid added, 'I thought he'd gone to Cardiff on important business today. I'm surprised he's still at home.'

Doris carried the coffee tray over to them and Cook placed the plate of biscuits on top of it.

'I heard the master talking this morning,' Doris chipped in, 'and he's asked Mr Anthony to take his place at the meeting today.'

'Oh, did he now?' Cook laughed. 'You don't miss much, do you, Doris!'

'Neither do you!' retorted the maid in a haughty fashion, her eyes flashing with indignation.

'Cheeky young whippersnapper!' Cook said good-humouredly. 'Now give that tray to Enid and get back to washing those pots!'

When the girl had left, Cook whispered behind her open palm, 'She's absolutely right – there's not much that bypasses me in this house!'

* * *

Later, Enid went to check on Maria where she found the girl on her hands and knees scrubbing the servants' corridor. As she stood there watching her, she noticed how red raw her hands were as she dipped a scrubbing brush into a pail of soapy water. Her long black hair had worked loose from her mob cap and had flopped into her face. It was then Enid realised what a chore it was for the girl as the pregnancy advanced and how much effort it took for her.

'Maria,' she said softly. 'Here, allow me to take over from you.'

Maria looked up at her, her huge, grateful eyes brimming with tears. Sniffing loudly, she said, '*Gracias*.'

'Have you informed Mrs Webster of your condition yet so that she gives you lighter tasks?'

Maria shook her head. 'No, not yet but most of the staff already know and some have offered me help like you are doing now.'

Enid nodded and she helped a puffing Maria up onto her feet. 'Now go and have a cup of tea in the kitchen with Cook while I finish this off for you. If Mrs Webster asks what you're doing in there, tell her I offered to help as you're on your monthly cycle and in a bit of pain.'

Maria nodded gratefully. 'I am so very sorry...' She wiped away a tear with the back of her hand. 'I feel... how you say er... remorseful now as I wasn't very nice to you when you first arrived.'

'I know,' said Enid, generously, 'but I realise the reason why – as I'd be sharing a room with you and you've been trying to hide your pregnancy all this time.' Maria smiled. 'Now then, go and have that cup of tea while I finish this off, then I'll come to see how you are. And if you like, we'll go to see Mrs Webster to explain what's happened. If you carry on like this you could harm yourself and the baby and you wouldn't want that, would you?'

Maria's eyes glistened as slowly she shook her head and turned to walk away.

* * *

Enid accompanied Maria to see the housekeeper to give the girl some moral support.

As they stood in the corridor lingering outside the housekeeper's office, she noticed Maria tremble. 'What's the matter?'

Looking at Enid she sighed. 'It makes me realise once I tell Mrs Webster I am pregnant and who the father is, it shall be a secret no longer…'

Enid laid a reassuring hand on Maria's arm. 'Believe me, you are doing the right thing, as the information you've kept inside will have to come out at some time in the future…'

Maria sniffed and then smiled at her.

Realising that the girl was close to tears, Enid knocked on the door.

Surprisingly, Mrs Webster wasn't angry with Maria but concerned for her well-being, telling her that now she had this information, the master and the mistress of the house both needed to be informed and a decision made regarding the girl's future welfare.

It had been an exhausting day and just as Enid was about to turn off the oil lights in the drawing room before heading off to bed, the door creaked open slowly and there in the doorway stood Anthony Clarkson, seeming a little unsteady on his feet, swaying from side to side.

As he approached her, she inhaled a strong smell of alcohol. What should she do now?

'Well, what do we have here?' he drawled, his voice full of surprise as though not expecting to see her there. She figured he was probably about to raid his father's drink trolley as there was all sorts on it: brandy, whisky and gin amongst other things.

Then she remembered he'd been out on business all day, so that's why he was in such a state. He'd obviously been wining and dining someone as he sealed some sort of business deal.

Enid stood frozen to the spot, her mouth drying up. She needed to keep her composure at all costs if she was to escape his clutches.

Anthony edged closer towards her and she flinched. 'You're a fine-looking young specimen, aren't you?' he said, and to her horror, he reached out and stroked her cheek. 'Untouched and untamed...' he murmured with a lustful look in his eyes. 'I can always tell the maidens.'

Now he was closer, Enid could detect a strong smell of something else that she couldn't quite identify and then she realised his hair was slicked down. He was wearing pomade to keep it that way. There were only two men at the house who slicked down their hair with pomade – the other being Phillip.

Enid swallowed hard. She didn't want to offend the young man but neither could she stand here trapped like a baby gazelle in the jaws of a lion. So, jutting out her chin, she stared him in the eyes and said, 'If you don't mind, sir, Mrs Webster is waiting for me in the laundry room. She sent a maid to summon me just before you arrived. If I don't appear there soon, she will come looking for me!'

That seemed to bring him to his senses as the lustful look faded from his eyes.

'Very well. Run along like the good girl I know you are, but soon, very soon, you'll not be untouched and untamed any longer – not if I have anything to do with it...'

Anthony's words left a bitter taste in her mouth as she fled the room, running down the corridor to the servants' staircase, not stopping until she got safely into her bedroom where Maria was sitting up in bed, seemingly waiting for her.

'What has happened?' she asked as Enid quickly shut and bolted the door, her heart pounding beneath her dress. She paused to catch her breath and then poured herself a glass of water from the jug on top of the cabinet, taking several sips to compose herself. When satisfied, she laid the glass down and lowered herself onto her own bed.

'It was horrible, simply awful,' she said, trembling. 'The master's son...'

'Sebastian?' Maria arched an eyebrow.

'No, Anthony. He's just returned from that business meeting in Cardiff. He's quite drunk and he intimidated me. Touched my face and said things so I lied and told him Mrs Webster was waiting for me in the laundry room. He stopped then but not before he told me that he intends to take my virginity, well, not in so many words but I knew what the implication was.'

Maria gasped. She got out of her bed and sat beside Enid, draping a reassuring arm around her shoulders. 'That man has got to be stopped,' she said.

Enid looked at her. 'Did he ever try it on with you?'

Maria nodded. 'Yes, but I've been fortunate as my father and uncle have made several visits to the house to see me. Anthony has seen them – they are well built and don't take messing from anyone. So he has backed off lately.'

Enid nodded. Pity she didn't have anyone to do the same for her. Jimmy would absolutely defend her honour but he was only a young lad and her father wasn't quite himself of late. There was no one to help her here but herself.

She paused for a moment as a thought occurred to her. 'Do you think I ought to tell Mrs Webster or Mr and Mrs Clarkson what just happened?'

Maria chewed on her bottom lip, deliberating. 'It *eez* difficult to know what to do in your case as you are on a trial here at the house. You might be sent back to... how you say? Something house?'

'The workhouse?'

'Yes, that is it.' She lowered her gaze. 'Anthony, he can do no wrong in his mother's eyes.'

'I suppose she wouldn't believe me if I told her. Maybe his father would though?'

'I'd just avoid Anthony for now until the family decide whether to keep you here or not, and if they do and he tries it again with you, then tell them. I have heard he has plans to go to London to work, so maybe he won't be here much longer.'

Enid nodded, relieved. She didn't see that much of him around the house anyhow. Maybe he'd acted the way he had because he'd been drunk. She hoped it would never happen again.

6

Maria was summoned to a meeting with Mr and Mrs Clarkson in the study to see what could be done about the predicament she found herself in. The father of the baby had been identified as a young gardener called Hywel Morris. The young man had shied away from his responsibilities with regards to marrying Maria. Understandably, Mr Clarkson took a dim view of this and said unless he did the decent thing and married her – to give the baby a father and a father's surname – then he would be dismissed forthwith. Mr Clarkson had gone on to say he would offer support if Hywel were to marry the girl and he would also arrange for them to have one of the small cottages in the grounds to live in.

With the threat of losing his job, public scandal and fear of Maria's father and uncle, Hywel Morris finally caved in and a marriage was arranged at the Catholic church.

Meanwhile, a letter had arrived for Enid. Phillip brought it to her at morning breakfast and she decided to save it for later to open when she was alone. The other servants seemed quite happy to read their correspondence at the table, excitedly discussing the contents of their letters with one another, but this was all too personal for Enid. It would be like telling the world her business or leaving her diary on the table for all to see. For now, she was savouring the fact Jimmy cared for her and she for him.

It wasn't until later that afternoon she was able to slip away and read the letter in the privacy of her bedroom.

Trembling, she used a silver letter opener to slit open the envelope, extracting its contents to read.

My dearest Enid,

I've been thinking about you since we last met and I can't get you off my mind – you're on it day and night. Mags says I'm lovesick for you as even she has noticed the dreamy expression on my face. Is it really possible to pine so much for someone? I was doing quite well until I saw you at the house and it was then I realised how much love I have for you.

When you're allowed an afternoon off I'd like to take you out for a walk somewhere. Maybe I could pick you up on the horse and cart and we could go to a tea room? Or Mags has even said she'd make tea and sandwiches for us.

Do let me know, my darling, where and when I might pick you up?

My beating heart awaits your reply.

Your loving suitor,

Jimmy

As she tried to put the letter back in the envelope, something fluttered onto the rug. She stooped to pick it up. It was some sort of dried flower. A rose by the look of it and a red one at that. Jimmy was showing her that he loved her and it filled her heart with a blossoming love for him too.

'Oh, Jimmy,' she whispered. 'If only you were here with me right now...'

She wondered if she'd have enough time this approaching Sunday to meet him. She could tell him to meet her directly after the church service, she supposed. But would any tea shops be open on a Sunday? Maybe not. Perhaps it would suit them better if he picked her up and took her to his home and Mags could make tea and sandwiches there for them. That way she'd get to see her old friends in China.

She slipped the rose in between the pages of the letter, folded it and slipped it back in its envelope and then placed it beneath her pillow. She'd reply tonight when she had more time.

The bedroom door burst open suddenly and Maria came in, looking none too pleased.

'Whatever's the matter?' Enid frowned.

'Oh, I don't know. It's just this wedding business,' she explained as she paced the bedroom floor. 'I feel Hywel doesn't want to marry me. He's being forced and I don't think I want to marry him either.'

Enid didn't know what to think. Society frowned on women who didn't have a father for their child and were unmarried.

'What would you like to do then?' she found herself asking.

Maria slumped down on her bed. 'I want to return home. There *eez* nothing here for me any more. When I was in *España* there was a young man. I loved him and he loved me. I think if our family hadn't come here we would have married.'

'So, how did you come to have relations with Hywel then?' It was a question that needed asking.

'I think I was a bit lonely. I used to walk around the gardens here sometimes, especially in the summer, and Hywel would be tending them. He'd take the time to talk to me and seemed to really care. He reminded me of Carlos back in San Sebastián.'

Enid nodded. 'But if you felt Hywel cared for you back then, why do you feel he no longer cares right now? He is young and maybe he fears being a father and taking on a wife, but it doesn't mean he won't care for you and the baby.'

At least that had given Maria something to think about. Enid had once glimpsed some of the gardeners who took their meals in the kitchen – always at a different time to the indoor staff. She'd been introduced to them all and, for some reason, Hywel had stood out in her mind. He was a quiet sort, seeming young for his age. Looking back on it, maybe he'd been so quiet as he had a lot on his mind – like fathering a baby – as no doubt, his parents would be mortified to discover their son had put someone in the "family way".

* * *

Enid couldn't wait for Sunday to arrive. She'd already written to Jimmy confirming she'd had permission to leave the premises on her half-day off. As the housekeeper had already met him and given her approval, he was allowed to collect Enid from the back of the house to take her to his home to have tea with Mags. Mrs Webster had stressed she hoped there would be a "chaperone" around, and Enid assured her there would. Enid could see that the housekeeper might have concerns after what had happened recently to Maria.

So that particular Sunday, Enid climbed on board the horse and cart and Jimmy took the reins as they headed towards Merthyr town.

'Well, look now, who's this smart young lady I see here?' Mags chuckled as Jimmy led Enid inside the house.

Enid giggled. It had only been a matter of weeks since she'd been at the workhouse but it might just as well have been months as she felt she'd really grown up of late, had to really.

'That's very kind of you to say so,' said Enid. 'How have you been coping since Elgan has been away?'

Mags shook her head. 'To be honest, it's been hard but I'm coping with Jimmy's help.' She glanced in his direction.

Enid smiled. 'That's good to hear.'

'Now I've prepared a tea for you both, just some cheese and cucumber sandwiches and I've baked some Welsh cakes for afters. I've put the kettle on to boil for Jimmy to brew a pot of tea...' She walked over to the door and pulled her cape from a hook, draped it with a flourish around her shoulders and then donned her bonnet. As she tied the ribbons beneath her chin, she added, 'I'm just nipping out for a while to see Mrs O'Connell from the market. She's not on her stall today of course with it being a Sunday but I've a little business to discuss with her.'

She nodded slowly and surreptitiously as though it were all hush-hush, then to Enid's surprise she winked at them both. Mrs Webster wouldn't be best pleased at the two of them being left alone in private together.

As Mags clicked the door shut, Jimmy grinned at Enid. 'Well, come on then, take off your jacket and bonnet and take a pew at the table, madam!'

It was so good to be in Jimmy's company once again and they spoke of all manner of things: how Mags was considering going into business, Enid encountering Betsan at the workhouse, Jimmy's funny stories of customers he met on his rounds, Enid's tales from the big house. And on it went. But there was something missing from all those accounts – how she feared being alone in the presence of Anthony Clarkson. His threat to her had been real enough at the time. If she hadn't had the presence of mind to intimate that the housekeeper would come looking for her, he might have tried it on there and then.

'What's the matter?' Jimmy asked, interrupting her thoughts.

She chewed on her bottom lip, deliberating whether to tell him or not. But if she did so then there was a strong possibility he might try to approach the man and she might not only face no more employment at the house, but there was also a probability the Clarkson family might retaliate and put out the word that Jimmy was unemployable or, even worse, the police might get involved. Poor Mags – her Elgan was already in prison and Jimmy was helping to pay the rent. No, she decided, she must keep the information from him at all costs. She must deal with this situation alone.

'There's nothing the matter,' she said, shaking her head. 'I'm just a little distracted, that's all, thinking of what I need to do tomorrow.'

Jimmy took her hand in his and gave it a gentle squeeze of reassurance. 'You're such a worrier, Enid. Now try and relax. It's your afternoon off from work – enjoy it.'

She nodded, realising he was right, of course.

**

The rest of the week at the house passed by without incident. The only times Enid encountered Anthony was in the presence of others and, even then, he didn't look her way. It was almost as if she were an invisible entity to him. She began to relax, feeling that night of his approach must have been because he'd been fired up from the drink.

It was a Saturday evening and dusk was beginning to fall. She thought she'd take a little walk in the grounds before setting off for bed. Collecting her shawl from the back of a chair, she whispered to Maria, who was already resting, 'I'm just going for a little walk. Would you like it if I brought you a cup of cocoa from the kitchen on my way back?'

Maria smiled and nodded gratefully at her. '*Sí*. Thank you.'

'I'll ask Cook if she's got any currant buns left over from earlier this afternoon,' she said with a giggle. Then wiggling the fingers of her right hand into a wave, she closed the door and headed for the garden.

All seemed quiet in the house. There were no sounds of chatter from the servants nor any sounds from the family members. It was eerily still. All that could be heard was the ticking of the walnut-encased grandfather clock in the hallway and the click-clacking of the tips of her boots on the marble flooring as she headed across the main entranceway towards the back door.

After walking down the dimly lit corridor, she approached the half-paned glass door and, for a moment, wondered if she had come all the way for nothing as Mr Dunbar might have already locked it for the night. But as her hand turned the brass knob, it opened easily. Still, she'd better not take too long just in case she got herself locked out. Quietly she closed the door behind herself.

In the distance, she noticed a couple of gardeners were just finishing off their work for the day, loading some trimmed shrubbery into their wheelbarrows. So with confidence and head held high, Enid descended the back steps and headed towards the vegetable garden, which was surrounded by a high stone wall. She'd been shown around there once. There was even a wooden bench inside and some small colourful flower beds. She'd sat there with Phillip and watched the glorious flutterings of several species of butterfly. That had been so relaxing and good for her soul. In the workhouse, they had daily yard exercise but there wasn't much to be seen there except for four high grey walls – this seemed a world away from all her troubles.

An arched dark wooden door was set into the walled garden. She opened that and glanced around at the garden's beauty. There didn't appear to be anyone around. All was still and tranquil, so she took a seat on the bench, closed her eyes and listened to the early evening sounds of the wind rustling through the branches of the trees. In the distance, a church bell chimed the hour.

The serenity of the garden and being away from the hustle and bustle of the big house soothed her. Then she startled as she heard a banging sound but realised it was only one of the gardeners returning his wheelbarrow to the tin shed and accidentally knocking into it. Noticing her, he smiled and doffed his cap. Sighing to herself, she realised she ought to return to the house.

Leaving the garden, she closed the door behind her and headed off down the other pathway that would take her through a circle of trees and past a small lily pond. She wasn't as familiar with this area of the garden but, through the trees, she could see the lights of the house in the distance.

An owl hooted from a tree branch, causing her to almost jump out of her skin. Realising she needed to calm herself down, she took several deep breaths, but then she heard what sounded like a twig snapping behind her. It made the hairs on the back of her neck bristle.

Quickening her pace, she told herself it was just her imagination at work as it had been that first day on the servants' staircase when the seamstress had followed her to return her bundle of clothing.

Then she felt it, the hand clamping roughly over her mouth, dragging her backwards. She tried to struggle free but was strongly in the grip of something – what, or who, she didn't know. But as she inhaled through her nose there was no denying the odour of pomade lingering in the night air. There were only two men at the house who appeared to slick their hair down with that – Phillip the footman and—

'Don't move a muscle or you're dead meat! I told you that you've got something I want to take from you and by heck I'm going to take it right now...' Anthony Clarkson's breaths were heavy, almost as though he were panting with lust for her. 'Do you understand me?' He growled as he held her so tightly, clamped to his own body with her back against his chest, she could barely breathe.

With tears coursing down both cheeks, she nodded. A shot of fear flooded through her body as she realised what was about to happen to her.

Oh, Jimmy, I wish you were here right now to save me!

Roughly, he pushed her face down on the ground so that the damp grass engulfed her and she inhaled the soft, mossy earth beneath it. None of that mattered right now. What did matter though was that life would never be the same for her ever again. He was going to rob her of something so precious to her, coveted by men, that once lost could never be regained.

Struggling onto her back and pushing herself backwards against the broken twigs, moss and grassy earth, she trembled violently. As she lifted her head to look up and face him, she saw his frame silhouetted against the silver moon. For the first time her fear choked her and all that seemed to emerge past her lips was a strange, strangulated cry that didn't even sound like her. It sounded like some poor animal yelping – in fear for its life.

One moment he was towering above her, the next he was on top of her, bearing down on her slight form. His face so close she could smell the alcohol on his breath. Maybe he'd even regret this act of degradation when he sobered up.

But for now, he had pinned her arms down above her head with one hand, the weight of his body crushing into hers while the other hand roamed freely beneath the folds of her skirts.

But why wasn't she kicking out and trying to scream? She seemed unable to do anything other than allow herself to be taken by him even though this was the last thing she desired.

Do something! Stop him! were the cries in her head. It was as if her subconscious were trying to inform her body to move, to react, somehow. But her body was refusing commands. Even when he ripped open her blouse causing the buttons to pop and scatter everywhere, and he lowered his head to suckle on her breast, she was numb. This wasn't happening to her, it was all happening to someone else and she was just observing.

The only time she felt anything was when he tore off her drawers with extreme force, murmuring and groaning as he spread her legs and entered her. It cut like a knife, a dagger driving home with each thrust as the pain ricocheted from one end of her body to the other.

He was building up into a frenzy, rhythmically moving back and forth, moaning, gasping, groaning. It seemed to go on and on and her only thought was: *This is happening to someone else...*

Finally, he sought his release as his body spasmed and he cried out, a low, guttural sound, almost animalistic, that sent some bird or another flapping its wings and flying from the branches above them; maybe it was the owl.

Then the next thing she knew, he was pulling away from her and lying beside her on the damp grass, panting, pleased with himself.

'You're no longer untouched and untamed...' he muttered as though he had done her a huge favour. 'Next time you have to learn to move around a little, buck your hips. It was a little like doing it with a bloody corpse!' He pulled himself up onto his feet, rearranged his clothing, and brushed himself down with the flat of his hand. Then, looking down on her, he added, 'You know your way back to the house.' Then he was riffling in his trouser pockets. He tossed some coins in her direction, making her feel like a cheap whore. 'I might have torn your drawers. Buy a couple of new pairs for yourself, Edith!'

She closed her eyes and blinked away the tears. He was more concerned with ruining her underwear than ruining her. It said a lot about him. The man who had taken her virginity so violently and in a cold-blooded manner didn't even know her name.

As she watched him walk away with a swagger, her thoughts turned to Jimmy and she wept bitter tears. Jimmy wouldn't want her now after this. He'd think she had loose morals and hadn't waited for him. No man would want her any more. What was she supposed to do now?

7

Time seemed suspended as Enid tried to process what had just occurred. About a quarter of an hour ago she'd felt at peace sitting in the vegetable garden with her eyes shut, enjoying the serenity of the moment. Now she was shattered into a million little pieces and she didn't know how on earth she was going to put herself back together again. She scrambled around in the dark to see if she could locate her underwear but she couldn't find her drawers anywhere, only her shawl. A voice inside of her seemed to be warning her to get back to the house. Unsteadily, she pulled herself up onto her feet, her legs feeling boneless as she staggered back to the house. Glancing down at her exposed breasts, she tied her shawl tightly around her. Nearly all the buttons had popped on her blouse when Clarkson had savagely ripped it open.

Huge sobs engulfed her, almost choking her, and she hoped upon hope that Mr Dunbar had not locked the back door before she got to it. She would hate to draw any attention to herself by knocking on it to summon help. She hurried along, bunching her skirts at her sides so they wouldn't get in the way to trip her up. Tears blinded her vision so she blinked them away. The house was getting nearer and nearer, until finally she found herself standing outside the back door. She twisted the knob and, to her utter relief, the door swung open, almost welcoming her inside.

She stood for a moment behind the closed door with her back pressed against it and took several deep, steadying breaths. She could have stayed there for longer to compose herself but didn't want to risk being spotted by any passing servants. So, she headed down the corridor in the direction of the kitchen, arriving just as Cook was emerging from it – no doubt about to return to her room for a well-earned rest.

Cook's hands flew to her face when she saw the state of Enid.

'My goodness me! You didn't half give me a scare there!' As Cook studied her she must have noticed something was wrong. 'What is it, *cariad*? Has something happened to you?'

Slowly, and unable to utter a single word, Enid nodded. She tried to speak but no sound was forthcoming.

'Now, don't strain yourself. I can see something's up. I'm just taking a break in my room, come along with me,' she said kindly. 'Hang on a mo, I'll ask Doris to send up a pot of tea for two.'

Enid nodded gratefully and then Cook left her side for a brief moment to give Doris her order. Enid was trembling violently and Cook was soon back at her side and taking her arm, escorting her down the corridor and up the backstairs to her room. When they got inside, she turned on the wall-mounted gas mantle over the fireplace to study Enid's appearance.

'You seem to be covered in small scratches and bruises.' She sniffed as gently she touched Enid's cheek.

Being covered in scratches and bruises seemed to be the least of Enid's problems. She just nodded and forced a smile.

'Now, I know you're badly traumatised by whatever happened to you and you're unable to speak for the time being,' said Cook, guiding her over to the neatly made bed and encouraging her to sit. 'So, just answer either yes or no by nodding or shaking your head, Enid love.'

Enid took a moment to compose herself before responding to the question.

'Has someone purposely hurt you?'

Enid nodded.

'Is it someone we both know?'

Slowly she inclined her head.

'Was it a member of the staff here from the house?'

Enid shook her head vigorously.

'Hmmm...' said Cook, rubbing her chin in contemplation. 'So, we've established it's not a member of staff, so I'm presuming it's a stranger?'

Enid shook her head.

Cook narrowed her gaze. 'You're not telling me it was a member of the Clarkson family who hurt you?'

Enid choked back a sob as she bit her lip and inclined her head.

'Oh, *Mam bach!*' Cook covered her mouth with the palm of her hand at the shock of the revelation. It was some time until she composed herself to say, 'Then I'm assuming it was Anthony Clarkson who hurt you?'

Enid nodded and tried to speak but failed again. And then, to her horror, she began to weep, producing huge, tremorous sobs that took over her entire being. Wave after wave that caused her body to shake violently.

Cook sat on the bed beside her and held her close, rocking her back and forth. 'There, there, good girl. You've done nothing to deserve this, whatsoever.' Then holding her at arm's length to peer into her eyes, she added, 'So then I'm assuming he's been improper with you in a sexual sense?'

Enid nodded and sniffed loudly. Cook rummaged in her pinafore pocket and handed her a clean handkerchief.

'Did he go as far as taking a married man's privileges from you?' At first Enid didn't understand what Cook was implying but then she said in a softened tone, 'Did he force himself on you, my sweet?' There were tears in Cook's eyes now as she uttered the words, almost as if by voicing them it was making things real for them both.

Enid studied the patterns on the rug beneath her feet. Watching the swirling, colourful shapes that it made. Then, taking a shuddering breath, she glanced up at Cook and nodded slowly. There, she'd indicated now what had occurred and she knew in her heart things would never be the same again.

* * *

After sipping a cup of sweetened tea at Cook's request, Enid was finally able to tell the woman what had happened to her.

Cook sat there, shaking her head in horror. 'It beggars belief he could do such a thing. I mean it's well known here amongst the staff at the house that Mr Anthony tries it on with the maids from time to time but no one has ever spoken of him violating them. Though there was one time last year...' Cook placed her index finger on her chin as she glanced up at the ceiling as though deep in thought. 'A new maid at the house left here almost as soon as she'd arrived. She'd hardly had time to settle into the position. She arrived on the Sunday teatime like yourself and had left here by the Friday morning. Now I had suspicions myself that Mr Anthony might have got a bit fruity with her, but that couldn't be proven. I kept my thoughts to myself about that.'

Enid nodded. Maybe Anthony Clarkson had tried it on with that particular maid but she hoped and prayed the young girl had left because she realised what might have occurred if she were to remain in service at the house. Why oh why hadn't she done the same thing? Her instincts had warned her. Instead, she'd been more interested in creating a good impression on the family than in protecting herself.

'Now, I tell you what we ought to do is go to see Mrs Webster about the situation. I'm sure she will want to inform Mr and Mrs Clarkson.'

'P... please, not like this,' pleaded Enid croakily, finally finding her voice. 'I feel so soiled.'

'That's to be expected,' said Cook. 'I'm glad you're finally able to speak to me. I'll get Alice to fill a bath for you in the servants' bathroom. There'll be no one in there this time of the night and it's far enough down the corridor for no one to even hear you in there. She'll give you soap and fresh towels and I'll loan you one of my spare nightdresses to wear to go back to your bedroom. Then in the morning, when I'm taking a break during the servants' breakfast, we'll go together to see Mrs Webster. Oh, and after you've had your bath tonight, I'll apply a little soothing ointment to those cuts and bruises. All right?'

Enid nodded gratefully, still feeling as though this were all some sort of dream. Soon, she'd wake up in her own bed and the nightmare would be over.

* * *

When Enid returned to her bedroom after taking a bath – no matter how much she scrubbed, she just didn't feel clean – she got into bed and drew the bed covers up over her head. The gentle sounds of heavy breathing came from Maria's bed. It was then she remembered she'd promised the girl a cup of cocoa last night. She must have got fed up of waiting for her to return with it.

It seemed to take an age to drift off to sleep and when she finally did, she had nightmares of being pursued through a wooded area by a pack of hounds led by a man on horseback who wore a top hat and hunting gear. When the man drew near and she was able to make out his face, it was Anthony Clarkson she saw there grinning and looking down, mocking her.

'No! No!' she shouted, causing Maria to startle and sit up in her bed.

'What's the matter, Enid? Are you having a bad dream?'

Enid awoke abruptly and sat up, her heart racing. The room was dimly lit but daylight was about to break. It would be time to rise soon, within the hour.

She deliberated on whether she ought to tell Maria what had happened last night. She didn't want to keep any secrets from her so she told her as best she could. This time she didn't break down in tears as she had in Cook's presence but she was aware that her voice had a catch to it.

'Oh, that's dreadful!' said Maria sympathetically. 'I never like that man; *eez* horrible. I try to, how you say?'

'Avoid him?' Enid offered.

'Avoid, yes. He scares me so.' Maria's eyes grew large. 'But what will you do now?'

'Cook has said she will accompany me later this morning to see Mrs Webster about it.'

Maria nodded. 'But how will you be able to attend to your work here first thing after what happened to you? It is something dreadful that has occurred. You should tell Mrs Webster straight away.'

'But Cook is too busy with the breakfasts right now. She said we'll go together when all the staff are busy eating theirs. Mrs Webster should be alone in her office then taking her own break.'

Maria nodded. 'I tell you what, when I go downstairs I will tell Mrs

Webster you're not well enough to work as you have an upset stomach, shall I?'

Enid smiled. It seemed the best solution all around. 'Thank you, Maria. You are a good friend to me.'

'Well, you did something like that for me the other day.'

After Maria had washed and dressed, she set out for Mass at the church and would return within the hour to begin work with the others. Her morning sickness appeared to have subsided, much to the girl's relief. Enid got herself washed and dressed and then lay on her bed in case anyone came to check. It seemed an age until Cook appeared at the door, knocking lightly on it before stepping inside.

'It's only me. Are you ready, Enid love?'

'Yes. I'm as ready as I'll ever be,' she said, before rising to her feet. She left the room with some trepidation as she realised a can of worms was about to be opened.

* * *

Mrs Webster looked Enid up and down over her spectacles. She was seated in her office behind a dark wood desk while Enid and Cook, standing before her, related the whole sorry tale of what had gone on the previous evening.

'So, you mean to tell me Mr Anthony was improper with you, Enid?' She arched a surprised eyebrow.

'Excuse me, Mrs Webster,' Cook intervened, 'but it's far more than him having been improper towards Enid. He attacked and violated her!' Cook pursed her lips, totally disgusted by what had occurred.

'So, he was physical with you, Miss Hardcastle?' the housekeeper asked, and Enid nodded.

'Not just physical – that can mean absolutely anything!' Cook spat out the words angrily. 'Rape! Mrs Webster! It was rape! He had carnal knowledge of the girl without her consent!'

Mrs Webster's eyes clouded over and she shook her head as she stared at the ledger in front of her for a few seconds as though it somehow held the solution. Then she stood, pressing her knuckles firmly into the desk so that they turned white. Fixing her gaze on Enid, she said, 'Now are you sure you didn't lead Mr Anthony on in any way? I have to establish the facts before I speak to the master and the mistress.'

'No, ma'am,' said Enid.

'For heaven's sake, woman!' Cook's eyes were on fire now. 'I saw the state Enid returned here in last night. She was unable to utter a single word at first. And look at the scratches and bruises on her face and arms! Her underwear was torn off her and is still missing. If you don't address this, I'm going to consult the constabulary, even if it means losing my position here! That's how strong I feel about it. A wrong has been committed and just because that son of theirs comes from what people would say is good stock that doesn't mean he ought to get away with it. He can't be protected just because they have more money than the rest of us!'

The housekeeper exhaled loudly. 'You've made your point, Mrs Shrimpton, and I do believe you. Both of you. I shall go and speak to the mistress. Meanwhile, Enid, have you had your breakfast yet?'

Enid shook her head. 'No, Mrs Webster. I don't have the appetite for it.'

'Well, at least go along with Cook and have a cup of tea and try a piece of toast to settle your stomach. Maria told me you weren't feeling up to it this morning and I can see why now.'

For the first time, Cook smiled at the woman, realising she was on their side about the matter. Then she draped a comforting arm around Enid and led her away.

What would happen next was anyone's guess.

***

Enid got through the best part of the day by keeping away from the rest of the household staff apart from Cook and Maria. She just had a feeling that if she encountered any of the others, they'd be able to tell by the look on her face that she'd been raped. She knew this was a foolish notion in reality, but she definitely was not the same person as she had been this time yesterday.

At four o'clock precisely, she was summoned to the drawing room where Mrs Webster explained that Mr and Mrs Clarkson would be waiting to speak to her. The housekeeper said the reason it had all taken so long was because the master had been attending to some business in Merthyr town and that he'd only just returned.

Mrs Webster accompanied her to the drawing room.

'How do you feel now, Enid?' she whispered as she touched her lightly on the shoulder as a show of reassurance.

'Frightened, I suppose...'

Mrs Webster nodded and then she knocked on the drawing room door.

'Please enter!' It was the mistress who spoke.

Enid's stomach flipped over as the housekeeper turned the knob and opened one of its double wooden doors.

Through the doorway, Enid could see Mr and Mrs Clarkson seated on the dusky pink velvet sofa with a low table in front of them and what appeared to be a tray with a pot of coffee and a stand of cakes on it.

'I've brought Miss Hardcastle to see you as requested, ma'am.' Mrs Webster inclined her head and Enid thought she'd better do the same. Both of them then walked towards the pair.

Mr Clarkson smiled absently at them as if he had no clue what was going on at all.

Enid's mouth dried up with apprehension.

'Thank you, you are dismissed, Mrs Webster,' the mistress said.

Mrs Webster turned and walked briskly across the room, her keys jangling from the chain around her waist, then she clicked the door shut behind her, leaving Enid with the Clarksons.

'Please do take a seat. Er, Enid, isn't it?' Mr Clarkson said.

Enid did as told, taking the armchair opposite. This didn't feel right, her sitting with the Clarksons as though she were a guest; she usually stood in their presence.

'Coffee?' Mr Clarkson offered while his wife just stared at her, making her shift about uncomfortably in the armchair. It was evident this was an awkward situation for both master and mistress.

'Yes please, sir.' Enid felt foolish as she was afraid to decline his offer for fear of causing offence, though a cup of coffee would moisten her dry mouth.

'Maria, will you do the honours and pour, then please leave the room?' Mrs Clarkson said, glancing over her shoulder.

Enid hadn't even noticed Maria had been stood quietly in the corner of the room. And now she was inches away but would not make any eye contact with her nor the Clarksons. Then she dismissed herself, closing the door.

All was quiet save for the sounds of the flickering flames of the fire in the hearth and the soft ticking of the mantel clock, which just served to increase Enid's trepidation.

Mr Clarkson glanced in her direction. 'Sugar?'

'Yes, please.' Enid sat forward in her seat, feeling most awkward taking coffee with the master and mistress.

Mr Clarkson added a couple of cubes of demerara sugar from a silver pot with a matching pair of tongs and handed her a cup with a spoon in its saucer.

'Thank you, sir.' She nodded as she took it from his outstretched hand.

He did not offer her a fancy from the cake stand though, and for that she was grateful, as she felt it might stick in her throat or she'd embarrass herself eating it in front of them.

She waited until Mr Clarkson took a sip of his coffee before mirroring him and taking a sip of hers, not even stirring her cup for fear of drawing attention to herself. Mrs Clarkson didn't appear to be drinking anything even though her cup was filled.

'Now then,' she said eventually, 'I've been informed by Mrs Webster that during the course of yesterday evening you encountered our son, Anthony, while walking in the grounds here at the house. Is that or is that not correct?'

'Yes, ma'am, it is correct.'

'And sometime later you told both Cook and Mrs Webster that Anthony behaved improperly towards you?'

'Yes, ma'am.'

Mrs Clarkson's words seemed to have an edge to them.

As if her husband realised this was the case, he intervened. 'Enid, I'd like you to think carefully when you next reply, as if you say the wrong thing or purposely tell a falsehood, it could have severe consequences for both our son and yourself. Do you understand me?'

Enid matched his penetrative gaze, feeling she had nothing whatsoever to hide. The sooner she got it all off her chest, the better. Even if the subject matter would cause some embarrassment for her – it needed to be said.

'I understand perfectly well, Mr Clarkson.'

Her nerves were beginning to get the better of her now as, trembling, she lifted her cup to take a sip and when she replaced it, it rattled in its saucer.

It was then Enid noticed what she thought was a little smirk on Mrs Clarkson's face.

'Then,' said Mr Clarkson, 'what exactly did Anthony say or do to you?'

Mrs Clarkson let out a slow, deliberate breath before saying, 'I think it's best you leave the room in case *poor Enid* becomes embarrassed, dear.'

Mr Clarkson nodded, his eyes widening with understanding. 'Oh, I see.' Then he rose to his feet. 'Yes, you're perfectly correct. You can fill me in on any details should I need to know later on.'

Once her husband had departed, Mrs Clarkson's manner changed. An icy chill descended on the room as the woman glared at Enid, making her feel much smaller than she already felt.

'What on earth is this nonsense that my son interfered with you?' The woman spoke sharply as if spitting out lemon pips from her mouth. Her sour expression was one of extreme distaste.

'B... but it's true, every word, Mrs Clarkson. He followed me, you see...' A lump had now formed in Enid's throat, which was making it increasingly difficult for her to speak, and unshed tears blurred her vision.

'Just because he happened to walk in his *own garden* does not mean he followed you, Miss Hardcastle!'

The mistress's eyes were dark and beady with anger now.

'He did, ma'am. Your son, Anthony, followed me and attacked me, throwing me to the ground!' Somehow she'd found her voice from somewhere. 'He ripped off my underwear, which I couldn't find afterwards and then he raped me...'

She swallowed the lump in her throat. It needed to be said.

Mrs Clarkson's nostrils flared. 'I've met your sort before! Little trollops who tease and tempt my son. What sort of *young lady* would go out walking alone at night, anyhow?'

Enid couldn't believe her ears. Mrs Clarkson was having none of it and blaming her for her son's behaviour! It was evident her precious son could do no wrong in her eyes.

'Well...' Mrs Clarkson said finally. 'It's obvious you can no longer remain in service here at this house after making false accusations, so you shall have to return to the workhouse. You are dismissed forthwith! Pack your bags. A coach will be ready to pick you up from the servants' entrance in one hour's time. You are not to speak to any of the servants before you leave here.'

Mrs Clarkson stood and pointed her long, slim index finger in the direction of the door.

It was the final humiliation. Slowly, and unable to comprehend what had just occurred, Enid stood, her legs feeling like jelly. Normally, she'd have curtsied or at least nodded her head at the woman as a mark of respect, but instead, she held her chin up high and said, 'Although you seem to think the best of your precious son, he is not the person you think he is. He threatened to rob me of my virginity last week on the night he returned from that meeting in Cardiff. He was drunk then and I believe he'd been drinking last night too!' Then she turned her back on the woman and walked with as much dignity as she could muster out of the room.

It was only when she got outside in the corridor the tears began to flow.

8

As soon as Enid alighted from the coach at the workhouse gates she was met by Mrs Parry-Jones, the supervisor, who strangely seemed to be expecting her. She quickly ushered her inside.

'We've been informed of what's happened, Enid,' she said curtly.

Enid raised her brows. 'But how?'

'A letter was sent here from Mrs Clarkson about a quarter of an hour ago. That's how I knew to be here to meet you.'

Enid could barely believe that it had all happened as fast as that. So now her version of events would not be listened to?

'Look, come into my office for a moment and then you can tell me what happened before I take you to see Master and Matron Aldridge. They'll have to make a decision about whether you are to remain here or not.'

This was so unfair. What had she done that was so bad for people to treat her as though she were a common criminal? They walked across the yard to the entrance block and turned left at the laundry room, taking the corridor down to the supervisor's office. Mrs Parry-Jones opened the door and offered Enid a seat. Enid placed her parcel of belongings on the floor and sat on a hard-backed chair.

The supervisor did not sit herself, instead preferring to perch against her desk with her arms folded.

'So, what's your version of events, Enid? Because Mrs Clarkson has described you as being a "wanton young woman" who is a mischief-making liar. If true, I have to admit I'm sorely disappointed in you.'

'But it's a lie, miss! I was r... raped by their son – Anthony! Mrs Clarkson won't hear a bad word said against him.'

'All right,' said the supervisor, 'I've not known you to lie before and if you are telling the truth, then I'm very sorry for what has happened to you. Unfortunately, I'm not the one making any decisions here. Now I can speak in your favour to the master and matron about your previous good character and conduct, but in all honesty, that's all I can do. It sounds as though they are ready to transfer you elsewhere, Enid. My hands are tied. You do understand that, don't you?'

Enid inclined her head and stared at the parquet floor. She supposed she did understand, as Mrs Parry-Jones had her own position to think about. She thought at least if she returned here, she'd have her family and her friend Betsan for support, but now it seemed they wanted for her not only to be banished from their home but from the Merthyr workhouse too.

Yet, what had she done that was so wrong? Nothing whatsoever. Her only crimes were that she was female and had been in the wrong place at the wrong time.

* * *

Mr and Mrs Aldridge took a very dim view of it all, refusing to take Enid's account of events on board, insisting the Clarkson family were of good character – after all, they donated well to the workhouse and employed inmates at their home from time to time. Indeed, their benevolence held no bounds.

The master paced the floor with his hands behind his back. The mirror above the fireplace was directly behind him, so that every now and again Enid caught sight of the bald patch at the back of his head in the reflection. Funny, she'd never noticed it before.

Matron didn't say much. She just sat upright in the wing-backed armchair and agreed with every comment her husband made.

'And so,' said Master Aldridge finally as he wiped some imaginary flecks of dust from the sleeves of his long jacket as though contaminated by Enid's presence, 'I think it is in the best interests of this institution and the Clarkson family, who have many useful ties here, that you be transferred to the Cardiff workhouse first thing in the morning, Miss Hardcastle.'

'But… but will I be able to say goodbye to my parents first and my friend Betsan, too? She's in the girls' dorm.'

'I shall arrange with Mrs Parry-Jones that you see both of your parents before leaving here. But you shall not return to the girls' dorm. You'll be kept in a private room where you shall receive your meals. Then first light you'll be dispatched to Cardiff…'

Enid gulped. 'But it's not fair. I haven't done anything wrong!'

Mrs Aldridge looked at her and she could tell by the expression on the woman's face she was convinced of Enid's innocence. Had it happened before then? To that maid Cook told her she had her suspicions about?

She supposed it didn't matter. The Aldridges knew where their bread was buttered – by the Clarkson family who had them in their pockets! Maybe the family was paying for their silence with a sizeable donation to the workhouse. They didn't want to make waves. It all made sense now.

Enid sighed. What she did know was that she was paying for a crime she hadn't committed. It was so unjust.

* * *

Jimmy was wondering why he hadn't received a reply to his last letter from Enid. He was hoping they'd be able to meet up again soon. He had thought she'd enjoyed the Sunday afternoon they'd spent together and she'd seemed to be settling in nicely at the Clarkson house. It was hard work but she got on well with the staff there, particularly Cook and the Spanish girl she'd initially had trouble with, called Maria.

'What's the matter with you, lad?' Mags broke into his thoughts. She was seated at the treadle sewing machine in the corner of the living room, running up petticoats for Mrs O'Connell's market stall. She'd put the proposition to her that afternoon she'd left Jimmy and Enid alone. And very nicely she'd been doing and all. They needed every penny now that Elgan was in prison.

Jimmy was supposed to have been brewing up a pot of tea for them both but his mind had wandered.

'Sorry, what was that you said, Mags?' He turned to face her.

'You just proved my point there, Jimmy. You're moping around the place and your mind is elsewhere lately! I've been waiting for my mid-morning cuppa for ages. It's not like you to be off the mark...' She turned away from the sewing machine to gaze at him.

Jimmy let out a long sigh. 'It's Enid. She hasn't been in touch since we last met. I've posted two letters to her since but got no reply.'

'Maybe they hold back letters to the staff at that posh house?'

Jimmy shrugged. 'I don't think it's that. She told me staff are allowed postal mail. In fact, it seems encouraged to keep their spirits up.'

'Ever thought she might have returned to the workhouse?' Mags sniffed loudly.

He honestly hadn't even considered that. 'I suppose she might have if they didn't want to keep her on.'

'But I thought you said they seemed pleased with her work?' Mags frowned.

Jimmy nodded. 'Yes, by all accounts they were. It doesn't make sense.' He scratched his head.

'Well, the only way you'll find out is either to call at one of the houses – the Clarkson house or the workhouse. Betsan and her father are still interned at the spike. They should be home soon; maybe she'll know something of what's gone on.'

'No,' said Jimmy firmly, 'I'll take the horse and cart up to the Clarkson residence and ask if they need any more shoe repairs done. The housekeeper seemed happy with my handiwork. I'll see if I can either have a word with her on the quiet or maybe with Cook. Perhaps I'll be allowed to speak to Enid even, like I was the last time.'

He reached for his jacket from the peg on the door.

'Hey! What about my cup of tea?' Mags yelled, but Jimmy was headed out the door, all thoughts of brewing up disappearing into the ether.

* * *

Jimmy pulled up the cart at the back door of the big house. There'd been no bother this time gaining access to the property as the lodgekeeper now knew him and was friendly towards him. Maybe Jimmy had even repaired his boots with that last order for shoe repairs.

He settled the horse, tethering it to a wooden post. 'There you go, boy. I won't keep you too long.' Then he knocked softly on the back door leading to the kitchen.

There was no reply but from inside he could hear the sound of voices, the clattering of pots and pans and movement. It was around half past eleven so he guessed they were in full swing, busy preparing luncheon for the family, so he rapped louder.

A young girl in a mob cap and pinafore, appearing to be around eleven or twelve years of age, came to attend to him. The smattering of freckles over her nose and cheeks made her look quite cute and cheeky, Jimmy thought.

'Hello,' he said, politely removing his flat cap and stuffing it in his jacket pocket. 'Is Cook around? I'm Jimmy Corcoran who repairs shoes for the family.'

The young girl beamed at him, leaving the door ajar as she shouted excitedly, 'Cook! Cook! It's that cobbler's apprentice you told us about!'

Jimmy grinned. It sounded as though he'd made quite an impression.

Mrs Shrimpton appeared in the doorway, her face flushed and her mob cap slightly askew on her head.

'Hello, young Jimmy, what can I do for you?' The woman smiled.

'Good morning, Mrs Shrimpton. I've come to see if I might have a word with Enid?'

Cook's eyes seemed to cloud over and the previous smile on her face had all but vanished. Something was up. He felt his heart slump.

'What's wrong?' he asked in barely a whisper.

'I'm sorry, lad,' said Cook shaking her head, 'Enid doesn't work here any more.'

He blinked. 'What happened?'

Cook glanced over her shoulder at the kitchen as if she feared being overheard. 'If I had more time I'd invite you in, Jimmy, but we're in the thick of it here at the moment. All I can tell you is Enid was dismissed from here the Sunday before last...'

Jimmy frowned. 'Dismissed?' This just wasn't making any sense to him. 'But what did she do that was so wrong? I can't imagine she'd steal or anything like that. She's as honest as the day is long.'

Cook pursed her lips. 'Between you and I, she did nothing wrong. Nothing whatsoever. There was, how shall I put this? A misunderstanding on the mistress's part. Now I can say no more as I might lose my job for speaking about it. Do you understand me?'

Jimmy nodded, mouth agape. 'So was she sent back to the workhouse?'

'As far as I know, yes. I've heard no word since.' She lowered her voice, as if being cautious about speaking to him. 'Sorry I haven't any better news for you, Jimmy. You're always welcome to call into the kitchen for a cup of tea if you're picking up or delivering shoes. Best call when it's quieter though. Ten o'clock in the morning or around two or three in the afternoon.'

Jimmy nodded. He'd arrived at the worst time for Cook and he appreciated she'd taken the time to speak to him at all, even briefly. 'Thanks for explaining things to me, Mrs Shrimpton.'

She nodded and he pulled his flat cap from his jacket pocket, replacing it on his head.

It was a full five days until Jimmy discovered Enid had been sent to the Cardiff workhouse.

But why? he wondered. Why hadn't they allowed her to stay at the Merthyr one?

'Betsan said something happened that made the matron and master send Enid to Cardiff,' Mags said, after passing on the news to Jimmy. 'It seems to be something to do with an altercation between her and one of the Clarkson family. She never got to see poor Enid as she was sent off early the following morning – never even got to say goodbye to the girl. I'm so sorry, Jimmy.' Mags shook her head in disbelief.

Jimmy rubbed his chin, wondering what on earth might have occurred to warrant Enid being sent away like that.

* * *

Enid had settled into the Cardiff workhouse regime, which was the same as the Merthyr one. Somehow the familiarity of it felt good to her, providing some level of security after what had gone on. The food though was a little better than at the last place and she wondered if that was down to the cook. Even the sloppy grey gruel tasted better here.

To her relief, she'd been welcomed into the dorm by an Irish girl of around the same age as herself: Connie O'Mara. Connie, along with others, had travelled over by ship from Cork to Cardiff.

Unfortunately, plans had been made by the authorities to ship all the men back home again. Some of the men had absconded from the workhouse as a result. They obviously had no intention of returning to their native homeland, which left their wives and children in dire straits. Who would provide for them now?

Some were from huge Catholic families, and there always seemed to be trouble brewing from the warring families who disliked one another. It wasn't unknown to find two or three women scrapping in the corridor, yelling insults and obscenities, tearing at one another's hair until sections came out from their roots. The women at the workhouse seemed louder and more aggressive than the men.

Connie, though, was not like that at all – she was a gentle soul who sought peaceful means to resolve any conflict that came hurtling her way. Enid was lucky that she took her under her wing.

'So whatcha be doing here, anyways, Enid?' she asked one afternoon. They were both seated on a wooden bench in the outside compound. The inmates had been handed an apple each courtesy of a kind local benefactor who owned a greengrocery business. It was a rare treat indeed.

'I suppose it's a bit complicated...' Enid paused for a moment as her stomach lurched at the thought of what had happened at the Clarksons'.

Taking a bite of the juicy green apple, she closed her eyes, savouring its sweet taste. She hadn't eaten an apple in ever such a long time. She hoped Connie would stop asking questions and leave her to her apple but the girl persisted.

'I've got time to listen,' she said softly, her beautiful violet eyes glinting. The sun was high in the sky behind her and seemed to illuminate her chestnut-brown hair, giving it an ethereal glow, making her appear almost angelic.

Enid took a shuddering breath. 'I was raped,' she said bluntly.

Connie's mouth popped open in shock. 'At the Merthyr spike?' Her eyes were wide now.

Enid shook her head. 'No, it was while I was sent into service at a big house in the town. The master's son did it.'

Connie laid a reassuring hand on Enid's shoulder as she began to sob. Life had changed for her since that evening. It wasn't just that she was no longer a virgin, it was the terrifying recurring dream that often disturbed her during the night: a man on horseback who was tracking her down with a pack of hounds. Not a night went by when her sleep wasn't interrupted by the memory of her attack and the beast who had done that to her.

Connie spoke gently. 'That must have been horrible for you. Are you scared in case there's a baby on the way now?'

Enid nodded and sniffed to stem the tears. 'Yes, I've not had my monthly yet so I don't know if I'm pregnant or not.'

'I see. What I don't understand though is why you were sent here. You've got no family in Cardiff, have you?'

Enid shook her head. 'No, I don't know anyone living here at all – not a soul. I have my suspicions that I was sent here as Master and Matron Aldridge wanted to keep Mr and Mrs Clarkson on side as they donate an awful lot to the workhouse. I wouldn't be surprised if Mr Clarkson is one of the guardians.'

'Doesn't seem right though, does it? We have a saying back in Ireland: *"You'll never plough a field by turning it over in your mind."'*

'Eh? What on earth does that mean?' Enid wrinkled her nose.

'What it means, and 'twill make sense when you consider it, is that just thinking about things won't get you anywhere. You have *to do* something!'

'But what?'

'Well, if it were me, I'd have a word with Master and Matron Finchley here. They're fair-minded sorts. Maybe they'd write a letter to the master and matron in Merthyr, or the Clarksons even? That family owe you something for the pain and distress caused, and if it turns out you're now pregnant by that son of theirs, 'twill be even more they owe you! They'll owe for the baby's upkeep as well as to keep any scandal at bay!'

Enid nodded slowly as she digested all that Connie had said. She hadn't looked at it in that light before.

'You're absolutely right!' she said, swallowing and then taking another bite from the apple as she thought things through. No point in just fretting about it at all.

Connie's words resonated with her: *"You'll never plough a field by turning it over in your mind!"*

* * *

The following day, Enid found herself being interviewed by Matron who shook her head and frowned as she listened to Enid's account as though she were sympathetic to the position Enid now found herself in.

'The way I see it is this,' said Matron finally, taking a peppermint cream from a pink candy-striped paper bag on the desk and offering one to Enid, who gratefully accepted and popped one into her mouth. 'There has been some sort of great injustice here, grant you, but I don't think we'd get very far contacting the master or matron at Merthyr. A rum pair they are by all accounts. I've had dealings with those two before now. They're as slippery as a pair of eels!' She pursed her lips. 'It might be best that I don't get overly involved in this as it doesn't directly concern me nor my husband. I'm only hearing your tale second-hand...'

Enid's spirits began to plummet but then Matron's tone lifted as she continued.

'However, I don't see why you shouldn't write to that Mr Clarkson yourself. You said he was easier to talk to than his wife?'

'I don't mind doing that, Matron,' Enid said, nodding, 'but I wouldn't quite know how to put things to him. Mind you, he never heard the full story at the time, as Mrs Clarkson sent him out of the room and I gave her the details.'

'You can write a letter though, can't you?'

'Oh yes. I used to write to my friend, Jimmy, while I was at the house...'

She failed to inform Matron that Jimmy had been much more to her than a friend; he'd been her sweetheart too.

'Then what is it that scares you so? For that's what it is: fear!'

'That I wouldn't be able to put myself across in the way I wanted to, as it's a delicate matter.'

'I'm quite sure Miss Goodman, the schoolteacher here, might help you apply yourself.'

Enid's face grew hot. 'Oh, I wouldn't be comfortable with Miss Goodman knowing about my circumstance…' She bit her bottom lip.

'I see. Well, I shall endeavour to help you then. If you write the letter in the first instance and I think it needs a little tweaking or amending here and there, you can rewrite it, but it will be mainly in your own words. Please don't concern yourself with worries about sending the letter to the man. You have nothing to lose as the worst has already happened to you.'

Enid smiled ruefully as she realised full well that maybe the worst hadn't occurred for her as yet.

At the moment, she didn't know whether she was pregnant or not.

* * *

Enid studied the letter she'd written to Mr Clarkson. It was the hardest thing she'd ever had to write in her life. She'd spent ages poring over it, changing words and rewriting sentences. Then she'd had to copy it all out neatly, but it needed to be just so. Her intention was not to sound sorry for herself or like a victim but to spell out the hard, cold facts that the man's son had raped her.

It was a full fortnight later before there was word from Mr Clarkson. His letter was difficult to decipher as the tone suggested he would very much like to arrange a meeting with her to discuss the situation. He wanted to know whether it was agreeable or not to her. That she hadn't been expecting at all, and her stomach flipped over at the thought of it. She'd imagined he'd either be angry with her for daring to contact him or perhaps he'd try to buy her silence. But meet with the man?

Matron thought it a good idea as long as it was a supervised encounter where she was present throughout. What a difference between Mrs

Finchley and Mrs Aldridge. They were like chalk and cheese! It was obvious the former had Enid's best interests at heart and the latter thought only of her own self-interests.

So, Enid found herself agreeing to the meeting, which would take place the following Monday morning before Mr Clarkson had business to attend to in Cardiff that same afternoon. Enid did wonder if the man was tying in his visit with her on the same day so his wife or son did not know about it. Or, in the worst case, maybe they knew all and had some input in what he was to say to her.

* * *

Enid's eyes scanned the exercise yard to find Connie and tell her the news about Mr Clarkson's impending visit.

She found the girl sitting alone on a wooden bench while the rest of the girls from the dorm were standing around chatting in various groups. It concerned her greatly that when she wasn't around, Connie was a loner. What was it about her that stopped her mixing with the others? Enid wasn't as friendly with the rest of the girls as she was with Connie but she did make an effort to speak to them and they seemed to like her. Whereas, if Enid wasn't around, no one approached Connie except for an Irish girl called Bridie who she'd been surprised to see whispering something to her in the dorm one time. Enid formed the impression Bridie was being secretive and acting in a surreptitious manner, which she didn't much care for. When she'd asked Connie about the girl, she'd just shrugged absently, making out that it was something and nothing though she was vague and never explained really what the girl had said to her. But Enid had a feeling Bridie was bad news. She came over as being quite a precocious sort and she'd once noticed her trying to sidle up to one of the men in the dining hall. What was her game?

'Are you all right, Connie?' Enid said as she sat beside her.

Connie lifted her head and turned it in Enid's direction. 'Yes, of course I am.'

'Why aren't you chatting with the other girls?'

'I'm not in the mood today. I just wanted some peace on my own. Time to think.'

Enid nodded. She well understood that. 'Do you mind me talking to you, then?'

Connie smiled. 'Of course not. I always have time for you, Enid. You're my best friend in here.'

It warmed Enid's heart to hear Connie say that.

'I've got a bit of news,' she said finally.

'Oh yes?'

'Remember what you said? That I have to do something about my situation?'

'Huh?' Connie furrowed her brow.

'That Irish saying you mentioned about ploughing the field? I took some action. Mr Clarkson is coming to the workhouse to see me soon – he replied to my letter!'

'Really?' Connie's eyes enlarged and she seemed to come alive. 'To be sure, it's what you deserve. That family owe you so much after all you've been through.'

Enid guessed they did but somehow she doubted things would turn out well for her. What if there was a hidden agenda behind this?

* * *

All that weekend, Enid struggled to finish her meals, her appetite being poor. Usually, she ate well, consuming anything laid before her. She wasn't at all fussy but this was something else – it was because she dreaded Monday morning as it fast approached. Not only that but her monthly still hadn't arrived. It was usually like clockwork and the fact it was delayed troubled her.

When the morning arrived, Enid took special care to ensure her appearance was as neat and tidy as possible. She'd bathed and washed her hair, trimmed her fingernails and donned a clean uniform, pinafore and well-starched cap for the occasion. Thankfully, when she'd arrived at the Cardiff workhouse, no one had insisted she be deloused again so now her hair was growing nicely. The little she did have, which was now collar-length, was neatly pinned up beneath her cap.

Enid waited with some trepidation with Matron in the office. A reply had been sent to Mr Clarkson, giving him the time and who to ask for on his arrival. But maybe he wouldn't show up?

'Don't fret so much, Enid,' said Matron. 'It's a long way from Merthyr. And there might have been a lot of coaches and carriages on the way in first thing what with people setting off for work and to conduct business. It is Monday morning after all!'

Enid guessed Matron was right. She was sitting on her hands to stop herself fidgeting but even so, it didn't stop her dangling her legs from the high-backed chair. Matron was seated behind her desk with an air of authority, attending to some paperwork, while the armchair nearest the hearth was reserved for Mr Clarkson. Cook had baked a special sponge cake and a young kitchen maid was ready at hand to provide a pot of coffee or tea at a moment's notice for them.

Enid glanced anxiously at the wall clock. Its hands now read ten minutes past ten and Mr Clarkson hadn't arrived as yet. What if he didn't show up at all? What if it was all some sort of a ruse or act to appear as though he were affable and compliant but he said one thing and did another? There were so many "what-ifs" circulating around in her mind.

But just as she was about to give up hope, there was a loud rap on the door and Mr Brownlow, the entrance porter, popped his head around the door.

'Excuse me, Mrs Finchley, I've got a Mr Clarkson here, says he has an appointment to see you.'

Mrs Finchley smiled and nodded but she did not stand to greet her visitor. She gestured with the palm of her hand for Enid to remain seated too.

As Mr Clarkson entered, he removed his top hat and placed it on the table. All the while, Enid's heart beat a military tattoo. But she needn't have concerned herself as he was all smiles and apologies. There was nothing to suggest he had any tricks up his sleeve.

'Do forgive me, Mrs Finchley,' he said, smiling. 'The traffic was heavier than usual this time of the morning. I've just discovered there was some sort of crash on the way into Cardiff. Apparently, a coach veered into the path of another and two horses were injured, by the seem of it. I do hope those poor beasts won't need to be put down...'

And just like that, Mr Clarkson had charmed Mrs Finchley and won the woman over.

Enid, herself, was understandably wary of the man, but by the time he was asked to take a seat and coffee was served, it was evident he hadn't a clue just how serious an allegation was being made regarding his son's behaviour and that of his wife for that matter. He had come to realise that she had duped him to save their son's skin.

It was only then that Enid felt able to release a long, slow breath.

'You have been treated most unfairly. So, how can I make things up to you, Miss Hardcastle?' he asked.

For the first time, Enid realised she had some traction here. Her first and foremost need was to see her parents and siblings again.

'I'd like to visit my family at the Merthyr workhouse as they need to know I'm safe and well here,' she said curtly.

'Consider it done, my dear. As long as it's all right with Matron?' He glanced in Mrs Finchley's direction and the woman nodded and smiled at them both.

'I would consider transferring you back there, Enid,' said Matron, 'but Merthyr is full to bursting at the moment and you have told me conditions are better for you here?'

Enid nodded. It was true enough. Things were better for her here overall and she'd formed a very close friendship with Connie. Matron, too, was easier to confide in than the matron at Merthyr.

When Mr Clarkson departed with a promise he'd return the following week with Matron's permission to take Enid to Merthyr, Matron settled back in her chair, a little smile dancing upon her lips.

'At least the gentleman is attempting to make amends to you, Enid,' she said. 'That's more than many might do in his position.'

She supposed the woman had a point.

* * *

Enid caught up with Connie on their way to the dining hall for their midday meal. Today it was minced meat in gravy with potatoes. The girls didn't mind too much as somehow the cook here managed to make things far tastier than they were at the Merthyr spike. Maybe Cook used herbs and spices to give the food more flavour?

'So how did your meeting with Mr Clarkson go?' Connie asked, as they stood in the queue with their tin plates in hand.

Enid clasped her plate to her chest, her eyes shining. 'Absolutely marvellous, Connie! I shouldn't have been so worried about meeting the man. He's on my side about things, for sure. No wonder his wife sent him out of the room while she had a private word with me!'

Connie wrinkled her nose. 'How'd you mean?'

'Well, she didn't want him to get the full picture of what had gone on with his son, did she? Wanted to warn me off. I think he had no idea she'd sent me back to the workhouse with instructions to transfer me here. Anyhow, the upshot is he wants to rectify things.'

'Get you moved back to Merthyr?' Connie frowned.

'Er, no. Not exactly. He asked me how he could make things up to me so I told him I'd like to visit my family at the Merthyr workhouse. Not only that but he's going to take me there!'

'That's wonderful news. I'm so pleased for you!'

Enid realised the girl meant every word.

'There's no luck with being transferred back to Merthyr at the present time as Matron reckons the workhouse there is full to bursting at the seams.'

Connie shook her head, her expression sad now. 'If you leave here, I don't know how I'll ever cope.'

Her friend's voice sounded so flat that it pulled at Enid's heartstrings. 'But you would manage, I'm sure. You get along with people well enough here, don't you?'

Connie looked at her as she blinked away tears. 'I suppose I'd have to, but that lot I came over with from Cork are so loud and always picking fights. At least with you I feel safe.'

'What about that Bridie one though? She seems to be trying to get in conversation with you a lot lately? I hope my suspicion about her being up to no good is unfounded and she has your best interests at heart.'

Connie's face flushed pink. 'Oh, I've never forgiven her for taking my lad from me on the boat over here. She's trying to make amends 'tis all.'

Enid blinked – this was news to her. 'What happened?'

'He was my sweetheart and we planned to marry someday, but as soon as he saw Bridie Hennessy, something seemed to come over him, as if she'd cast a spell. He was bewitched by her he was. And she did nothing to stop it, even though she knew he was supposed to be mine an' all.'

Her voice now had a catch to it, which concerned Enid. For a moment she thought the girl might cry, so she felt it best to give her something to hope for. 'Well, I'm going to make you a promise here and now, Connie, if I ever leave here I will keep in touch with you. And if I get a job somewhere, I'll even try to get you one there too – wherever I happen to work.'

Connie swallowed and smiled, nodding at her friend. 'That would be grand, sure it would.'

'You never know, either one or both of us might get boarded out somewhere soon.'

They'd both reached the front of the queue so their conversation ceased and they held out their plates as dollops of minced meat in gravy with mashed potatoes were ladled onto them. Enid had hated to hear Connie speak that way and guessed not only was the girl feeling out of things here at the workhouse, but she was also homesick for Ireland.

* * *

The following Monday, Mr Clarkson returned early to escort Enid to Merthyr.

'I've taken the liberty of making an appointment for you to see an outfitter here in Cardiff first,' he said. Then turning towards Matron, he smiled. 'If that's permissible, that is? I'd like to fit Enid out for some new clothing for when she leaves here and begins work elsewhere.'

Enid frowned. Leave here? New outfits?

'Enid, Mr Clarkson and I just had a discussion before you joined us and he says he can get you work at another big house. This time it's in Cardiff,' Matron enthused.

Enid gasped with surprise. 'Work, Mr Clarkson?'

'Yes, my dear. A friend of mine has just purchased a house in this vicinity. In fact, that's why I was able to arrive here early this morning. I stayed there last night. He's seeking reliable, hard-working staff. All he has employed there at the moment is a cook and a housekeeper who are pitching in to do everything. Now, you don't have to accept but it would be a good opportunity for you and your family.'

'My family?' She pressed the palm of her hand to her chest and blinked several times. What did they have to do with it?

He nodded. 'That's right. There's an apartment that goes with it attached to the main house. Now, I could arrange for your father to have employment there as a general caretaker. Maybe arrange work for your mother as well. The apartment would be big enough for the whole family.'

Enid could hardly believe her ears. She found herself taking a seat in the armchair without even asking permission from Matron while her mind absorbed what he'd just told her.

With tears in her eyes, she gazed up at him. 'What have I done to deserve any of that, Mr Clarkson?'

To her surprise, Mr Clarkson knelt beside her and patted her hand. 'My dear, you have been badly wronged by my son. I banished him from our house, much to my wife's chagrin. I no longer want him under my roof. He can make his own way in this world. It's you who is the important one right now. And if you are with child as a result of his actions then I shall make amends there also.'

'I really don't know if I am or not,' she said, which was perfectly true. Her monthly still hadn't arrived though.

'We'll cross that bridge if we come to it,' said Matron brusquely. Then, turning her attention on to Mr Clarkson, she asked, 'So what time do you envisage returning my charge here? And have you informed the Merthyr workhouse of her visit?'

'It will be sometime tomorrow. I've made arrangements for Enid to stay overnight at a local hotel in Merthyr. Then I'll return her to you the following day. As regards the Merthyr workhouse, yes, they're amenable to the visit. I shall accompany Enid and have a word with her parents about those jobs in Cardiff if they want them. I'm sure they won't turn them down as the living quarters are an attractive proposition.'

Enid smiled at the thought of returning to Merthyr once again. She hadn't seen Betsan since the day she left for the position at the Clarkson house when the girl had presented her with the rose brooch for luck. She still had it in her possession, safely pinned to the inside of her dress. She couldn't afford to leave it hanging around in case it got nicked by one of the inmates. There were lots of nifty fingers inside the walls of a workhouse.

9

'This won't take long, miss,' said the female assistant, smiling at her.

Enid was stood perched on a wooden box while the woman hemmed up the skirts of her dress with several silver pins.

Mr Clarkson had insisted on buying Enid a whole new wardrobe of clothing in preparation for her working at the new house, along with some fashionable day dresses with matching jackets and a selection of stylish hats. It all seemed unreal to Enid. She was being treated like a princess. She wondered if his wife was aware of how he was spending their money.

The only garment available to be taken away and worn immediately was a heather-coloured dress and matching short jacket with felt hat. Oh, she did feel grand on Mr Clarkson's arm as he escorted her to his awaiting coach. There was plenty of time to enjoy the view out of the window on the way to Merthyr and to chat about all manner of things. He didn't say where his son had gone to, now he'd been banished from the family home, but she guessed he'd have been paid a pretty penny to leave. Part of her felt a little sorry for him but she realised, with his education and social position, he should soon gain employment somewhere of note.

Once in Merthyr, Mr Clarkson booked her into a hotel on the high street, causing the landlady to raise a curious eyebrow in their direction. It was then Enid realised maybe the woman recognised him and thought he was conducting an affair with her. She'd hardly be his daughter staying at that sort of establishment, would she? Nevertheless, they had coffee and sandwiches in the dining room and took a stroll around the town itself. Their appointment at the workhouse had been arranged for four o'clock sharp and it was only a quarter past three.

Strangely, although she hadn't been away all that long, it felt different. Yes, things seemed familiar to her, like the open-air market and the costermonger barrows and carts clattering up and down the high street. *She* felt different. Her clothing was high quality now and thanks to her benefactor she was moving on to a new life.

'Enid?' Mr Clarkson's voice intruded into her thoughts, bringing her back to reality. 'I think we'll take the coach up to the top of the town. There's a place where you can purchase er... how shall I put it? Lady's garments for your night's stay at the hotel.'

It was a moment before Enid realised what he meant. Of course he was referring to nightgowns and that sort of thing, maybe underwear too. Her cheeks blazed but she tried not to show her embarrassment. 'That sounds a good idea. Thank you, Mr Clarkson.'

* * *

Enid's breath hitched in her throat when she and Mr Clarkson were taken into a private room to meet with her family. Her mother, who was seated with Baby Jonathan on her lap, rose as soon as she saw her. She handed the baby to Enid's sister, and then hugged her daughter, the two of them openly weeping together.

Arthur, though, had a steely look in his eyes as he glared at his daughter's companion. 'What's he doing here? The father of the man who ravaged you?'

How did her father know who Mr Clarkson was? That puzzled her.

'It's all right,' Mr Clarkson said in a calm manner. 'I know you don't think much of me from that last visit I had with you...'

Last visit? That was news to Enid. So Mr Clarkson had gone out of his way to speak to her father? Maybe to apologise for his son's attack?

'But I've had a good idea that might suit everyone. I can't change what's happened and my son has been sent away never to return to my home again, but I do plan to make amends to both your daughter and yourselves.'

'How the blazes can you possibly do that?' Arthur tilted his head to one side and frowned.

'It just so happens that I have a friend living in Cardiff who has taken charge of a big house. He needs staff. Now he's happy to take your daughter on as a housemaid and will provide you with employment too as a caretaker, which means you can also all live free of charge at an adjoining apartment.'

Martha's eyes brightened as she smiled. 'Really?'

Mr Clarkson nodded. 'Yes, really. I daresay there'll be a job there for you if you want it as well, Mrs Hardcastle.'

Before his wife had the chance to say anything, Arthur butted in.

'What's the bloody catch?'

'There is no catch, Mr Hardcastle. I'd just like to make amends for my son's misdemeanour, that's all.'

'You mean like tarting my daughter up with your money? Whoring her out to another house?' Arthur scoffed, his eyes dark and beady-like now, which Enid understood meant one thing: anger.

'I haven't tarted your daughter up, as you put it, Mr Hardcastle. I just thought it would be nice for her to have some new clothing. She looks like a respectable young lady to me.'

'And me and all!' yelled Martha in his defence. 'Don't take any notice of your father's remarks, Enid. He's hurt, that's all.' She reached out to pat her daughter's forearm.

'Don't you all bloody see? She's ruined forever!' shouted Arthur. 'Will be no good for another now that son of yours has had carnal knowledge of her. No decent man will look twice at her. She'd just as well walk the streets to ply her trade now that she's been broken in!'

A stunned silence shrouded the room as if no one knew quite what to say.

Enid's heart began to race and, suddenly, she felt she couldn't get any air into her lungs. Is this what it had come to? Her father thinking she'd be better off working as a common prostitute? She became aware of someone crying, then she realised the sound was emanating from within herself. It was like the night of her rape – she was violated then, physically, but now she felt violated by her father's cruel words.

'I bet you led him on!' he began to shout at her again as he stood and jabbed a finger in her direction. 'A man of his class wouldn't do something like that unless you'd been flirtatious with him. Enjoying his attention a bit too much, were you? And no doubt that Jimmy one has been dipping his bloody wick and all!'

'Arthur!' yelled Enid's mother. 'Not in front of the children, please!'

This didn't sound like the father Enid had known. Losing his job and being in the workhouse seemed to have changed his personality.

'Aye, well, she'd just as well drop her bloody drawers for any man now! She's ruined for life!'

The next thing Enid knew she was in Mr Clarkson's arms, almost unable to stand as he tried to support her small frame.

'Mr Hardcastle, you are being most unfair to your daughter. She behaved impeccably as a maid at my home!' shouted Mr Clarkson as Enid sobbed on his shoulder.

'Daughter?' Arthur scoffed. 'I no longer have a daughter...' Then he turned his back on them all, walked out the door and slammed it behind him.

'I don't know what to say, Mrs Hardcastle...' Mr Clarkson shook his head and patted Enid on the back gently. 'The intention of this visit was to bring the family together not to divide it. I think we'd better leave now. I give you my word that Enid shall have that new job if she wants it and I will look out for her with her future prospects in mind.'

'Oh, Enid love,' said her mother, weeping now. 'I'm so sorry about your father. I'm sure he doesn't know what he's saying.'

Oh, he knows all right, thought Enid as she drew away from Mr Clarkson's embrace, the tears blurring her vision.

* * *

Enid barely remembered the coach journey back to Cardiff the following day, feeling numb and disorientated. She'd slept fitfully at the hotel. If things had gone differently with her father and he'd been pleased with the offer for jobs for the family and a home to live in, then she might well have enjoyed her overnight stay. As it was, her heart was broken by his vicious tongue.

'I'm truly sorry, Enid,' Mr Clarkson said when he dropped her off at the workhouse later that day, regret in his eyes. They were stood outside the big wrought-iron gates of the building. 'I feel this is all my fault for going to see your father that first time without your knowledge. It was obvious he dislikes my family for some reason as well as for what my son did to you. He seems to have taken exception to me.'

Mr Clarkson placed the palms of his hands on her shoulders in a fatherly fashion. 'Please don't allow any of this to deter you though. There's a position waiting for you at Beechwood House. I hope you'll still consider taking it?'

Silently, Enid nodded. For a moment, she considered asking if Mr Clarkson thought that he could get employment at the house for Connie too. The words were on the tip of her tongue but then she stopped herself from asking. This wasn't the right time. She'd see how she got on there herself first and then ask if there was a position for her friend.

Dropping his hands to his sides, he said, 'Now, it'll be a few days until it's all sorted, so meanwhile, after you change back into your workhouse uniform, give your new outfit to Matron for safekeeping. You can wear it when you arrive at the new house to create a good impression. I'll arrange for the ladies' outfitter to send the rest of the clothing I purchased on to the house ahead of your arrival.'

'Thank you, Mr Clarkson,' she said gratefully. And then, quite naturally, she stood on tiptoes to plant a kiss on his bewhiskered cheek. 'Oh, I'm so sorry...' she said quickly, realising she might have crossed a boundary with the man.

'Please don't concern yourself.' He waved a gloved hand of dismissal. 'That display of affection was rather lovely. It's good to be appreciated for a change.'

It was then she wondered who it was who didn't appreciate him – his wife or his daughter? Maybe both of them?

'Now you'd better run along as I've taken up quite enough of your time as it is. I don't want Matron getting cross with me.' He chuckled as he playfully wagged his index finger.

* * *

Jimmy had been to the Merthyr workhouse to see if he might speak to Enid's parents but he wasn't permitted to visit her mother and, to his disappointment, Arthur Hardcastle refused to meet with him. He just couldn't make it out at all. Arthur had always been a fairly affable sort who had greeted him kindly in the past when he'd visited their home. He racked his brain wondering if he'd offended the fellow in some way.

'You don't want to worry your guts out over something like that,' Mags said. 'I've known that happen in the past – folks' personalities changing after they go inside those places. You mustn't forget the man has lost his job and all. My guess is he feels humiliated as he can no longer provide for his family. You're better off forgetting about Enid, I think, lad.'

But he didn't want to forget about Enid. How could he? She meant so much to him.

'Mags, Enid means the world to me. I don't think she'd purposely leave like that without telling me.' He tilted his head to one side, trying to fathom the whole situation. 'I need to know what's happened to her. Don't you see? We were brought up here in China together. In the old days my mam was friendly with hers until...'

'I know, lad...' Mags shook her head sadly. 'Until that tragic event happened to your mother. In the old days this was a real community here. Everyone pulled together. But lately, people seem to be moving on elsewhere. I put it down to unscrupulous landlords like Richards getting too greedy and hiking up rents. If he'd given Arthur a couple of weeks' grace with his rent then the man might have got himself another job and continued renting that property.'

Jimmy frowned. 'I dunno though, Mags. From what Enid told me, her father was always behind with the rent. I expect Richards had given him so many chances and in the end, he'd had enough. The man was living on the bones of his arse!'

'Jimmy! Stop using that sort of language!'

'You're a fine one talking. Well, not so much these days but you used some choice language when you were making visits to that gin house in Georgetown!' He glanced at her and seeing his comment had brought her near to tears, added, 'I'm sorry, I'm just worked up about Enid. Doesn't make any sense whatsoever to me.'

'Me neither but about my drinking… You know I don't do that sort of thing any more, even though I've been tempted a time or two since.'

He nodded. 'I know and it was unfair of me to throw it in your face. The reason you drank in the first place was because you missed your twins, but now you've got them back with you again!'

'That's very true. Life felt empty without those little darlings.'

Jimmy had seen a vast difference in Mags since Betsan had brought Alys and Aled back into her life.

* * *

The day came when Enid had to leave the workhouse for good. Matron had given her a pile of books to take with her on loan and she'd packed them well in brown paper and tied them with string. They'd said their farewells in her office with a promise that Enid would remain in touch and let her know how she was progressing. She had so much to thank the woman for.

Then the time came for her to say goodbye to the girls in her dorm, and finally to Connie who was seated on the bench in the exercise yard. She stood when she saw Enid approaching. Enid's new employer, Mr Darling, had sent his coach to collect her – the books and her luggage were already safely stowed on board.

Enid gazed at her friend for the longest time with a lump in her throat. Then they were in one another's arms, Connie clinging on to her for dear life.

'I'm going to miss you so much!' Connie wailed as her body was overtaken with convulsing sobs.

Enid had never seen the girl quite so emotional. 'Don't worry, I'll write to you and we'll get to meet up. I can visit you here too.'

A soft frown creased Connie's forehead as tears of emotion welled up in her eyes. 'If I stay in here after you've gone, I'll fall apart. I'll never cope here without you.'

'Ssshh! Don't go upsetting yourself. You'll manage.' But deep down, Enid wondered if the girl would; she seemed so forlorn since Enid had mentioned going to work at the house. 'And don't you forget I'm going to try to get you a position working with me as a maid,' she added brightly.

Connie forced a smile. And then out of the corner of her eye, Enid spotted someone she hadn't expected to see: Bridie.

'Now youse don't want to go worrying about Connie!' she said with a glint of mischief in her eyes. 'She'll be having a high old time of it when you've left here.'

Connie shot the girl a withering glance, which made Enid wonder what all that was about, but there was no time to hang around as the coach driver had made his appearance and was taking out his pocket watch from the inside of his coat pocket and checking the time as if to say: *Hurry up now, we need to be on our way!*

Ignoring Bridie, Enid hugged her friend one more time and whispered in her ear, 'Don't you fear, you'll be with me again soon enough. I'll write to you and I'll not let you down!'

Connie nodded, seeming a little more in control now. Enid turned to head towards the coach and when she reached the workhouse gates, she glanced behind to wave to Connie, to see Bridie now had her arm draped around the girl's shoulder, with a smile of satisfaction on her face.

10

Beechwood House wasn't the sort of place Enid had been expecting. She stood on the street gazing up at the cream-coloured house with its huge sash windows and black wrought-iron railings. Although a very smart town house within a street of similar properties, which no doubt also had servants to attend to their owners' needs, this wasn't at all what she'd imagined. It wasn't quite as big as the Clarkson residence but it was impressive nevertheless, built three storeys high with attic rooms on top of those. The kitchen, which was located in the basement, led directly out on to the street above via a set of stone steps.

The Clarkson residence had been peaceful as it was set well away from the road and other houses, but here it was noisy and bustling as a plethora of wheels clattered over the cobbles. There was a lot of traffic both on foot and by carts, coaches and carriages. But the strange thing was at the rear of the house there was a lot of land and at the end of that, a stable for the horses. The back entrance was where deliveries, wagons and carts might draw up, not visiting guests who would enter the dwelling directly from the pavement at the front.

A shiny brass plaque to the right of the black solid front door, which was located by way of a series of steps, read, "Darling Residence, Beechwood House".

Enid had taken a hansom cab to the house and now the driver was unloading the few bags of luggage she had to bring with her, including the pile of books tied up with string loaned by Matron from the workhouse library. The books had such titles as: *A Guide for Housemaids*, *Social Etiquette for Young Ladies* and *Mrs Branston's Book of Practical Household Tips*. Matron Finchley was leaving nothing to chance by the looks of it. She was aware the woman had thought of just about everything and, silently, she thanked her for that.

* * *

Enid stood before the housekeeper, Mrs Sowerberry, who was a tall, spindly woman with her hair severely scraped back and pinned neatly beneath her well-starched white cap. Her dark navy dress fitted her form well. Expecting her to be as severe in personality as her appearance, Enid was in for a surprise as the woman was extremely welcoming towards her.

'I'm really pleased someone else has come along to help us here at last,' she enthused. 'It's far too much for me and Cook to run this house alone, though Mr Darling has this very day employed a gardener and just yesterday a butler. He's also been in touch with a servants' employment agency, so hopefully more will arrive soon.'

Enid nodded sympathetically, understanding all too well the demands of a big house, though this one would fit into a corner of the Clarkson House back in Merthyr. 'Yes, it must have been hard work for you both,' she agreed.

'Now then, your position here for the time being, until more staff arrive, will be maid-of-all-work – both kitchen and domestic duties. Hopefully, within a week or two, there should be some new maids in attendance if that agency can arrange it.' She sniffed loudly. 'I understand that you have some domestic experience?'

'Only a little, ma'am – I worked at a big house in Merthyr for Mr Donald Clarkson.'

'I know of the man. Doing what exactly?' She lifted her brow.

'No kitchen duties as such, other than taking serving dishes upstairs to the family. Mainly it was lighting fires, helping in the laundry, cleaning and polishing the furniture, that sort of thing. Oh, and serving in the dining room when required.'

'You've had a good grounding then, by the sound of it. Now if I send you to help in the kitchen you might have to peel vegetables, check on the ovens and hob, those sorts of tasks. Are you able to cook if required?'

'A little, ma'am. I used to help my mother at home before we entered the workhouse.'

'All to the good. I'm sure you'll get along magnificently here. Come with me, I'll take you to meet with Cook.'

Enid hesitated.

'Anything wrong, Miss Hardcastle?' the housekeeper asked, a look of concern on her face.

'No, not really. I was about to ask if my friend at the workhouse might be interviewed for a position here. She's a good worker and…'

'Oh, I'm sorry but this is most irregular.' The woman's forehead furrowed into a frown. 'Mr Darling has made it plain that all the staff employed here are to come from the employment agency as they're properly vetted that way. I don't doubt what you're telling me about your friend, but it's really early days and you haven't settled in to work here yourself as yet, have you?'

Enid's face grew hot. 'I'm sorry for asking, but it's important to me. I didn't like leaving her there.'

Mrs Sowerberry smiled. 'Look, there's been an exception made in your case as you've been highly recommended by Mr Darling's friend – Mr Clarkson. Give it a while to find your feet in here and if any more vacancies arise in the future, then maybe we can think about it.'

Enid's heart sank, but at least the woman wasn't telling her "no" indefinitely. Meanwhile, she could write to Connie and maybe visit her at the workhouse in a week or two. But she really did have concerns for the girl's welfare in there, particularly as it appeared as though that Bridie might be taking her under her wing.

'Come along, Enid,' said Mrs Sowerberry as though trying to gee her up after her disappointment. 'I'll introduce you to the cook here, Mrs Betsy Appleton. I'm sure you'll both get along famously!'

* * *

Mrs Appleton seemed to live up to her name with her rounded figure and her plump persona. She beamed when she set eyes on Enid. Looking nothing like Cook at Hillside House, Betsy Appleton was much shorter-set and walked with a waddling gait as though maybe she had something wrong with her hips. Her bright sapphire-blue eyes were kindly with creases at the sides and she seemed so passionate about her position at the house.

'I think you'll get to like it here,' she told Enid, peering at her over her round silver-framed spectacles, her frilled cap moulded to her head.

'Mrs Appleton doesn't just cook excellent, wholesome fayre,' extolled Mrs Sowerberry, 'she's... well, you tell the girl, Mrs Appleton...'

Cook beamed as she clasped her hands together. 'When I was young I worked in France and was trained by a chef there. He taught me how to make choux pastry, how to cook classic French cuisine, how to bake and that sort of thing,' she said, speaking quickly, slightly out of puff in her excitement to relate the tale.

Enid could well imagine that the woman loved to tell the story to everyone she encountered but that didn't deter her from listening with interest. 'So, how did you end up living there then, Mrs Appleton?'

'It was due to my father, you see. He was a butler whose services were very much in demand. English butlers are revered around the world, you know, thought to be the best. Anyhow, we were living in London when we upped sticks to move to France. The Dordogne region. Mother wasn't keen on living there though. She stuck it out for as long as she possibly could, but in the end we returned home and settled here in Cardiff. That, she didn't mind too much as some of her relatives were Welsh, but her home had been in London. I think she found the Welsh way of life a little unusual, especially when people forgot she was present and spoke in their native tongue.'

'So, you had two years of good training there, didn't you, Cook?' Mrs Sowerberry said.

'Oh, yes.' Cook had a wistful look of longing in her eyes. 'Except I'd fallen in love with a young Frenchman who worked at the house as a gardener...'

'Oh?' said the housekeeper, looking startled. 'Well, you've never mentioned that before!'

'No.' Cook shook her head. 'I don't talk about it much but it broke my heart to leave Anton behind. We wrote to one another for a time but then his letters became less frequent and one day, I received a letter from one of the maids at the house who told me he had passed away. He was killed in a terrible train accident, just like that out of the blue...' She placed the heel of her hand to her chest and gasped as though the pain of it after all these years still wounded her deeply.

'You sit down and I'll make us all a cup of tea,' said Mrs Sowerberry tactfully.

Cook nodded as though in a daze. Then a little brass bell from the set on the wall clanged loudly.

'It's the master,' said Mrs Sowerberry. 'He'll be wanting his morning elevenses. If I brew up, can you take a tray of tea and a plate of biscuits up to him, Enid? It will give you the chance to introduce yourself.'

Enid smiled disconcertedly at the thought of introducing herself to the master of the house, having noticed that things were less formal here than at Hillside House. 'Yes, of course, Mrs Sowerberry.'

The housekeeper quickly brewed up as Cook composed herself by taking a seat at the table. Then Mrs Sowerberry handed the tray to Enid.

'There'll be a cup in the pot for you when you return,' she whispered. 'I'm just going to see Cook's all right. I've never heard that sad story from her before but, then again, I've only been working here this past month.'

'Where do I go?' asked Enid.

'He's in his study, turn right down the corridor until you arrive at the entrance hall then take the next corridor and it's the second room on the right.'

Enid nodded, her breath hitching in her throat. Suddenly, she felt very nervous of meeting her new employer.

The entrance hall wasn't as grand as at Hillside House but it was impressive, nevertheless. It had a curved mahogany staircase leading upstairs and black and white marbled tiles on the floor. Several stylish-looking leafy plants in large plant pots adorned the place and colourful gilt-framed paintings were displayed on the walls. High on the ceiling was an elaborate crystal chandelier that glittered as prisms of light projected, reflecting into a spectrum of colours.

Taking the next corridor, Enid paused outside the study. Should she knock on the door? Or just enter unannounced? But her hands were full as she was carrying the tray. After deliberating for a moment, she engineered it so that the tray rested on her forearm as she supported it against the door and knocked with her free hand.

Relief flooded through her when the occupant answered. 'Please enter!'

Huffing out a breath, she turned the doorknob and pushed the door open.

The man, who was standing with his back to her, staring out of the window, was much younger than she had imagined him to be. She estimated him to be in his early thirties perhaps and, when he turned to face her, she saw he had mysterious-looking green eyes, a strong, chiselled jaw and thick, wavy dark hair. He was astonishingly handsome to behold.

'Hello, you,' he said warmly as he beamed at her. 'I take it you're Miss Enid Hardcastle, are you?'

'Yes, sir.' She bobbed a curtsy and set the tray down on his desk in front of him, realising she wasn't wearing a maid's uniform as yet – she was wearing the heather-coloured dress and jacket Mr Clarkson had purchased for her. She was all too aware of how odd it must appear, her bringing in the tray dressed like that.

He pulled out his leather-backed chair from the desk to take a seat.

'Would you like me to pour for you, sir?' she asked.

He nodded. 'Thank you, that would be most welcome.'

She did as told, her hand trembling slightly as she poured the tea into the awaiting cup.

'I'm pleased to have you on the staff here, Enid.' He beamed at her. 'Mr Clarkson speaks very highly of you.'

Enid felt her face flush pink and she hoped Mr Clarkson had not mentioned anything else about her, like the rape, for instance. She'd be mortified to find he had.

'Thank you, sir.'

He dropped two sugar cubes into his cup and added a splash of milk from the jug. Stirring his cup carefully, and looking up at her as he did so, he said, 'You're a keen worker – I'll give you that. You're not due to begin work until tomorrow.'

'I don't mind pitching in, sir.'

He grinned, revealing a straight set of ivory-white teeth. 'I can well believe that. Although it's been hard on Mrs Sowerberry and Mrs Appleton, even though I'm the only occupant here and the most eligible bachelor in Canton, Cardiff!'

She giggled, once again realising that formalities at this house were more relaxed than at Hillside.

'Now I won't detain you, young lady. If I know Cook and Mrs Sowerberry, they'll be keeping a cup of tea for you in the kitchen.'

'They are, sir. And thank you.' Smiling, she bobbed another curtsy before leaving the room, thinking she was going to enjoy working at this new house.

* * *

It was a full week before the master received a full complement of staff. Enid had half hoped they'd have trouble getting all the people needed; that way Mrs Sowerberry might have given Connie a chance, but that did not happen. The positions at the house were easily filled as people were keen to work. A butler, gardener, a gardener's assistant, kitchen maid, parlour maid, laundress, two footmen and a stable lad had been employed. During that time, as maid-of-all-work, Enid had been expected to sally back and forth between the kitchen and other domestic duties, so if she wasn't found clearing out the coal grates, she'd be located serving in the dining room. Pinafores were changed for the occasion. Sometimes she'd find herself up to her elbows in soap suds in the laundry room. But now her role in the house needed defining.

Mrs Sowerberry called Enid into her office one afternoon, quite out of the blue.

'Please close the door behind you, Enid,' she said with a little smile on her face.

Hesitantly, Enid clicked the door shut behind her. What was going on here?

'It's come to my attention,' she continued, in a most solemn fashion, which caused Enid's heart to pound erratically, 'that...' She paused before adding, 'you're doing very well here at the house.'

Enid could hardly believe her ears.

'Am I, miss?'

'Yes, you are. Now that we've got enough staff on board for the time being, I'd like to give you a piece of good news!'

'Yes?' She blinked several times.

'I'd like to appoint you to the role of upper housemaid. This shall mean you are in charge of the other maids. It is you they'll turn to if I am not around. If neither myself nor Mr Tatton are available, then you shall answer the front door to callers.'

'But me, Mrs Sowerberry? Why? Two of the new maids are older than me.' This all seemed a bit premature to her. After all, she hadn't been at the house for very long.

The woman sniffed loudly. 'They're not that much older than you and, besides, neither has any experience of working in a big house. One previously worked as a cleaner and the other at a factory. I'd like you to be upper housemaid as I see something in you that they do not possess. You are quick to catch on and you use sound judgement about various matters.' The housekeeper's eyes were shining now. 'So will you accept?'

Enid lifted her head and held her chin upright. This was the first time in a long while that she felt proud of herself, that she'd achieved something of note, and it felt pretty good to her.

'Yes, ma'am. Thank you for your consideration.' It made no sense whatsoever to Enid that one of the young women had no experience. Connie would be more useful as she'd cleaned back at the workhouse, helped occasionally in the kitchen and cleaned out the grates in Mr and Mrs Finchley's quarters. She was beginning to wonder whether she was marked because she was a workhouse girl.

'Now, I'll announce it to the rest of the staff later. Also you're now eligible for a small wage increase.'

Enid hadn't even considered that; the mention of the new position offered had astounded her too much. Everything seemed to be going swimmingly.

'Thank you, ma'am.' She nodded at the woman.

'You're dismissed for the time being. Return to your bedroom and write a letter about your good news to whomever!'

Who could she write to though? Not her father, for sure – he no longer cared. Jimmy! She could write to him telling him where she was and that she was safe. But if she did that surely he'd try to find her and no matter how much she longed to see him, she could never lie, not to Jimmy. He'd find out about the rape and she didn't want that. If he didn't know where she was, he couldn't contact her and, given time, it would leave him free to find someone else. No, it just wasn't possible. She'd have to write to her mother, as Mam was still on her side and would welcome the good news. Maybe she could write to Connie too about how well she was settling in here, but what could she tell her about the expected position at the house? Maybe Connie's luck might have changed by now, and she'd be boarded out soon anyhow.

It was while she was walking up the backstairs to her room that she felt an awful cramping sensation that doubled her up in agony. She'd never experienced anything quite like it before and it robbed her of all breath.

Beads of perspiration broke out on her forehead as she managed to stagger towards her bedroom and, as soon as she got inside, she lay on her bed with her legs drawn up in a foetal position. It was then it dawned on her: her monthly still hadn't arrived. Was she having a miscarriage? Oh hell no! This was the last thing she needed right now. All sorts of thoughts were swimming around in her mind. She'd had no real signs of being pregnant though other than no monthly.

'Aargh!' She let out a loud, guttural sound, which brought the housekeeper bursting into the room.

'What on earth's the matter, Enid? I was just following you up the stairs to tell you something I'd forgotten to say when I heard you cry out.'

Enid lifted her head from the pillow. 'I'm not sure if I'm having a baby or not.' She managed to huff out the words.

The housekeeper's eyes enlarged with horror. 'I'll see if I can summon a doctor,' she said, 'meanwhile, I'll fetch one of the maids to sit with you.'

True to her word, the woman disappeared and one of the new maids, Penny, appeared. The girl's forehead creased into a concerned frown as she approached.

'Mrs Sowerberry said you were having bad stomach pains and I'm to sit with you until the doctor arrives,' she said timidly.

The girl looked a little uncertain about what she ought to do in such circumstances.

Enid nodded gratefully. 'Thank you, Penny.'

'Is there anything I can fetch for you? Maybe a glass of water? I won't be long.'

Enid lifted her head off the pillow but was so exhausted, she lay back down again. 'Please...'

Penny left the room for a couple of minutes then reappeared, handing a glass to Enid who sat up and took some slow sips. Her breathing had now returned to normal and the pain had subsided somewhat. Then she felt it, something warm oozing from between her legs. But she wasn't passing any urine – this felt beyond her control and she knew without a doubt it was blood.

'Can you leave me for a couple of minutes?' she asked. 'Just pass that flannel from the washstand, please?'

Penny nodded. 'Would you like me to wet it for you? For your forehead, is it?'

Enid shook her head, wishing the girl would leave. At the workhouse they were given rags to wear – pieces of towelling that could be washed and reused – but she hadn't thought to ask if she could bring any with her.

'I think my period has just arrived suddenly,' she said.

'Oh, I see,' said Penny. 'Shall I pass you a clean pair of bloomers as well?'

'Yes, please.'

When the girl had departed to stand outside the door, Enid removed her drawers and mopped up the blood from between her legs with them, then she discarded them under her bed for the time being. Next she placed the flannel in her clean drawers to line them until she could ask Mrs Sowerberry what was the best thing to do.

Voices outside the door startled her, and then she heard the housekeeper dismiss Penny before someone with a deep, resonant male voice spoke as he entered the room.

Doctor Elwyn Lloyd was a middle-aged man with bushy grey sideburns and a full, rounded face. He smiled when he saw her, placing his leather Gladstone bag on a chair beside the bed. 'Now then, young lady, what's been going on here?'

Enid explained all about the rape and how she thought she might now be miscarrying as a result, as her monthly hadn't arrived.

The doctor nodded with a grave expression on his face. 'Let's examine you, then, young lady,' he said softly. 'If you can lift your dress and petticoat, so I can palpate your abdomen?'

She did as required of her and lay back on the bed. He removed his bowler hat and jacket and placed them on the chair and then rolled up his shirtsleeves to the elbows.

'My hands shouldn't be too cold,' he said, as he began. 'Tell me if you feel any pain or tenderness anywhere I touch.'

Then he began to gently palpate her abdomen with his fingertips and the flat palm of his hand.

'I forgot to mention to you, Doctor, after having that bad stomach cramp earlier, I started bleeding.'

He nodded and carried on palpating her abdomen.

'It's slightly tender there.' She indicated in the middle of her stomach, just beneath her navel.

He stopped what he was doing. 'I'd be inclined to think that maybe as you've been very stressed with goings-on lately regarding what's occurred, maybe that's messed with your usual menstrual cycle. You'll need to rest for a few days.'

'But they need my help at the house,' she protested.

'Now, don't you concern yourself about that,' said the doctor kindly. 'I'll explain to the housekeeper and I'll warn her to be discreet. She can always tell the staff you have some sort of stomach bug and you need to keep away from the rest of them for a few days.' Then his eyes took on an expression of sadness. 'My dear,' he said, sitting on the edge of the bed, 'you've been through a huge trauma of late and as you're experiencing more period pain than is usual, I'll just keep you on bed rest for now.' He winked at her, rolling down his shirtsleeves and, donning his hat and jacket and lifting his bag, he left the room.

Enid heard him speak briefly with Mrs Sowerberry outside the door, then there was a light knock on it as the housekeeper emerged.

Enid swallowed. Would the woman be cross with her as she couldn't work for a few days? Would she chastise her in some way as her father had, as if the rape had been her own doing? But no, she was sympathetic, asking how she was feeling and offering to send up a cup of warm milk and a cheese sandwich.

'Enid,' she said softly, her hand on the doorknob, 'I'll delay informing the rest of the staff about your new appointment for now until you're up on your feet again, you know... just in case.'

Enid knew all too well what the woman meant. Just in case she *was* pregnant after all. There was still a slim chance no matter what the doctor had said.

* * *

On the fifth day of bed rest, Doctor Lloyd came to examine Enid and after asking her a few questions, he was convinced that what she had experienced was a particularly heavy monthly period, which had now ceased.

She felt so much better physically as well as mentally and could now recommence her duties at the house. She'd never forget what had happened to her that fateful evening in the grounds of the Clarkson house but she had no intention of allowing it to define her nor for it to mar the rest of her life. So the following day, Mrs Sowerberry summoned the rest of the staff in the servants' dining room to inform them that Enid was being made upper housemaid. There seemed no objection to this and no one except the housekeeper knew Enid's secret.

The two things that still haunted her were being disowned by her father and breaking off contact with Jimmy. At least she had her work at the house to keep her busy and, from time to time, Mr Clarkson called and took her to visit her mother and siblings in the Merthyr workhouse, but it was upsetting Dad turned down the opportunity to see her. It was such a shame that her father hadn't accepted that caretaker job at the house. Then they might have all left the workhouse, but pride came before a fall.

It was on one such visit that Enid was astonished to discover that her father was no longer an inmate.

'I don't know where he is,' said Mam, sadly shaking her head. 'He's not the man we all once knew. He's had no interest in me nor the kids for ages. I heard a whisper he's been hitting the bottle but where he's getting the money for it with him being out of work, I just don't know.'

It was extremely concerning but Enid had an idea. She stretched out her hand across the table to squeeze her mother's in reassurance. 'How about I try having a word with Mr Darling to see if I can get you some work at the house and maybe some living quarters too? After all, Mr Clarkson originally reckoned he could get you somewhere to live with Dad as caretaker, but maybe Mr Darling would consider taking you all without Dad? I've heard the laundress might be leaving soon as her husband has found work in another town and they'll have to move away.'

'Oh, will you? There's good you are to me, our Enid.' Mam sniffed and she wiped away a tear with the back of her hand.

And so it was arranged that Martha move into the apartment with the other children, where she'd work in the laundry room. Childcare was required and when Enid herself couldn't step in, then the other maids did it, until Mr Darling secured the services of a nanny, paid for by the generosity of Mr Clarkson.

During that time, Enid watched all three siblings become healthier-looking as they gained weight. They had rosy complexions now instead of that sallow colour she'd noticed at the workhouse. Her mother too, although working hard in the laundry room, had put on a little weight and seemed so much happier, although from time to time Enid noticed a wistful, faraway look in her eyes as if her mind was elsewhere. She guessed her mam was thinking about the man she'd married. He should have been here with them all, not getting himself drunk in some pub or backstreet somewhere, but as Mr Clarkson had told her, maybe it was his way of coping with life. He'd recently endured losses and maybe life was all too much for him right now.

Mr Clarkson reassured her he'd do all he could to trace him.

Enid had to remind herself that it was not that unusual for men to abandon their families at the workhouse as they became both physically and emotionally separated from them. Even those men from Cork had abandoned their families almost as soon as they'd arrived at the Cardiff workhouse. What happened next though took Enid's mind off these things that concerned her, even her father.

11

A new member of staff was employed as a footman at the house. Mark Simpson, the one who had originally been taken on, had left to work elsewhere and Enid thought maybe he'd been made a better offer. So in his place was a brand-new footman who was introduced to the staff over breakfast one morning by Mr Tatton.

As soon as Enid laid eyes on him, she felt something stir inside of her. What was it? Interest? Excitement? Maybe a little of both?

Samuel Banks was in his early twenties, going by his appearance. He wore a navy jacket, short at the front and tailed at the back. It was embossed with gold buttons and matching below-knee breeches. A dogtooth checked waistcoat and high-collared pristine white shirt with a gold tie at the neck completed the outfit. His jet-black hair was slicked down. But it wasn't just his uniform that was so striking, it was his face too, for he had what Enid would have described as "smiley eyes" and a broad grin. It wasn't even as though he were conventionally handsome either, as his ears stuck out a smidgeon, but he had such charisma and, when he spoke, he had a way of fluttering his eyelashes, as though he were a little abashed, which endeared him to Enid.

Samuel, or Sam, as he was less formally addressed by the staff, became a firm favourite with everyone, particularly Enid. Compared to Jimmy he seemed to be more polished and refined. He doubled at times as a gentleman's valet for the master and seemed to know all manner of things, like which knives and forks were used at various meals, the special way of laying them out on the table, the protocol of fine etiquette. All in all, he was an impressive young man who had taken the eyes of all the maids at the house. As he was that much older than Enid though, she didn't see herself in with any sort of chance. In any case, what man would want her now she was no longer a maiden?

Although she'd decided against contacting Jimmy following the rape, there was a question that needed answering. If he cared so much about her then why hadn't he tracked her down by now? It would only have taken a visit to the workhouse where someone in authority might have given him the information or even if he had asked to speak to either her mother or father they would have put him in the picture. That there'd been no contact from him was sad in itself.

Enid wasn't seeking any sort of romantic relationship with Samuel and for some reason that seemed to draw him towards her. One morning, she was seated on the wooden bench at the back of the property as she was prone to do when she needed to think, when he approached.

She looked up at him and he smiled at her.

'Mind if I join you?'

Returning the smile, she shook her head. 'Not at all, but why aren't you still with the others at breakfast?' Enid hadn't much felt like eating that morning and sought some fresh air.

'I might say the same thing about you!' He chuckled as he took a seat beside her. 'Why did you excuse yourself from the table?'

'Oh, I'm not all that hungry. I got used to eating little at the workhouse, I suppose, particularly at breakfast time. And you, what's your excuse?'

'Feeling out on a limb, I suppose.'

She blinked. 'Really?'

'Why do you seem so surprised, Enid?'

'Well, all the maids here seem taken with you.'

He didn't smile nor chuckle, instead his face took on a serious expression. 'To be truthful I find their company a bore. I'd much rather speak to you instead.'

'Now you do surprise me! What do I have that they don't?'

'Intelligence and interesting conversation...' he said, drawing closer to her.

Realising she had to put a firm boundary between them, at least for the time being, so they both knew where they stood, she said, 'Yes, it would be good to be friends here, wouldn't it?'

He swallowed and nodded and moved slightly away from her. 'Yes, I suppose it would as that way we'll both have an ally in one another at the house.'

She nodded at him.

They sat in companiable silence for a couple of minutes, until Sam rose from the bench and said, 'Right, I'd better leave you to it, Enid. If I stay out here much longer, Mr Tatton will come looking for me!'

She smiled as she watched him leave. That was an unexpected but rather nice encounter, which gave her a warm feeling inside.

12

Enid had been working at the house for a few months when, unexpectedly, Mr Darling's sister, Eliza, arrived to stay complete with several trunks and her own personal maid. Young, vivacious and full of life, Eliza was like a breath of fresh air as she breezed through the place. Her enthusiasm knew no bounds. She enchanted the staff, particularly Samuel whose eyes seemed to follow her around wherever she went. Enid noticed how the young woman dallied with him too, toying with his emotions. He was not of her class, not her station in life, so nothing could possibly come of this idle flirtation, but still, it was hard for her to witness first-hand.

The only way something could come of it was if Eliza was prepared to run off with him and settle for a mundane life of mediocrity. A life of hardship even, if Samuel couldn't afford to support them. Then Eliza's beautifully manicured nails and soft lily-white hands would end up roughened and calloused from washing clothing, scrubbing floors and chopping sticks for firewood. Maybe her health might be ruined too if she had to work long hours in a factory to earn a living to help to support them and any children they might have.

'A penny for them?' Mrs Sowerberry intruded into Enid's thoughts. She was in the drawing room on her hands and knees, setting the fire, her hands and fingernails caked in coal dust.

Enid, still on her haunches, turned her head to look at the woman and shot her a rueful smile. 'I doubt they're even worth that.' She sighed, clambering to her feet. Although the fire had been set, it would be later in the day when it needed to be lit as it wasn't all that cold now the weather had broken. It was mid spring, where some days could be quite chilly and others almost summer-like, except for the evenings when the temperature dropped. Today was one such day.

Mrs Sowerberry smiled. 'It's Samuel, isn't it?'

For a brief moment, it felt as if the woman had read her thoughts, but that was fanciful thinking. An impossibility. A guess at best. Deciding honesty was the best policy, Enid nodded.

'Yes.' Her mouth was dry now.

'I've noticed how Miss Eliza acts around him in such an improper manner. You like him, don't you?'

She nodded. 'Is it that noticeable then?'

'Not to everyone else, but to me, yes. He's a handsome young man – not of the same social standing as Miss Eliza, nevertheless, she enjoys the interaction.'

'And he with her, no doubt!' Enid's voice was clipped.

'Yes, I'd imagine so but if it carries on he'll end up hurt by it. If Mr Darling were to discover what's going on...' The housekeeper paused.

'But I've noticed Miss Eliza never flirts with Samuel in front of her brother.'

'Then she's very clever by all accounts. I've asked Mr Tatton to have a word with him as a warning.'

Enid nodded. Why should she care anyhow? Why indeed?

Because you have feelings for him, a little voice inside her said.

'Now I won't keep you any longer, Enid. You've been through a lot this past year or so on a personal level. I'd suggest you distance yourself from Samuel if you don't wish to get hurt yourself.'

Tears pricked the backs of Enid's eyes, threatening to well up and spill down both cheeks. Realising Mrs Sowerberry made an excellent point, she swallowed hard to compose herself. She wiped her dusty hands on her pinafore and nodded at the woman as she mouthed, 'Thank you, ma'am.'

It was time to return to her bedroom anyhow to clean herself up and change to her white pinafore before joining the rest of the staff for breakfast. Mrs Sowerberry had given her something to think about, if she wasn't careful she might end up getting hurt herself.

* * *

Mags startled, imagining she was seeing things. The man sitting slumped against the front door of the Hardcastles' old house had a bottle in his hand and he hiccupped loudly. She rubbed her eyes as if they might be playing tricks on her. It was twilight and she could have sworn that was Arthur Hardcastle. But surely that couldn't be the case as he and his family were now at the workhouse? It didn't look like the father of the new family who were now living at the house either; he was a larger-framed chap.

As she approached, she called softly, 'Arthur? Arthur, is it you? It's me, Mags Hughes.'

'Mags!' he cried as if pleased to see her.

'What are you doing back here?'

He looked up at her with large, doleful eyes. 'Came to see what I've lost,' he said, his voice morose.

'But why are you no longer at the spike? And where are Martha and the kids?'

'Gone!' He let out a long groan. 'I left the workhouse for a while and when I went back there, they'd all gone.'

'Gone? But where to, my love?' She stooped low to speak to him.

'Some big house our Enid is working at in Cardiff or some such place... at least that's what I was told.'

Now he sounded like he might cry. Mags laid a hand on his shoulder.

'Come with me,' she said. 'Let's get you sobered up and something to eat inside of you. You'll feel better afterwards and we can talk properly then.'

'I need to tell them all how sorry I am,' said Arthur, shaking his head. 'Particularly Enid. I misjudged the girl and said some terrible things...'

'You're not making any sense, Arthur. Now come with me and we'll talk more when you've sobered yourself up.'

He nodded and Mags offered him her arm to help pull him to his feet.

He didn't smell none too fresh either. Oh well, he could have a good wash and she'd loan him some of Elgan's clothing. Elgan wouldn't be needing it where he was right now. Thankfully, Jimmy had taken the twins over to visit Betsan, so they wouldn't see the man in this state. Hopefully, he'd have sobered up before their return.

Funny how the cards life dealt you could make or break you if you allowed them to.

* * *

Following a good meal, wash and brush-up, Mags could glean from Arthur that something bad had occurred for Enid while she worked at the Clarkson house. Betsan had also indicated that but had not gone into any detail, but Arthur eventually told her that Anthony Clarkson, the son, had carnal knowledge of his daughter. He admitted that he'd misread the situation and that he hadn't believed Enid's account at first, thinking she'd been loose with her morals.

'I can't believe you'd have thought such a thing of your daughter,' said Mags, shocked. 'Why, even my Jimmy could have told you Enid is a lovely girl. I think she was sweet on him and he on her but nothing ever happened between them. He treated her like a little lady...'

'Oh, I realise that now,' said Arthur as he looked down at his feet and blew out a hard breath. 'If only I could take back those cruel, hurtful words. Someone at the spike had smuggled alcohol in and I wasn't in my right mind at the time. To be truthful, it weren't even her I was angry at, it was the situation we all found ourselves in. Instead I took it out on all of them...'

'Take it from someone who knows,' Mags said sagely, 'the bottle won't do you the slightest bit of good.'

Arthur nodded and then continued, 'To make matters worse, I'd been offered a job myself at this big house in Cardiff. Could have been a caretaker or something but I turned it down in anger. We'd have got rooms there an' all. The whole family might have stayed together but I had to spoil it for them. Martha was all for it. I hurt them all,' he said sadly. 'My flamin' pride got in the way.'

'Well, pride comes with a pinch, they say, maybe it's not too late,' Mags said optimistically. 'Why don't you try to have a word with that Mr Clarkson? You're looking a bit tidier now after that wash and brush-up and changing into my Elgan's clothing. Go up there first thing tomorrow and ask to see him.'

'Aye, maybe I could,' said Arthur, cheering up a little now. 'I haven't got anything to lose. I already have nothing.'

'That's the spirit. Just one thing...'

He angled his head to one side as he looked at her. 'Yes?'

'Don't mention any of this to Jimmy. The lad's upset enough as it is that Enid's gone someplace he doesn't know, and I think things are best left as they are, as he seems to be slowly getting over it all. He knows nothing about what happened to her and it would upset him so.'

'I feel bad now as the lad turned up at the workhouse asking to speak to me but I refused him.'

Mags nodded. 'Aye, we all have regrets. He might be back at any moment now though.' She bit her lip as she glanced at the clock on the mantelpiece.

'Then I shan't keep you,' said Arthur, standing. And then he hugged Mags. 'Thank you,' he whispered in her ear.

'It's all right. I've been down on my luck a time or two and hit the bottle like you as well, so I know what it's like.'

He nodded then pecked a kiss on her cheek.

She dipped her hand into her pinafore pocket and handed him a silver shilling. 'Use this to get a bed and breakfast somewhere overnight. Get a good rest before you see Mr Clarkson. There's a nice lodging house in the Pontmorlais area run by a Mrs Gladys Thomas. She doesn't charge much either. I've scribbled the address down for you.' She riffled in her pinny pocket and handed him a scrap of paper.

Arthur looked at her with tears in his eyes as he nodded his thanks.

'Good luck to you,' she said, shaking his hand.

And then he turned his back and was gone out into the night. For a brief moment, she wondered if she hadn't dreamt it all.

* * *

Enid could feel Mrs Sowerberry's eyes on her from an upstairs window as she sat in the back garden. Samuel had followed her out here and was now seated on a bench beside her.

'Mr Tatton had a word with me this morning,' he said, lowering his head and avoiding eye contact.

'Oh?' Of course she knew very well what he was referring to, but he didn't know she knew. He was waiting for her to ask, but she didn't.

There was a long pause, as if neither knew quite what to say, and then he said, 'He reckons I'm acting improper with Miss Eliza.'

'And do you think you are, Sam?' said Enid as she emitted a soft sigh.

He drew in a breath and let it out again. 'No, not really. We like talking to one another. I love hearing what she has to say about all her trips to places like Paris and Milan and the society balls she's attended.'

'Sounds pretty boastful to me!' scoffed Enid.

He looked at her, making eye contact for the first time. 'But don't you think she leads an interesting life?'

'No, not really. All the things she's able to do are because she has money. She's pandered to and precocious and not only that, she's toying with you, Sam!' Enid raised her voice, surprising herself with its venomous tone. It was so unlike her to be nasty or spiteful but she felt it now. Felt it for the man who was being used as a poodle by some pampered female!

'Toying?' He said the word as though it were alien to him, almost as though he'd never heard the word in that context before. Looking directly at her, he frowned. There was a hurt expression in his eyes and, no, she hadn't meant to injure his pride, but it had to be said. 'What the devil do you mean by that?'

Enid sighed. 'She's playing around with you, Sam. Do I have to spell it out to you? Like a cat plays with a mouse, patting and prodding it. Haven't you ever noticed she doesn't even address you when the master is around? Then when he's no longer here, she makes a play for you? In any case, playing with you or not, what are your intentions towards her?'

He cleared his throat. 'I've a little money saved. I'd like to take her out to the theatre maybe one evening.'

'And you think she'll be satisfied in the cheap seats and walking back home with a meat and potato pie from the shop afterwards? I think not!' she said scornfully. 'Miss Eliza is used to the finer things in life.'

'Well, I'm going to ask her anyway. I like her and I believe the feeling is mutual.'

Although Enid liked Sam a great deal, she didn't have such strong feelings for him that him pursuing a life with Eliza would break her heart. Anyway, she still had feelings for Jimmy, which she'd shifted to one side following the rape. Thinking on, she said kindly, 'Do as you must, but take care. If the master gets to hear of it, you might end up losing your position here.'

She patted his arm affectionately and rose from the bench, glancing up at the bedroom window where the housekeeper was still watching them.

Once inside, Enid had a lump in her throat, feeling helpless to save Sam from the clutches of a little madam who just viewed him as some sort of tin soldier to do her bidding. To take out of the toy box and play around with and then to return when she'd got fed up after having her fun.

Later that evening, Enid explained to Mrs Sowerberry what Sam had told her.

'Mr Tatton hasn't got through to him, I'm afraid. He intends to ask Miss Eliza to accompany him to the theatre.'

'Really?' The housekeeper raised her brows. 'Then we have done what we can to warn him off and I'm afraid the rest is down to him. I'm quite sure Mr Darling would be furious if he ever found out.'

Enid dreaded to think of the consequences if that should occur.

* * *

'So you're Enid's father,' said the cook who had introduced herself as Mrs Shrimpton to him. She handed Arthur a cup of tea, strong and sweet as he liked it. It must have been a quiet time for the woman as it was mid-morning. He'd spent last night in that guest house Mags had recommended and very comfortable he'd been there too, though he'd hardly slept a wink as his mind had been on this morning and righting a wrong. He'd eaten a little breakfast a couple of hours ago, so the cup of tea here was most welcome.

The staff dining table appeared to have been cleared away and, in the distance, he heard the sounds of pots and pans clanging and cutlery clinking.

'Aye, I'm her father, for my sins,' he said with a tone of regret to his voice.

Cook tilted her head to one side as she studied him. 'And what's so wrong with that?'

'Oh, nothing. Nothing whatsoever, only I've let her down lately. You know what happened to her here, don't you?'

Cook nodded. 'Yes, but apart from the family and the housekeeper, I'm the only one who does.'

'I'm glad of that.'

'But you indicated you let her down, Mr Hardcastle?'

'I did. You see, I didn't take her word for it.' He lowered his voice. 'I didn't immediately believe that she was raped. In my head I thought maybe she'd been a party to a liaison between them as I've been told the young Mr Clarkson is a very handsome man.'

'I can assure you she was telling the God's honest truth, Mr Hardcastle. I was the first one to see her following the awful event – she couldn't even speak for the first half-hour or so. She kept trying to get her words out but they wouldn't come. I had to get her to answer my questions with a simple yes or no – that's how traumatised she was, you see. She was trembling too!'

The woman spoke with passion, closing her eyes for a brief moment as she recalled that awful night.

Arthur shook his head and, with his eyes brimming with tears, looked across the table at the woman. 'Thank you for what you did for my daughter that night.'

'It's all right,' Mrs Shrimpton said, her tone level now. 'Your daughter is a very brave girl. You ought to be proud of her.'

'I am,' said Arthur, wiping away a tear with his hand.

'Now, finish your tea and I'll fetch the housekeeper. She can take you to Mr Clarkson. He's a good, kind man and I'm sure he'll help to reunite you with your daughter.'

'God bless you, Mrs Shrimpton.'

She smiled at him and, through his tears, he watched her leave to go in search of the housekeeper.

* * *

Samuel, dressed in a smart striped blazer, white shirt and cravat, tailored trousers and sporting a straw boater on his head, entered the kitchen.

'Where you off to then?' Penny asked him.

The staff were seated around the table enjoying an afternoon tea of miniature cucumber sandwiches, scones and a large pot of tea.

Samuel removed his hat and placed it on the table in front of him before seating himself. There was a spare spot as Mr Tatton wasn't present, which Enid thought was just as well as the man had warned him about his recent behaviour.

She wondered how Samuel would answer the question.

'I'm going to see a theatre performance tonight,' he enthused but did not add anything further.

'To see what?' Penny wasn't giving up.

'There's a play on called *Off to the Seaside*. I've been wanting to see it for ages.'

Samuel obviously hoped it would be enough to put the girl off but she persisted in grilling him.

'Who's going with you then?'

Samuel tapped his nose with his index finger. 'Mind your own.'

He chuckled as Penny's face flushed at the thought of being labelled a nosy parker, so she said no more on the matter and instead began to spread some strawberry jam onto a scone.

Though all the way through tea, Enid could tell that Sam was nervous as he ate very little and seemed quite tense. It was a relief when they all left the table.

'Where are you meeting her?' Enid asked later when they were alone in the corridor.

'At the end of the road. She's going to slip away without telling her brother.'

'I hope you know what you're doing, Sam.'

He shot her a cheeky grin. 'Please don't worry about me, Enid. You are a good friend, but I'll be all right.'

Good friend or not, she'd hate to see him lose his position at the house.

It was with some trepidation later that evening that she watched him leave, ready to meet with Miss Eliza at the end of the road.

So it was surprising to her when she found the young woman seated in the library some twenty minutes later, sprawled out on a chaise longue, reading a book with a glass of sherry in her hand.

Eliza raised her eyes from the page she was reading as Enid entered, fixing her with a questioning gaze. Should she say something to her or not? But if she reminded her she was to meet Samuel that would draw attention to the matter and, in any case, it was none of her business. He'd made it quite clear he had designs on Eliza and not her.

'Hello,' said Eliza, smiling as she closed her book, laying it down on the small table beside her.

'Hello, miss,' said Enid, wondering if the young woman was being genuine with her or not. 'I'm sorry, I didn't realise anyone was in here. I just came in to borrow a couple of books. Mr Darling said I could.'

'Oh, Edmund sent you, did he?' Eliza nodded approvingly. 'So, you're rather a bookworm, are you?'

'Yes, miss.'

'And what sort of books do you read?'

'Thomas Hardy or anything by the Brontë sisters – that sort of thing.'

'Oh, me too,' said Eliza, her eyes shining bright. 'Perhaps we're both romantics then if we like the Brontë sisters?' She fluttered her eyelashes in an amused fashion.

Although Enid would have loved to have discussed this topic of conversation with anyone else, when it came to Eliza, she felt guarded. She didn't want to overstep a boundary with her betters as Samuel was doing.

'It's all right,' said Eliza softly. 'You go ahead and choose. I'll go back to my books – they fill an empty evening.'

As Enid turned away to search the walnut bookcases, she wondered if Eliza was just saying that to throw her off the scent and that she would later sneak out and meet Samuel. Or was she just being cruel, leading him on, maybe?

By the time Enid had made a selection of books to take back to her room, Eliza had left her position on the chaise longue so she assumed she had gone off to get ready for her assignation with Samuel. Her heart slumped at the very thought of it.

After depositing the books in her bedroom, she went to the kitchen in search of Cook, as they were going to have a cup of cocoa with one another before bed. Although Mrs Appleton was doing the very same thing with Enid here as the cook at Hillside House had done, they were both entirely different sorts. Mrs Appleton was quite ladylike in manner and could turn her hand to anything, even the finest of dishes, particularly anything French. Whereas Mrs Shrimpton liked a little drink and was more slap-dash. Nevertheless, she'd warmed to the pair of them and wondered would they like one another if they were ever to meet? But she just couldn't imagine Mrs Appleton kicking off her shoes to reveal a big toe poking out of one of her stockings!

Enid had almost dozed off in the rocking chair near the hearth when Mrs Appleton startled. 'What's that?'

'I didn't hear anything,' Enid said, but realised she might have been asleep and not heard it.

'There's someone knocking on the back door!' Cook furrowed her brow. 'Now, who on earth can that be at this hour?'

For a moment, Enid wondered if it was Samuel returning home, so she rose from her chair offering to answer, much to Mrs Appleton's relief.

As Enid unbolted the heavy door and drew it open, she said, 'So, how did it go th—?'

But she didn't get to finish her sentence. She'd thought it would be Samuel but, instead, the man who had been facing in the opposite direction now turned slowly to face her, and she almost fainted to see who it was standing there.

13

'Dad!' Enid's hands flew to her face.

Her father, blinking for a moment, looked at her with such sad, doleful eyes. 'Can you ever forgive me, Enid? I've been such a fool to ever doubt you. I should have realised you were telling the truth all along.'

That's all she'd needed to hear – that he believed her about the rape and was seeking forgiveness from her. The next thing she knew she was in her father's arms and they were weeping openly together.

Mr Clarkson seemed to appear from somewhere then. Where he'd been she had no clue, maybe he'd hidden in the shadows or just emerged from his coach.

'I've brought your father to you,' he said jovially. 'He came to see me to ask for forgiveness and I'm going to have a word with Mr Darling to see if he will still employ him as a caretaker here.'

'That's wonderful news!' Enid gasped. And before too long all three were seated in the drawing room with Mr Darling, who was equally happy to take her father on.

The only concern was if Enid's mother would feel the same after he'd abandoned the family for months on end. It was discussed and all agreed it would be best not to wake her as it might disturb the children. So Arthur was given something to eat by Cook who was pleased to be introduced to him and then he was given a bed in the men's quarters for the night. There would be time tomorrow to be reacquainted with the rest of his family. Meanwhile, all thoughts of Samuel and Miss Eliza flew out of Enid's head.

* * *

At staff breakfast the following morning, Samuel was nowhere to be seen and Enid wondered why. Where on earth was he? Hadn't he returned from last night's jaunt? And was Miss Eliza missing too?

It was a full hour before she discovered what had happened when she found Sam taking a break on the garden bench.

'What happened last night?' she asked.

He sighed loudly. Then he turned to face her. 'She didn't turn up, that's what. I waited for over a half-hour and then this morning she informed me a guest had called at the house unexpectedly. Couldn't be helped, I suppose...'

Enid realised full well there had been no guest the previous evening except for her father's arrival, which, besides, was at a late hour, so it wouldn't have concerned Miss Eliza anyhow.

She could sense how sad he was. Poor Sam had built himself into believing something magical was about to happen. Now his hopes had been cruelly dashed by a little madam who was toying with his affection. How cruel of her!

Evidently, Eliza had been lying to Sam but Enid didn't want to hurt his feelings by telling him that.

'Oh, sorry to hear that,' she said sympathetically, choosing her words well. 'But why didn't you come for breakfast? Cook was asking about you.'

'I just didn't feel hungry,' he said, shaking his head.

'Why don't you go and get something now instead? I'm sure Mrs Appleton will oblige. Or even just a cup of tea and a piece of toast to keep you going until the next mealtime?'

He nodded. 'Yes, I think I will, thank you. Why do you care so much though, Enid?'

She swallowed. 'Oh, I'm like that with everyone,' she said so as to sound as if her feelings for him weren't really all that special. And then she changed the subject. 'Hey, you'll never guess what happened last night.'

'What?' His eyes widened now with interest.

'My father turned up here out of the blue. He's going to take the caretaker's job after all.'

'That's good news, Enid!' Sam enthused. 'I know you missed him so much.'

Enid still didn't know how her mother had taken the news and, by now, surely they would have had the chance to talk? Her mother tended to have breakfast in the apartment with the younger children. Hopefully, she wouldn't send him packing – that would be intolerable. If Enid could forgive her father then surely her mother would too?

It wasn't until the afternoon that Enid had a chance to speak with both her parents. To her utter relief, her mother was allowing her father to stay in her apartment, though she sensed an air of uncertainty between them. Hopefully, given time, things would slowly return to normal, especially now he had his pride back at having a job and them all having a roof over their heads at long last. From now on, they weren't going to be ejected every so often with their key taken off them for good measure, either. And the children were thrilled to be reunited with their father too.

Yes, things were definitely on the up.

Arthur Hardcastle proved to be an asset to the house as he was able to turn his hand to many things. If he wasn't fixing furniture, then he was able to touch up the paint on the walls, mend anything that had broken, even attend to minor shoe repairs, which made Enid think of Jimmy. She had toyed with the idea of writing to the lad but there'd been a lot of water flowing beneath the bridge since that dreadful incident at the Clarkson house. She had no wish to overturn Jimmy's world as she guessed he'd been dismayed at her sudden departure.

Another person she had on her mind was Connie. She'd kept in touch with her since leaving the workhouse via letters back and forth, and she'd managed just one visit, where she'd been dismayed to see the girl seemed unlike herself, appearing distracted and edgy somehow. So far the girl had no luck getting away from there – she hadn't even been boarded out anywhere as yet. So when the opportunity came up of a kitchen maid's position at the house again, as a maid called Dora was leaving to get married, Enid suggested Connie.

'But what do we know of this Connie you speak of? I remember you telling me about a friend at the workhouse the day you arrived here.' Mrs Sowerberry peered at Enid over her glasses. They were in the housekeeper's office where she'd been poring over a large ledger of accounts. It was neatly kept as the woman had beautiful penmanship. 'Is it the same girl?'

'It is. What I do know of her, Mrs Sowerberry, is that she's a good worker and one of the few inmates there whom I trusted. Many were on the rob. I trusted Connie so much that she even knew where my special rose brooch was hidden and she never even took it nor borrowed it, not once in all that time. I'm ever so worried about her welfare in that place since I've left.'

'She's not as tough as you, by the sound of it?'

Enid shook her head. 'No, she's not.'

Mrs Sowerberry smiled. 'If that's the case, and I trust your judgement, then I'll write to the workhouse and request she comes for an interview and offer to send Mr Darling's coach over. You can even accompany your friend here.'

Enid beamed. 'Oh thank you, ma'am. You won't regret this!'

'I sincerely hope not!' said the housekeeper with a note of mirth to her voice.

* * *

'I've not heard back from the workhouse,' said Mrs Sowerberry a few days later. 'You'd think that they'd be glad of us offering an inmate a position here at the house!'

Enid frowned, also knowing that offering a workhouse inmate a position like this was as scarce as hen's teeth.

She was in the midst of instructing Penny how best to clean up the drawing room after the chimney sweep had swept the chimney there. Thankfully, they'd used lots of dust sheets and newspapers and the sofa and chairs had been draped in old blankets, so neither furniture nor rugs had been ruined.

Enid, dismissing herself from Penny's side for a moment, fixed her gaze on the housekeeper, tilting her head as if deep in thought.

'That's most odd, Mrs Sowerberry. Matron isn't one to rest on her laurels and I know she was delighted when I was given the opportunity to work here. There must be a good reason for her not replying.'

'That's as may be but if we don't hear back soon, I'm going to have to advertise the position with that staff agency. Cook is finding it hard to cope in the kitchen now that Dora has left to get wed and she's not getting any younger. Her hips are playing up something rotten.'

'Leave it with me. I have to go out on an errand later in the morning so if I call to the workhouse while I'm out and about, I'll try to find out what's going on.'

Mrs Sowerberry nodded. 'Very well. But do bear in mind every day that passes by is more difficult for Mrs Appleton.'

Enid considered the dilemma for a moment. 'I'll tell you what, as soon as Penny and I finish here, I'll send her to help Cook in the kitchen.' She raised her voice and looking in the girl's direction said, 'You like working in the kitchen, don't you?'

Penny smiled. 'Oh, yes. Cook likes feeding me up an' all as she reckons I'm far too thin!'

That was true, though Enid had never seen someone stuff her face as much as Penny and not seem to gain an ounce of weight. She was just one of those energetic sorts who seemed to burn it all off very quickly.

Mrs Sowerberry nodded approvingly. 'I'll leave it to you to sort out then, Enid.'

She realised the woman had a lot of faith in her and it made her feel good about herself. There weren't many who could say they'd reached the level of upper housemaid at such a young age and in such a short space of time. Sometimes she might even have to step into Mrs Sowerberry's shoes if she were taking leave of absence or was taken ill. Well, she reckoned she knew enough about the running of the house now to do that. The only thing that concerned her were the accounts that needed keeping but the woman assured her that it was all pretty straightforward and that she could teach her all she needed to know in an afternoon.

* * *

The following morning, Enid set out with a spring in her step to head off to the workhouse. As she strolled along the streets, enjoying the beautiful day, where the sun was high in the sky and created a dappled effect of the leaves of the trees on the pavement, she thought she saw a familiar figure striding towards her. Her breath hitched in her throat and she froze for a moment as a feeling of dread seeped into every pore of her body.

No, it couldn't possibly be! Not him!

Enid's heart began to pound and her mouth dried up as she turned away to pretend to search for something inside her reticule. No, she must surely have been mistaken. She watched the man as he passed by and headed towards a tobacconist shop at the end of the road. He looked so much like Anthony Clarkson but she hadn't seen his face close up as she'd purposely glanced in the opposite direction. Maybe she ought to have taken a chance and looked directly at him to see if he really was the man. But who knew what might have occurred if it was and he recognised her?

She assured herself she must be imagining things as his father had told her his son was in London, training to be a lawyer. It must have been someone who resembled him, she thought as she watched the top-hatted man step inside the shop.

If it had been Anthony Clarkson, surely he'd have recognised her? But then again she was wearing a bonnet and his father had informed her Anthony wouldn't know where she now resided.

No, she decided her imagination was just playing tricks on her – that was all. Taking a moment, she inhaled a composing breath and then exhaled.

* * *

The porter at the workhouse door was happy to allow Enid entrance once recognition dawned and she'd explained her reason for being there. So she was ushered to Matron Finchley's office where the woman ordered a pot of coffee for two to be served as they discussed matters. Matron was delighted to see her again and hear she had settled well into life at Beechwood

House. But the woman's face clouded over at the mention of Connie O'Mara.

'Connie left here a few weeks ago...' she explained as she inclined her head to stir her cup of coffee. Then she glanced up to meet with Enid's curious gaze. 'Didn't she inform you? I understand you kept in touch with one another?'

'Oh, we did.' Enid frowned in disbelief. 'But I didn't realise it was more than six weeks since I'd last heard from her. She owes me a letter. Have you any idea where she might have gone to, Mrs Finchley?'

The woman shook her head. 'It was a strange thing as she said she'd like to get herself a job and then, one morning, the supervisor went to check the girls had all risen from their beds and Connie was missing. In fact, it appeared as though her bed hadn't even been slept in.'

Enid took a moment to digest the news. 'But wouldn't any of the girls in the dorm have known of her plans or seen her leave the workhouse?'

Matron Finchley chewed on her bottom lip. 'Apparently not. Well, if anyone knows anything, they're keeping tight-lipped about it for some reason. The one person who might hold the key to all of this is Bridie Hennessy but she won't tell me anything. I'm convinced she knows something.'

Enid could well imagine – she was a sly one, that Bridie.

'Might I have a word with one or two of them?' Enid asked. 'Is Maisie or Annie still in the dorm?'

'No, I'm afraid not,' Matron said almost in a whisper now. Enid could detect a sadness behind the woman's eyes. 'Maisie was taken by a sudden fever a few months ago.' She swallowed as if composing herself for a moment. 'And Annie has now left. All above board that was. She's working in a tea room now and lodging nearby.'

'Any idea of her address?' Enid asked hopefully, lifting her brow. 'If anyone knows anything it will be Annie. Connie often mentioned her in her letters.'

'I can give you her address but it will probably be useless. She left here well before Connie's departure so I can't see her knowing anything, but you never know, I suppose.' Matron rose from her chair and went to the cupboard to remove a heavy navy ledger, which she set down on her desk, flipping through it as her eyes scanned its pages. She ran her index finger down row after row of inmate names. 'Ah, here it is, Ivor Street. It's between the gaol and the railway station.'

Taking a pencil and a sheet of paper, she scribbled the address down and handed it to Enid who folded the sheet and placed it safely in her reticule. It wasn't much but at least it was something to go on.

'Oh, I almost forgot.' Enid dipped her hand into her wicker basket and handed Matron a pink candy-striped paper bag. 'Peppermint creams for you. I remember how much you like them!'

'For me?' Matron looked overwhelmed. 'I'm touched you remember but what have I done to deserve them?'

'I'll never forget your kindness – it was you who encouraged me to contact Mr Clarkson in the first place and I thank you for that.'

Matron smiled a smile that lit up her hazel-brown eyes. 'Think nothing of it. And I'm so pleased to hear things are going well at the new house for you, Enid.'

'Oh yes, they are. My parents and my brothers and sister are living there with me. They have an apartment there. Dad's employed as a caretaker and Mam works as the laundry mistress.'

'Oh, quite a family affair then!'

Enid smiled with satisfaction, realising just how lucky the whole family was after all that had occurred.

* * *

The light was beginning to fade as Enid arrived on Ivor Street that evening. Although she knew it would be foolhardy to go to a strange area alone, she just had to find out what happened to her friend.

A crowd of young children who had been playing hopscotch on the pavement scattered as she arrived, almost as though any strangers in the area brought bad news with them. And no doubt they were used to the local constabulary telling them off or clipping them around the earhole for some misdemeanour or another.

She fumbled in her reticule for the slip of paper Matron had given her.

She'd remembered the street name but not the number. Ah yes! Number 19.

The front door of the lodging house had obviously seen better days as the brown paint appeared worn and scuffed, though lace curtains hung from the windows, making Enid wonder whether maybe the proprietor wished it to stand out from the other dwellings, which were equally as shabby with no lace curtains.

Before knocking, she cleared her throat. She lifted the knocker and rapped three times. Presently the door was drawn back by a middle-aged woman, smartly dressed in a high-necked blue and white pinstripe dress, which to Enid spelt efficiency.

'Hello, miss,' the woman said. 'If you're looking for a room I'm afraid there are no vacancies at the moment.' She spoke in a highly refined voice, which made Enid think she'd put it on. 'But I can recommend Mrs Clancy's lodging house just across the street.' She pointed a long, bony finger in the general direction of the house.

Enid smiled. 'Er, no, thank you though. I'm looking for someone who lodges with you. Annie... Oh dear.' She bit her lip. 'I don't remember her surname...'

Why on earth hadn't she asked Matron when she was at the workhouse?

The landlady narrowed her eyes with suspicion.

"Ere, what's your business?' She looked Enid up and down. 'Not snooping around, are yer?'

Funny, the woman had slipped back into her real accent now, forgetting herself for a moment.

It was then Enid realised the woman suspected her of having ulterior motives. Cook had already warned her people in the area were suspicious of the police and the press due to nefarious deeds committed in these parts.

'Oh please, I am sorry. It's just I'm searching for a friend of mine from the workhouse. She went missing recently and Annie might know of her whereabouts. Do you have anyone staying here who came straight from there?'

The woman sniffed loudly. 'I might have...'

She wasn't making it easy for her. 'How about I give you a description then?'

The woman's features seemed to soften. 'Very well, go on then...'

'She's about my height and has dark hair with a swarthy complexion, brown eyes, round face and around my age too.'

'Yes, there is a young woman from the workhouse of that description. Been staying here for a few weeks but her name ain't Annie.'

Enid frowned. This was making no sense whatsoever. 'What's her name then?'

'It's Lilian. Look,' said the woman, sighing now, 'it'll be easier if I go to fetch her than playing twenty questions on the doorstep, then you'll see it's not the girl you're after.'

Enid nodded her thanks as the woman left her on the doorstep. There was the exchange of voices from inside and then, as if by magic, Annie appeared at the door.

'Hello, Enid!' she greeted, looking genuinely pleased to see her. 'But what are you doing here?'

The landlady stood open-mouthed for a moment.

'So, you are this Annie this young lady is seeking?'

'Oh yes.'

'But you told me your name is Lilian!' she said in an accusatory tone as if it was the worst sin in the world.

'It is. Annie is my nickname!'

'Oh,' said the landlady, laughing now. 'Well, come inside, dear. You can both catch up with one another in the parlour.'

As the pair waited for Mrs Bray, the landlady, to fetch a tray of tea, they made small talk.

'So, you really like it at the tea room?' Enid asked.

'Oh, yes. It's better than being at the workhouse at any rate!' Annie chuckled. 'And Mrs Bray here is ever so good to me.'

It sounded as if the girl had settled well but Enid had come here for a reason. 'The reason I've called is that I've lost touch with Connie. I had hopes of getting her a job as a maid at the new house where I work, but I sent a letter to Matron requesting her permission and there was no reply so I showed up there yesterday.'

'And?' said Annie as Mrs Bray set a tray of tea on the table for them.

'Matron said she left in the middle of the night and no one has a clue where she's gone to. Her bed wasn't even slept in. Did she ever say anything to you about her future plans?'

Annie shook her head, looking troubled for a moment. 'Let me just pour the tea or it will be getting stewed and then I'll tell you something odd that occurred.'

Enid raised a curious brow as she watched Annie pour the tea, the steaming brown liquid filling up the teacups just enough to add a splash of milk from the jug. She guessed it was the girl's vast experience of working at the tea room that made her so precise.

'Sugar?' Annie looked at her.

'Yes, please. Just one spoonful.'

When the teas were ready, both sat at the table and sipped them slowly.

'This is what was so strange,' began Annie. 'Just before I left the spike to come here, one night I was disturbed. Something kept hitting the dormitory window. Oh, nothing heavy, it sounded like small chips of stone or gravel – nothing that would break it at any rate. As my eyes became accustomed to the light, I noticed Connie at the window giving some sort of signal to someone outside. A thumbs up or something like that. She'd lifted the sash window and was leaning out of it. 'Course she couldn't shout to whoever it was as she'd have woken us all up. Then she disappeared. She was gone for ages and my heart was racing. I debated whether to go and see Miss Perks as I was that scared something had happened to her.'

'Who's Miss Perks?'

'Oh, you wouldn't know... We had a new supervisor; that's her name. Anyhow, I was just about to get out of bed and summon her when Connie turned up looking like she'd been pulled through a hedge backwards.'

'Did she know you were on to her?'

'Sure she did, as I asked her afterwards. She claimed she'd been down near the docks as there's lots of sailors down there who'd like to take a pretty girl out for the night. Reckoned they spend lots of money on them. She even asked me if I'd like to go with her one night but I refused. Maisie went, but once seemed enough for her. Did Matron tell you she's since passed away?'

Enid nodded sadly. 'Yes, I was ever so shocked to hear that. Some kind of fever, weren't it?'

'Yes. It was never explained but the workhouse doctor examined her. The rumour was that she'd caught some sort of pox from one of those sailors.'

Enid's hands flew to her face in horror. Now she was beginning to get it. 'So, do you think that's what Connie is doing? Selling herself to men?'

Annie nodded. 'I've no doubt of it. Some bully or another was running her for immoral purposes and sending a cab to pick her up some nights, I reckon, or he was transporting the sailors to the workhouse and taking her from there to be used. I've no doubt that's why she never returned.'

'It's inconceivable and extremely sad. Connie is so beautiful and such a kind soul,' Enid said, shaking her head in disbelief.

'She seemed to go off the rails once you left the spike. Several times she was so tired she could hardly perform her workhouse duties. One of the other girls found her curled up under the stairs on more than one occasion, fast asleep she was – out for the count.'

'So, if I need to find her I need to scout around the docks?'

'Aye. Bute Street. It used to be Charlotte Street and Whitmore Lane where all the goings-on took place – Mrs Bray told me so – but now most of the action is in the Bute area from Bute Street down to the bay. Loads of pubs there and where there's loads of pubs there's loadsa hungry and thirsty sailors with an appetite for more than a pie and a pint! If you get my drift?'

Enid nodded. 'I'm going over there now when I've finished this cup of tea.'

'Oh no, don't be silly, Enid. Don't go alone.'

'I have to, Annie. I want to take her back to the house with me.'

'Then let me come with you...' Annie stood and looked at her friend with concern in her eyes.

And so it was decided that Annie would accompany Enid in her quest to find Connie.

* * *

Annie led Enid down an alleyway and along several dimly lit streets. Darkness had fallen and, as it was a cloudy night, only the light emanating from the several gas lamps, dwellings and pubs was visible.

'Give us a kiss, darlings!' A man emerged from a tavern, invading their space as he swayed back and forth precariously. For a brief moment, Enid froze, feeling rooted to the spot. It reminded her of when Anthony Clarkson had forced himself on her; that sickening mingle of pomade and alcohol had sent her senses reeling as she'd inhaled the odour and a primeval fear took over her body.

'Get out of our way!' shouted Annie in a fierce voice that Enid had not heard previously from the girl. She stepped forward and pushed him, unafraid of the encounter.

Surprisingly, the man stepped out of their way, hiccupped and apologised. After being put in his place, he'd gone from a raging beast to a gentle lamb in seconds. Although Enid marvelled at her friend's command over the man, she realised they might not be as fortunate the next time, especially if they were to encounter two or more men on their crusade. Men would be on the prowl around these parts, seeking females to spend the night with. A quick fumble or a knee trembler in a dark alleyway, for a fee, of course.

Enid closed her eyes for a second to blot out the memory of Anthony's attack. How could Connie sell herself like that, especially when she knew that Enid had herself been taken by force, her body ravaged against her will? It also reminded her of what happened to Jimmy's mother back in Merthyr. If she hadn't been plying her wares that fateful night she might still be alive today.

'Are you all right, Enid?' Annie's voice was full of concern. Of course she didn't know anything about Enid's rape, wouldn't realise how intimidating that incident had been for her.

'Thank you. I'm all right. I just wasn't expecting that man to get so familiar with us, that's all. But thinking about it, he was looking for easy pickings, I suppose?'

'You suppose right. I don't know what's the matter with half of these men. They've most likely got a wife and kids back home.'

'The trouble is their wives are too shattered to see to their needs, most probably.'

Enid realised some wives would be like her mam, always seeming to have a baby hanging off them. Forever having sore breasts, lack of sleep and lack of inclination to have sex with their husbands. So those men sought other means. It was even rumoured that the customer who had been with Ginny, Jimmy's mother, not long before she died had been married. Her father said it was thought he was someone from the ironworks. It was a rum life indeed.

Many of the pubs they passed were rowdy, with raucous noise emanating from within, uproarious voices, cheers, laughter, even songs belted out from one or two establishments.

And all the while, Connie was out there, somewhere.

14

Cardiff had grown into the world's busiest port for exporting goods, and as coal and iron were shipped via the canal from Merthyr, the area attracted sailors and dock workers from all over the world to the bay. Tiger Bay comprised the dockland area, including the infamous Bute Street. The area had fast gained a notoriety for its criminal activities including murder and prostitution. So the idea that Connie had taken it upon herself to work in such an area horrified Enid.

Annie was now taking Enid by the arm to guide her through the busy streets, but she paused for a moment.

'Hey, they look like a couple of working girls over there,' she whispered as she nudged her with her elbow.

Enid scanned the street and found her eyes resting on a house at the end of it, the door ajar with a shaft of light projecting out onto the pavement. Outside stood two women, gaudily dressed, their backs slumped up against the wall, their breasts almost spilling over the low necklines of their dresses, their hemlines riding high to display their calves. Disgusting, her mother would have called it. She could just hear her voice saying, "A fine pair of trollops!" Thank goodness Mam didn't know where she was right now.

Before she had a chance to ask Annie what she thought they were up to,

Annie said, 'They're plying their trade. Trying to nab any passing man who will pay for the privilege of their company. It must be a brothel.'

A shiver coursed down Enid's spine. 'So you think Connie might be working from someplace like that?'

'No doubt about it,' Annie said, shaking her head. 'Come on, let's ask them if they know her.'

They crossed the street and stood before the women, who eyed them up curiously. ''Ere, whatcha staring at?' asked the taller of the two.

Under the street lamp Enid could see she had a dark, alluring look about her, but seemed hard-faced. In contrast, the other was shorter and blonde-haired. Both were attractive sorts but didn't look decent to Enid. Their frilled petticoats were raised too far above their ankle boots for her liking.

'Hello.' Enid smiled, tentatively. 'We're looking for a friend who was in the workhouse with us. Connie O'Mara? Would you happen to know of her?'

The woman stared for such a long time that Enid began to feel uncomfortable, but then she said, 'No, can't say I do. And you think she might be in the profession, like?'

'Aye, we do. We know it for a fact,' said Annie.

'She might well have changed her name then to do the business.' The blonde woman spoke for the first time. 'What's she like?'

'She's Irish. About my age,' Enid said. 'Very pretty, long chestnut hair. She's got beautiful violet eyes. Quite a calm, serene sort of person.'

'Don't sound like anyone we know, does it?' the tall one said, now throwing back her head and laughing. 'Most of the sorts we know are very feisty. They fight in the streets, not calm and serene for a moment!'

The blonde one though seemed to be deep in thought. 'I do know someone who's Irish who might fit that description. She works in The Blue Anchor as a barmaid, has done for a few weeks now.'

'So she's not on the game, then?' Enid raised a surprised brow.

'I didn't say that now, did I?' said the girl. 'The landlord there, called Cornelius Sharpe, runs some of the girls if not most on the side. It's an extra way of making up their wages, taking a sailor or dock worker upstairs. He's a right 'un, mind you. You wouldn't want to cross him, let me tell you.'

'How'd you mean?' Annie stepped forward with interest.

'Well, he leaves the girls to drink with the fellas then they go upstairs when they get them pie-eyed drunk. The girls have been warned by him, see. They're not to drink too much alcohol. By morning, the men have often been robbed blind. One man, all he had left was his kegs! Try explaining that to his wife. You could enquire there for a start but don't be surprised if no one wants to speak to you; they rarely do to outsiders.'

Enid nodded gratefully. 'What are your names? I'm Enid and this is Annie.'

'I'm Flora and this is Rosa,' she said, gesticulating her hand in her friend's direction in a theatrical fashion.

'Thanks for your help.'

'Don't say you was speaking to us, mind,' said Rosa sharply. 'We might get in trouble for it with the landlord. Sometimes he puts a bit of work in our direction.'

'No, we won't,' Enid reassured her, and when they walked away she turned to Annie and said, 'Nice of them to give us their names like that!'

'Nice?' Annie scoffed. 'They're bloody made up, those are, to sound exotic for the punters! They're probably called Gladys and Mabel!'

For the first time, Enid laughed, tickled at the thought of it.

'Now how do we find The Blue Anchor?' she asked when the merriment had subsided.

As they drew nearer to the wharf, Enid heard men's voices drifting towards them, discussing the cargo being loaded on the ship. It sounded as if they'd be setting sail soon. It was amazing to think that ship might be sailing as far away as Africa. The tall mast was silhouetted against the sky as a full moon had emerged from behind a cloud. Didn't the sailors use the stars and moon to navigate their ships? There was so much noise and clatter going on that you wouldn't think it night-time at all.

A sudden thought gripped her. 'What if Connie's stowed aboard a ship like one of these and has gone to another country?'

'It's possible I suppose but not probable. I don't think she'd want to leave while her family are in Cardiff. She wouldn't want to be parted from her mam and sisters.'

'Maybe not but what if she was forced on one of those ships by sailors or one of the bullies? They might well take working girls with them on their voyage.'

'I've no doubt they do – men have their desires after all,' said Annie in a matter-of-fact tone. 'But we have to hope that she's here, somewhere.'

Finally, after asking one of the sailors about The Blue Anchor, he directed them to the pub in question.

As they stood outside, two sailors emerged and a strong smell of alcohol permeated Enid's nostrils. The sailors didn't try to bother them at all and Enid wondered if they'd already been with working girls and that's why they didn't show any interest, their urges now fully sated.

The bar area was crowded as a group of men tried to catch the bar staff's attention.

'Over here when you have a moment, Mr Finley!' one man shouted, holding up a pewter tankard.

'Come on, darlin', I ain't got all night!' shouted another to a girl serving drinks.

Enid scanned the bar and couldn't see who the barmaid was for a moment, until eventually she was rewarded with a glimpse as the area cleared. But it wasn't Connie. This was a very young girl of about thirteen years of age and the way Mr Finley was tapping her on the head, she wondered if maybe it was his daughter helping out.

Then over in the far corner, Enid heard a ripple of applause and her eyes were directed to a small stage, framed by red drapes. As they were pulled back, there she saw a well-endowed woman in a low-cut dress. The men began to cheer and whistle as she sashayed across the stage, wiggling her hips in a provocative fashion and blowing them a kiss.

Then she began to sing.

> *He was only a cheeky sailor,*
> *Only the tar for me,*
> *Only a cheeky sailor,*
> *Who wanted to go to sea...*
> *Only a cheeky sailor,*
> *Only the one for me,*
> *He left me at the dockside,*

Riding those waves from me!

The song seemed to delight the men as she stepped down from the stage, plonking herself seductively on one man's lap, pressing her enormous bosom into his face then covering him in kisses, as the rest egged him on. Enid wondered if maybe she was also a working girl or was she just a singer sent out there to ramp them all up so that they'd spend their hard-earned money on booze and women?

Following a few performance songs of the same ilk, as the male pianist bashed away on the piano keys with great aplomb, the woman left the stage to rapturous applause and shrill whistles, and then someone else emerged through the curtain.

There, on the stage in a white satin dress with her dark chestnut hair falling in waves on her shoulders, was Connie, appearing virginal and meek. A stark contrast to the last performer. For a moment, Enid felt like calling to her and waving her arms to attract her attention but it was obvious she was about to sing as the pianist struck up "The Rose of Tralee".

> *The pale moon was rising above the green mountain,*
> *The sun was declining beneath the blue sea;*
> *When I strayed with my love to the pure crystal fountain,*
> *That stands in the beautiful Vale of Tralee...*

Enid marvelled at her friend. The girl sang so beautifully you couldn't hear a pin drop. The men were spellbound by Connie's singing, which sounded so clear and angelic. Enid noticed one man rubbing his eyes and saying to the fellow beside him, 'This always reminds me of my family back in Ireland, so it does!'

This was what Connie was up to, then. Enid hoped upon hope the girl wasn't working as a lady of the night as well.

Mr Finley passed around a bucket for the men to drop their spare coins into and, going by the chinking noises, it sounded like a lot. But as soon as the performance had ended, to deafening applause and appreciative murmurs, there was a deathly silence as all eyes turned to the man emerging from the back room. He had an air of arrogance about him and he walked with a swagger. He wore a well-tailored long jacket, white shirt and navy cravat neatly held in place by a gold pin. His pinstriped trousers and shiny, well-polished shoes gave the appearance of wealth. It was then she realised that this was the landlord the girls spoke of and not Mr Finley like she'd earlier assumed. This man had an angry look on his reddened face as he strode towards the stage.

Grabbing the bucket from Mr Finley, he said, 'I've told you before I don't want any of those soppy, sentimental songs in this establishment!'

Mr Finley's hand trembled and a nerve near his eye twitched. 'Sorry, Mr Sharpe. It won't happen again. It's just some of the Irish in here like a little taste of home and they always put a bit extra in when the lass sings.'

'Well, she can sing all right, I agree,' he said, nodding at her. 'But you hear, young lady? You're to sing more lively songs for the men.' Then he stage-whispered in her ear, though so loudly Enid managed to work out what he said, 'The idea is to get them upstairs in the bedroom not wanting to throw themselves off the dock outside!'

Connie nodded, the whites of her eyes on show. It was in that moment Enid could tell how petrified she was of the man as he roughly grabbed hold of her arm, putting pressure on it with his fingers. In an instant, Enid made to barge towards her friend and confront the bully – something she wouldn't normally do – but in the nick of time, Annie pulled her back.

'Don't!' she whispered. 'We mustn't draw any attention to ourselves as who knows what might happen otherwise. Connie doesn't even know we're here. We'll come back another time to rescue her.'

In the moment, Enid felt too fired up to want to return another time but as her heartbeat returned to normal, she could see the sense of Annie's suggestion. In amongst the melee, the pair quietly slipped away back out onto the pavement outside.

'What now?' asked Enid.

'I think we ought to get out of here. We'll hail a cab around the corner. You can't walk all the way home in the dark; it's just not safe. The cab can drop me off on the way. Don't worry, I've got enough money on me.'

Enid was thankful for her friend's suggestion. She barely had enough money on her to pay for a cab.

'At least we now know where Connie is and roughly what time she performs at the pub,' Annie added.

That was some consolation at least.

* * *

When Enid returned to the house she was surprised to find Sam sat at the kitchen table drinking a cup of tea, all alone. None of the kitchen staff was anywhere to be seen so she guessed they'd already retired for bed.

'Hello,' she said tentatively, wondering what sort of response she'd get. The last time she'd had any conversation with him had been when he'd been let down by Miss Eliza.

He looked up as she approached and his eyes said it all. They appeared hollow somehow. 'Hello,' he sniffed. 'How are you up so late?' Then noticing something, he said, 'You've got your jacket on? You been out somewhere?'

She nodded. 'Went in search of a friend. Any tea left in the pot?'

'Yes. Help yourself.'

She went to fetch a cup and saucer and poured herself some of the brew. It looked strong, which wasn't usually to her taste, but she didn't mind too much as she felt she needed it right now after the night she'd had. When she'd poured for herself, she topped up Sam's cup.

'What's wrong, Sam?' she said in a sympathetic tone of voice.

'Oh,' he sighed deeply. 'You were right about Miss Eliza – she was playing me all along.'

'How do you know that?'

'That night she didn't show up to meet me for the theatre, I discovered from one of the maids, she took herself off to bed early and then the following morning there was a gentleman caller at the house for her.'

'That's strange. I never saw him but then again I did have an errand to run.' She realised it must have been the morning she went to see Matron at the workhouse. 'What was he like, this gentleman?'

'Tall, dark and handsome, the usual cliché...' He laughed in a scornful manner.

'I know the sort. And you think they are romantically involved?'

'I should say so. Penny overheard their conversation. He's in some sort of training to be a lawyer, I think, but marriage plans were discussed...'

Enid's eyebrows shot up in surprise. 'Well, who'd have thought it!'

'Who indeed! Not muggins here!' He pointed a thumb at himself. 'I feel a complete fool, Enid. I allowed myself to get carried away with all the things she was saying to me.'

'You won't be the first one that's happened to, Sam, and you certainly won't be the last. Just chalk it down to experience.'

'I know you are right. But why did I ever think such a thing was possible in the first place? Miss Eliza is of a different world to me, another class...'

Enid had to agree. She knew what that felt like. 'I wonder if her brother knows about this man?'

'Evidently not, according to Penny. He arrived at the house the morning Mr Darling left for a few days away in London on business!'

'Very convenient. She wouldn't dare bring a man to the house if her brother was here. Not unless she sought his approval beforehand. But thinking about it...' She chewed on her bottom lip. '...if she's practically engaged to be married that makes what she did to you even worse in my book, Sam.' She glanced in his direction to witness that his face had creased with pain. Now she wished she hadn't said what was on her mind at all.

They sat in companiable silence for a while. She yearned to tell him all that had happened tonight but he was hardly in a fit state to listen and surely wouldn't take it in anyhow. It was obvious he'd had some sort of infatuation for Miss Eliza and was broken-hearted. She quietly washed her cup and saucer and excused herself from the kitchen.

Oh, Sam, why did you have to fall for that young lady of all people?

15

The following morning, Enid was able to put thoughts of Connie and Sam out of her mind as the house was abuzz with chatter and speculation regarding Miss Eliza and her mystery beau. So far, only Mr Tatton and Penny had caught sight of the man. But today, Miss Eliza had informed them her gentleman would be arriving at the house for afternoon tea, which was to be taken in the drawing room. She gave Mrs Sowerberry special instructions for how the room was to be cleaned, the furniture was to be rearranged at her behest and a small table with the best linen and two matching chairs were to be sited near the long French windows. Also, she suggested particular floral displays to be arranged: pink and white carnations for the table and for the flower stands. In the corners of the room, she requested seasonal spring flowers, which co-ordinated colour-wise with the table.

Miss Eliza seemed to be going to an enormous amount of effort for the young man. Was he about to propose to her like the rest of the staff at the house appeared to think? Yet this was the first Enid had heard of such a liaison between the pair. And wouldn't Mr Darling be annoyed if he returned from London to discover this was so? In any case, she couldn't see how this could possibly happen without him requesting permission from the head of the house in the first instance. Their father might have passed on some years since, but Mr Darling had taken his younger sister under his wing.

By early afternoon, Penny and Daisy seemed to be strung up about it all.

'It's just not fair,' Penny moaned to Enid, gesticulating as she threw up her hands. 'Miss Eliza asked me to wash all the downstairs windows for a second time today! Nothing seems good enough for her!'

'Aye, and she'd been in the kitchen laying down the law and all to Mrs Appleton. Cook's not best pleased. She said she has enough to contend with without baking fancies on top of everything. Of course, she knows of Cook's background with the French baking, and she's out to impress a certain someone. Can't wait to see him though! You've already seen him, you lucky dab!' Enid shot an interested glance in Penny's direction. 'Tell me again what he looked like?'

'Dark-haired, very tall and broad-shouldered. Incredibly handsome. He fair took my breath away!'

Enid smiled. It appeared as if Penny was smitten by the man. She was looking forward to seeing him herself now after all the build-up to it. Understandably, the one person who wasn't looking forward to this was Samuel, who was walking around with a glowering expression on his face, so much so that Mr Tatton had pulled him up about it in the corridor.

The time for the gentleman's arrival was to be three o'clock precisely. Penny and Daisy kept peeping by the drawing room window for the arrival of his carriage while Miss Eliza told them she would wait in the library to be summoned when he called. She obviously didn't wish to appear to be too keen, waiting around for his arrival. A wise move, Enid thought, but she guessed the young woman wouldn't be able to concentrate on one of her books, more likely reading the same page over and over again in anticipation at their assignation.

'He's here!' shouted Daisy and the staff sprang into action as his carriage drew up outside. Mr Tatton waited behind the door for the knock, his back stiff as a poker as both maids stood outside the drawing room door with Mrs Sowerberry and Enid. Samuel, though, was nowhere to be seen.

'Good afternoon to you, sir!' Enid heard Mr Tatton greet the man. 'I'll just send one of the maids to let Miss Eliza know you have arrived.'

Some pleasantries were exchanged as the butler took his cape, top hat and cane, and then Mr Tatton summoned Penny to fetch Miss Eliza. The gentleman was stood behind the butler, and Daisy almost wet herself with the excitement of it all, but as soon as Mr Tatton stepped away, Enid stared at the man in horror.

It was him!

She'd not been wrong that morning; it hadn't been her imagination at all. It was Anthony Clarkson himself who was Miss Eliza's suitor!

The entrance hall seemed to swirl around her as the colours mixed and matched and fine crystal drops from the chandelier above seemed to sparkle like stars in the sky. And then she was lying on her back with Mrs Sowerberry gazing down on her. Somewhere in the distance, she heard Mr Tatton ushering Anthony into the drawing room. Had he spotted her?

Someone was kneeling beside her, tapping her cheek. 'Are you all right?' It was the housekeeper.

'No, not really,' whispered Enid. 'It's him…'

'Who, dear?'

'The man…'

Enid wasn't sure if the woman realised what she was referring to but the next thing she knew she was being helped to her feet and told to go and lie down in her bedroom.

'I'll be with you in a few minutes after I've supervised in the drawing room,' Mrs Sowerberry said tactfully. 'I'll ask Daisy to make you a cup of tea and then we can chat later.'

Enid nodded, and shakily she made her way to her bedroom, ensuring she took a firm hold of the handrail on the way up. Was this some kind of a joke? Mr Clarkson had made it sound as if she'd never have to see Anthony ever again, so why was he arriving at the house and wooing the master's sister of all people? It made no sense whatsoever.

As she reclined on the bed and tried to relax, all of a sudden she sat bolt upright. *The master!* If she, herself, had been raped by Anthony and goodness knew if there were others too, then what about Miss Eliza's safety? She'd be safe here at the house but what if the man offered to take her somewhere unaccompanied? Without her brother's presence, was she safe?

Enid's heart began to pound at the implications. What on earth could she do about this?

A few minutes later Daisy knocked on the door with a cup of tea for her. 'I hope you're all right, Enid,' she said softly as she laid it down on the bedside table. 'You're not feeling unwell like the last time, are you?'

'Last time?' Enid blinked.

'You know, when you had that sickness and had to stay away from the rest of the staff here?'

Enid noticed the girl had stepped well away after placing the cup and saucer down on the bedside table. Was she afraid she was going to catch something from her? It was then she realised what Daisy was implying. Of course, Mrs Sowerberry had made it known that Enid had some sort of sickness that time she thought she might be pregnant, ironically by the man downstairs now about to take tea in the drawing room with Miss Eliza.

'Oh, nothing like that.' Enid smiled at her. 'I'm just prone to fainting spells when I'm having my monthly, that's all.'

There was no use telling Daisy or any of the others about Anthony as they'd hardly believe her. She wondered if Mr Darling would either.

There was one person though who could deal with this and that was Mr Clarkson, senior. But to contact him would take time. Unless she sent him a telegram? But even then by the time he arrived here something might have occurred.

'You return downstairs, Daisy. I'm fine,' Enid said. 'And thank you for the tea.'

Daisy's eyes lit up. She was obviously dying to return to the drawing room to get a good gawp at Anthony Clarkson and eavesdrop on his conversation with Miss Eliza.

It was a good twenty-five minutes before Mrs Sowerberry turned up. She knocked softly on the door before entering and then sat on the edge of the bed, patting Enid's hand in reassurance. 'So, what you're telling me is that gentleman, if that's the right term for him, sitting downstairs with Miss Eliza is the same man who took you by force?'

'Raped me? Yes. It's him. I can't understand what he's doing here, as his father banished him from the home. I thought he might have explained all that to Mr Darling.'

'Maybe he already has,' said the housekeeper sagely. 'Perhaps he did exactly that but Mr Darling doesn't realise Eliza is seeing Anthony so wouldn't feel it necessary to inform his sister about the matter. But the problem is, now I have this information, what do I do about it?' The woman's forehead creased into a frown.

Although it wasn't her fault, Enid now felt guilty for laying the enormity of the situation at Mrs Sowerberry's door.

'When is Mr Darling due back here?' Enid asked.

'Not for two or three days. I've no way of contacting him either as he told me he would be staying at different hotels in London.'

Enid chewed on her lip. 'Oh dear.'

'Oh dear, indeed.' The housekeeper looked away for a moment as if trying to compose herself and then fixed her gaze on Enid. 'Now my immediate problem is what are we going to do about you?'

'Me?' Enid blinked.

'Well, yes. The man's presence is going to distress you – it already has. Would you rather say you're ill?'

'No, I will not!' said Enid, gritting her teeth. 'He's affected my life as it is. Maybe it would be a good idea for me to encounter him, show him my presence here at the house, and that way he may back away from Miss Eliza.'

'That's a possibility, I suppose, though I suggest you are never alone with him. I don't want to put you through something you're unprepared for.'

Enid was beginning to feel incensed at the situation now. All this time she'd felt saddened by it but now she was prepared to fight fire with fire.

* * *

Mrs Sowerberry dismissed Penny and Daisy from the drawing room, telling them that she and Enid would take their place. Both girls grimaced as they could no longer earwig. As Enid passed the maids as they departed, she noticed Anthony had his back to her. He was seated at the table in front of the French windows as Miss Eliza faced him across the table. Enid's stomach lurched violently as she took a position in the corner of the room, while Mrs Sowerberry sorted out some plates and small cake knives and linen napkins for the table, which she placed before them.

Then Penny arrived with a tray of tea, which she handed over to Enid. Mrs Sowerberry nodded at Enid, who worried now if she'd drop the tray she was that nervous, but instead her resolve took over as, with confidence, she placed the tray on the table and removed the china teapot, milk jug and cups and saucers in front of them, neatly arranging them before pouring. Initially, Anthony took no particular notice of her as his eyes were firmly fixed on Eliza, who spoke excitedly about her plans to visit Paris. He appeared quite smitten with her as he smiled at her rabid enthusiasm.

'Oh, I think Paris would be a fine place for a honeymoon,' he said. 'I went there about two years ago and visited Montmartre.'

Then, tearing his eyes from Eliza, he caught Enid's persistent gaze, and in that moment recognition dawned. He knew it was her.

Swallowing hard, he seemed flustered and had forgotten his train of thought as he averted his gaze back on to Eliza. 'Now, where was I?'

'You were telling me how you visited Montmartre,' she said in an amused fashion.

Normally, Enid would have stepped away from the table by now but she was enjoying making the man squirm. So she stood back just a little and continued to stare at him without Eliza noticing.

He placed two fingers beneath his shirt collar as though it were now too tight for him, and Enid could see the slightest trace of beads of perspiration on his forehead. Reaching into his top pocket, he extracted a handkerchief to mop his brow, replaced it and then took a long swig from his teacup, which must have gone down the wrong way as he began to cough and splutter.

'Are you feeling all right? You're looking awfully pale.' Eliza looked at him, her eyes full of concern.

'I'm f... fine, thank you.'

Enid kept her unwavering gaze fixed on him and as he glanced at her she smiled self-assuredly, causing him to immediately look away. It was obvious her presence made him highly uncomfortable. It was a particularly warm afternoon too, which couldn't have helped matters for him.

Finally, Eliza, who seemed terribly confused by her guest's behaviour, said, 'I'll tell you what, I have a special book about Paris in the library. I'll just go and fetch it for you...'

Maybe she was feeling uncomfortable now too, as surely she'd usually have asked Enid to fetch it for her.

Anthony nodded as she stood and left the table, Mrs Sowerberry making no attempt to intervene or offer to fetch the book herself.

As soon as Eliza was out of the door, the housekeeper stood there blocking it.

Anthony's eyes widened and then he stared down at the table, no doubt wishing Eliza would return as soon as possible.

'So, we meet again, Mr Clarkson,' said Enid as she moved closer.

He looked up at her and forced a smile. 'So, we do, er Edith, isn't it?'

'No, it's ruddy well not!' Enid raised her voice as she felt a vein pulsate in her neck. 'My name is Enid, E-N-I-D, not Edith like you called me the night you forced yourself on me! What's it called now?' She loomed over him. 'Yes, that's it! One word can describe what you did to me: rape! You're the bastard who robbed me of my virginity!'

He began to push himself away from the table as if unable to bear what he was being accused of. Then standing, he took several strides forward as if about to leave the room to find Mrs Sowerberry in his path.

'And where are you off to, Mr Clarkson?' the woman asked. 'Don't you think it rather rude to walk out on Miss Eliza when she has invited you for afternoon tea?'

'Just tell her I have business to attend to!' he snapped, but the woman didn't budge an inch.

'Oh no, you're not getting away that easily. There's a name for men like you!'

'Get out of my bloody way, you old crone!' he yelled as spittle sprayed from his mouth.

The whites of the housekeeper's eyes were on show now, the woman realising the seriousness of what was occurring. 'I'll only get out of your way if you promise to end things with Miss Eliza or...'

'Or what?' he sneered.

'Or she and her brother will be informed of what you did to Enid. That you, sir, are a rapist!'

He lifted his chin and sniffed loudly. Then shouted, 'Ha! Who do you think they'll really believe? Me or you pair? Eliza is besotted with me and she wants a ring on her finger, as for that brother of hers, he's too savvy to let a little thing like the rape of a paltry parlour maid – who, might I add, was panting for it – get in the way of me marrying his sister, you old fool!'

Then he grabbed Mrs Sowerberry and began to shake her violently as Enid, not knowing what to do now but overtaken by her anger, lifted the iron poker from the fireplace, rushed towards him and struck him on the back of his head. He dropped like a swatted fly onto the floor at the housekeeper's feet.

'Oh, Enid, what have you done?' Mrs Sowerberry's hands flew to her face in horror as she stared at Enid, who still had the poker in position above her head as if she was about to use it again.

The poker fell from Enid's hand with a clatter onto the floor as though it were too hot for her to handle.

'I think I've killed him!'

16

Enid held her breath and it felt as though time stood still, as the blood seeped from Anthony's head, pooling into a small puddle on the floor.

But then Anthony groaned.

He's alive!

'Quick, replace that poker by the fireplace!' shouted Mrs Sowerberry. Then she ran to the table to fetch some napkins and knelt to hold them to his head to stem the flow of blood. 'Grab that spare tablecloth on the unit there, Enid!'

Enid did as told and she managed to wipe the small pool of blood from the parquet floor. Then she helped Anthony, who seemed dazed by the event, onto his feet.

'Escort him to his carriage while I deal with this...'

Enid complied with Mrs Sowerberry's request as she took Anthony by the arm and led him to the door. She'd never have believed she'd be in such close proximity to him ever again. But she was no longer scared of him. He seemed a bit confused.

'Where are we going?' he asked.

'Your carriage is waiting to take you home,' she said sharply, and then she opened the door and led him down the small flight of steps and to his waiting carriage, where the driver seemed surprised to see him so soon.

'What's happened here?' he asked as he clambered down from his seat to help him on board.

'Mr Clarkson fell, suffering a blow to his head. We think it's best if he returns home to rest for now,' said Enid. It seemed the best way to explain things and as he wasn't complaining or resisting, she relaxed for a moment, letting out a little breath of relief.

The driver nodded at her and said no more, managing to seat Anthony inside the carriage, eyeing him up and down as he did so. 'We better get the doctor out to you when you get home, sir,' he advised.

Anthony Clarkson raised a hand of protest. 'No doctor, please.'

Then Mrs Sowerberry arrived with his cape, hat and cane and handed them to the driver.

'This is most unusual,' said the man, shaking his head.

'Nothing unusual about it at all,' said the housekeeper curtly. 'The maid told you, he fell and hit his head, best place is home right now.'

The driver's eyes widened in disbelief, but he said no more about it.

When he'd driven away, Mrs Sowerberry draped a reassuring arm around Enid's shoulders. 'Don't worry. I think it's just a surface wound. Hopefully, he won't remember too much about what happened and, in any case, how can he explain things after what he did to you?'

Enid's eyes grew large. 'Miss Eliza!' she said with some alarm.

'Don't worry. I've sent Penny to delay her in the library with a tale of Mr Clarkson asking her to look for a book I know we haven't got. She'll be there a while yet. Then when she does emerge, I'll give her a tale about how he had to leave suddenly as he'd forgotten he had an important meeting.'

Enid didn't know whether that would work or not but it was the best option they had for the time being.

'I'd better fetch a mop and bucket to clean that blood away properly from the drawing room floor,' she said solemnly.

Mrs Sowerberry nodded. 'Don't forget to clean that poker while you're at it and put the tablecloth and napkins to soak in the laundry room.'

It had been an eventful afternoon to say the least and Enid hoped it wouldn't get any worse than it already was. She glanced at her hands, which were now trembling, but although part of her regretted her actions against Anthony Clarkson, there was a part of her that said, *Good enough for him. At least I might have saved Miss Eliza from a fate worse than death!*

* * *

When Eliza re-emerged, Enid had bundled up the bloodied tablecloth and napkins and, thankfully, the floor and poker had been wiped clean.

'Oh?' said Eliza, her eyes widening. 'I haven't been gone all that long, have I? I couldn't find the blessed book for ages, so I pulled lots of books down from the shelves, then I remembered it was in my room all the time. After that, Penny arrived mentioning another book Mr Clarkson needed, but I couldn't find that one anywhere.' She sighed softly then frowned. 'But why have you cleared everything away? And where is Mr Clarkson? He hasn't left, has he?'

Enid was about to reply when Mrs Sowerberry entered the room, patting down her hair as if to compose herself.

'Yes, miss. Mr Clarkson suddenly realised he had an important meeting that had gone completely out of his mind. He sent his apologies before leaving. He left in haste as he was late for it.'

Eliza's face crumpled and, for a moment, Enid thought the young woman was about to cry, but then she took a deep, composing breath and said, 'I suppose it couldn't be helped. Hopefully he will return when the meeting has ended. Did he say he'd call back here?'

'No, miss,' Mrs Sowerberry said softly. Then as if to ease the situation she added, 'How about we make you a fresh pot of tea and serve up some of those cakes in the library for you? A good book will take your mind off things.'

Eliza nodded and smiled but Enid could tell tears weren't far away.

* * *

The laundry room was a hive of activity as Enid entered. She watched as Daisy dipped a couple of bed sheets into a large copper vat of bubbling hot water located at the far end of the room with the aid of a large pair of wooden tongs. The girl was so small, she had to stand on an old packing crate to do so. In another corner were two ironing boards where Penny was hard at it with a smoothing iron. It looked as if it was the master's shirts she was pressing there. But where was Mam? She needed to speak to her before anyone noticed the blood on that linen tablecloth and those napkins.

She finally noticed her mother seated at a small table, jotting something down in a hard-backed ledger.

She glanced up as Enid approached.

'Hello, love, need something from here, do you?' She smiled.

Enid shook her head. 'No, well, not exactly.' She lowered her voice. 'Can I have a word with you in private, please?'

Her mother nodded, unsmiling now, and she hated herself for having to trouble her about the issue, but in a way it was something that involved her too.

'Come on,' Mam said, standing, 'we'll go into the stockroom. No one will trouble us in there.'

Following after her mother, Enid left the laundry room and headed next door to the stockroom, where her mam took a large metal key from her pocket to open the door. It was well lit inside with a large window at one end. Shelf upon shelf of newly washed and dried and neatly folded items were stored there: bed linen, tablecloths, towels, clothing and all manner of things that had gone through the laundry room lay here waiting for collection from a maid or two.

'Now, what is it?' Mam asked, looking deep within her daughter's eyes.

Enid wrung her hands, not quite knowing how to put things. Whatever she said it would hurt her mother to hear that man's name mentioned. But what could she do? She couldn't lie. Taking a deep breath of composure and then letting it out again, she began.

'You know Miss Eliza had a special visitor here to the house earlier?'

'Aye, I should do and all, the way Penny and Daisy have gone on about the gentleman...' she said with a twinkle in her eyes. 'What of it?'

'Well, it was no gentleman, it was Anthony Clarkson!'

'Oh, good grief!' said her mother as she clamped her hand over her mouth in disbelief. Dropping it to her side, she asked, 'What on earth is *that man* doing here?'

'He's gone, thank goodness. He was taking afternoon tea with Miss Eliza in the drawing room when she left to fetch a book from the library to show him. Meanwhile, I ended up losing my temper with him so he got up to leave, but Mrs Sowerberry blocked his way out. She warned him to keep away from Miss Eliza or she'd inform her brother.'

'I should think so and all! Oh, Enid, he didn't hurt you, did he?' Her mother's eyes were full of compassion now.

'Oh no, nothing like that. He got nasty then and began to shake Mrs Sowerberry roughly. But, Mam, it was the other way around.'

'Other way around?' Her mother angled her head to one side.

'I feared for what he'd do to Mrs Sowerberry as she wouldn't move out of his way, so I did something stupid that I'm not proud of but if I hadn't done it, he might have hurt her.'

'Go on, what did you do then?'

'I picked up the poker from the fireplace and bashed him over the head with it!'

Mam opened her mouth to say something and closed it again, before finally saying, 'Well done you! Well bloody done, our Enid! He had it coming to him after what he did to you.'

'I thought that at first but then I looked at his crumpled-up heap on the floor and the blood was oozing out of his head. Mrs Sowerberry used the napkins to stem the flow of blood coming from his head and I used the tablecloth to wipe the floor until I could mop it up. This is what I'm saying. I've placed those in a bag in the laundry but I'm afraid in case questions are asked if found by Penny or Daisy or even someone else maybe.'

'Have no fear, I shall think of something. What was Miss Eliza told? I'm taking it that brute got back onto his feet again?'

'He did, yes, and he left before she returned. Mrs Sowerberry spun a tale about how he forgot he ought to be at a very important meeting. We told his driver he had fallen in the drawing room and hit his head.'

'Then that is what I shall tell them if they ask but I should be able to soak the items before they go into the copper and they'll be none the wiser. Where did you place the bag?'

'It's in that old cupboard at the far end of the laundry, I tucked it away until I could tell you about it.'

'Good thinking. I'm glad he's had his comeuppance and you've done a good thing. Now he should stay well away. Miss Eliza doesn't need bothering with the likes of his sort!' Martha spat out the words. 'One thing that does puzzle me though is how of all people he was courting her?'

'I've questioned that myself and the only thing I can think of is that as his father is friendly with Mr Darling, the two families might all know one another. Maybe he's known her for years.'

'I would have thought Mr Darling would have wanted to keep his sister well away from a rapist.'

'Maybe he doesn't know what happened to me.'

'I suppose that's a possibility.'

'One thing's for certain though, Mam. I am going to tell Mr Darling everything when he returns from London. It's too risky in case Anthony Clarkson contacts Miss Eliza, as she doesn't know what he did to me, or the lies to cover up what I did to him, attacking him with a poker come to that!'

Her mother, nodding her approval, looked away for a moment, and when she turned back to face her daughter, her eyes were glistening with tears.

* * *

'Miss Eliza hasn't left her room for a couple of days,' said Sam, frowning. 'It's most unlike her.'

'Haven't you got over her yet?' snapped Enid.

They were both in the kitchen preparing to take some trays to the dining room for the master's breakfast. He'd returned home from London late last night and Enid thought it would be a good opportunity to gauge what sort of mood he was in before approaching him about his sister. If the business trip had gone badly then no doubt it would be written all over his face and she'd be wise to approach him at another time.

'What on earth's got into you?' Sam looked mystified.

'I'm sorry, Sam, it's not you...' She huffed out a breath. 'It's something that happened recently regarding her and the gentleman caller.'

She had his interest now. 'Tell me later when we're on a break,' he whispered. 'I'll meet you at the bench outside.'

She nodded, now wondering if that may be wise, as how was she going to explain why he'd really left and that was the reason for Miss Eliza's upset?

When they arrived outside the dining room, Mr Tatton opened the door for them and Sam carried the silver salver over to the serving area to prepare. This morning, Cook had made a bowl of kedgeree, so wearing white gloves, he set upon spooning the dish onto a white plate, while Enid poured a cup of tea.

Mr Darling was in the middle of reading his *Times* newspaper as she approached with the smaller tea tray but he looked up and smiled at her.

'Good morning, Enid,' he said, and she could tell by his tone and manner he was in a good mood. That business trip must have gone well.

Mr Tatton appeared at the table with salt and pepper pots and when Sam placed the plate of food down, the butler looked at Mr Darling.

'Salt and pepper, sir?'

Mr Darling nodded his approval and all three staff members stepped away from the table. Mr Tatton busied himself, polishing some silver cutlery while Sam and Enid returned to the kitchen to fetch the rest of the breakfast, which this morning was a selection of cold cuts with bread and butter and a fresh fruit salad. It often amused Enid how much the master put away in the mornings for breakfast but, that said, he never ate at midday, instead preferring to wait until his evening meal. These breakfasts seemed to set him up for the day.

'Got time for a cuppa, you two?' asked Cook.

Enid nodded. 'A quick five minutes. Mr Darling will be a while yet.'

'Thumbing through *The Times* again, is he?' She chuckled.

'Yes,' said Samuel. 'I think he'll make a start on the crossword soon.'

'I've never known a man to take so long over his breakfast.' Cook smiled. 'But it suits me as I can have a break before I start cooking food for the staff. Now I've just brewed up, so I'll be mother and pour.'

'Thank you, Mrs Appleton.' Enid took a seat at the table while Sam followed suit.

She noticed how Sam kept glancing at her as she spoke animatedly with Mrs Appleton, mainly relating how she thought Mr Darling's London business trip must have gone well as he appeared in a good mood this morning.

It wasn't until later when it was their official break time as they sat on their favourite bench out the back of the property that he managed to ask her what was going on with Miss Eliza.

'Look, Sam,' Enid said softly, 'I am sorry I was a little sharp earlier with you but there's good reason I'm concerned about Miss Eliza and her suitor...'

He turned to face her. 'I was about to say the same thing. I glimpsed him on the way in and I didn't like the look of him. Seemed too self-assured to me.'

Enid huffed out a breath. Of course, no matter what he knew or didn't know about the man his view would be coloured anyhow as he desired Miss Eliza for himself. He had the young woman on a pedestal.

'Well, your powers of observation are founded, Sam.'

'You mean I'm right?' He blinked several times as though pleased with himself.

'I worked for his family in Merthyr before coming to Cardiff. In fact...' She hesitated before carrying on. 'He was the reason I was sent to the Cardiff workhouse before being employed here.'

Sam frowned. 'I knew I was right about him!' He slammed his fist down on the armrest of the bench and Enid could feel its vibrations. He gritted his teeth. 'So, what happened then?'

'Oh, it's a long story. Maybe I'll tell you some day but for now all you need to know is he's not a very nice person. I hadn't done anything wrong but his mother sided with him over something and saw to it I was sent back to the Merthyr workhouse. I was there with my family, see, because we lost our home. Then early the very next morning I was transferred to the Cardiff one.'

'But that still doesn't make sense why you ended up working for Mr Darling and how his sister knows the man?'

She shook her head as her eyes glistened with tears then, swallowing, said, 'It's because of Mr Clarkson, senior – his father. He realised an injustice had been carried out towards me and he offered to help me and my family get employment here with Mr Darling. He happened to be a family friend.'

'Oh, I see.' Sam took her hand in his own and gave it a gentle squeeze of reassurance. 'I don't know quite what happened to you there but it sounds as if lies were told to get you fired, Enid.'

He stroked the back of her hand as if only appreciating her for the first time as a young woman even though they'd been friends.

Enid shivered for a moment. She didn't know if she liked him touching her that way as it seemed so intimate after being Jimmy's girl. It wasn't just that though – she was jumpy these days in general since the rape as she couldn't be certain of any male attention directed her way.

'So, do you think I ought to go and see Mr Darling later to warn him about his sister and Anthony Clarkson?'

He nodded and then he brushed away her tears with the pads of both thumbs. 'Undoubtedly, yes. Yes, Enid, you really must.' Then he hugged her towards him.

From the window above, neither saw Mrs Sowerberry who had been watching the entire time.

The woman turned away from the window and smiled to herself.

17

Enid swallowed hard before knocking on Mr Darling's study room door.

'Enter!' he called out.

What if she was doing the wrong thing and he wouldn't welcome the news about Miss Eliza and that brute Clarkson? It was too late to back out now and she hoped she wouldn't lose her job over what she was about to reveal.

'Hello, Enid,' he greeted as she entered. 'What brings you here? Has Cook sent you to see if I'd like some refreshment?'

She shook her head. 'No, Mr Darling, though I can fetch something for you when I leave here after what I've come to tell you, if you like?'

His generous lips curved into a smile. 'That would be most welcome but do take a seat.' He was sitting behind his desk and he gestured to the empty chair on the opposite side of it.

The refreshment for her employer became forgotten about as Enid explained what had happened with Miss Eliza and Anthony Clarkson. He said nothing throughout, just listened and, at the end of it, his forehead creased into a frown.

'Now, are you sure about all of this, Enid? What you are saying about him being a rapist is a serious charge. I've known the family for years. Indeed, Donald Clarkson is my friend. Now, just who is this young lady his son raped who worked at the house last year? I may have to have a word with her as I don't want my sister put in any danger...'

Enid deliberated before telling him any more. Her plan had been to create a fictitious character so the shame of it all as the victim would not be cast on herself but now she decided that honesty might be the best policy. Her mouth felt dry, almost as though her tongue was enlarged, and she wished she had something to drink. Her eyes scanned the room and fell upon a jug of water on a glass trolley near the windowsill that Mr Darling used to add to his whisky.

'Please, Mr Darling, it's taking me a lot to tell you all of this. I barely slept a wink last night. May I have a glass of water before I explain?'

He nodded. 'Of course.' Then rising from his chair, he went over to the trolley and poured her a glass, before pouring himself a small glass of whisky from a crystal decanter. He placed both down on the desk and watched as she took several sips.

'The maid I told you about who was raped last year... I know so much about it because it was me.'

His eyes widened with the horror of it all and then, blinking, he said, 'Anthony Clarkson raped you, Enid? And you worked at the house?'

'Yes, sir. I was in the Merthyr workhouse back then and boarded out as a maid to the Clarkson house. It was made plain to me as soon as I arrived there that I was to watch out for my safety and take care not to be left alone in the same room as him and I'd been forewarned about him by one of the footmen. Then I was to find out for myself. One night, he returned late from a business meeting when I was in the drawing room. He smelled strongly of alcohol and told me then he had plans to rob me of my virginity. I managed to get away from him then, but had been put on my guard. But the night it happened I went for a walk in the grounds. It was a lovely evening and I had no idea he'd followed me to a wooded section where it all happened.'

She closed her eyes tightly at the shocking memory of it all.

'Oh, Mr Darling, it was dreadful. He pinned me down and forced himself on me and I couldn't do a thing. I couldn't even find my voice to cry out for help. Not that anyone would have heard me anyhow as the gardeners had just packed up for the evening, as it went dark.'

Mr Darling's eyes showed a great deal of empathy as, gently, he said, 'That must have been awful for you, Enid. I can't believe he'd do such a thing. But I do believe what you're telling me. Is that how his father arranged for you to work here?'

'Yes.' She nodded. 'Mrs Clarkson tried to cover it all up and told the matron and master at the Merthyr workhouse to transfer me to Cardiff, but her husband found out, banished Anthony from their home and started taking care of me. He promised to help my family after all his son had put me through...'

It was beginning to feel as though a burden had been lifted from her shoulders.

'What happened when he visited my sister the other day?' Mr Darling narrowed his eyes now.

'When Miss Eliza left the drawing room to fetch a book from the library, me and Mrs Sowerberry had a go at him. She warned him to leave your sister alone or else she'd tell you about what he'd done to me. She blocked the doors as he tried to leave but then he got angry with her and shook her. I don't know what came over me but I hit him on the head with a poker.'

Mr Darling's mouth popped open and he closed it again. 'Why, you do surprise me, Enid. But I think you did the right thing as he might have hurt Mrs Sowerberry. What about my sister? Does she know any of this?'

'No, not at all,' Enid said, shaking her head. 'Mrs Sowerberry felt it necessary to tell her an untruth that he'd had to leave as he had a pressing appointment he'd forgotten all about. She seemed to believe that. But of course she was badly disappointed. I think she hoped he'd return to see her following the so-called meeting. Mrs Sowerberry put her straight on that though...'

Edmund Darling rubbed his chin. 'How do you mean?'

'She made it clear that he wouldn't be calling here.'

'That's good and that's how it shall remain. I never want him to set foot near my sister or this house ever again. I've a good mind to go to the police about all of this but then I don't want to lose my friendship with his father...' He trailed off, as if deliberating.

'Maybe someone else needs to do it,' Enid said candidly.

'Or just maybe someone needs to teach the brute a lesson he'll never forget!' Mr Darling stood and walked over to the window, his whisky glass still in hand. What was he thinking about?

Enid sat in silence as she finished her glass of water. Then she stood and said, 'Thank you for listening to me today. Would you like that cup of something now, sir?'

Turning, he shook his head. 'No, thank you, that won't be necessary now. I think I'll stick with something stronger.'

18

Enid felt a sense of reassurance now that she'd informed Mr Darling about the troubling issue regarding his sister. Strangely enough, Miss Eliza no longer seemed to be upset and later that day could even be heard singing to herself, which puzzled Enid greatly, but thinking no more of it, she explained all to Sam without telling him it was she who had been raped at the Clarkson house.

'I'm not convinced it's over between the pair,' Sam said.

They were in a room that was used for cleaning boots and shoes. Sitting at an old table and holding a duster and a tin of black polish, he proceeded to rub away at the master's boot. He was wearing an apron, which reminded Enid of Jimmy, of what he wore when he was polishing and mending shoes. Here, her father usually did that sort of thing, as the general caretaker and handyman, but today, he was excused from that particular duty as he'd been asked to ferry Mr Darling into Cardiff on a business meeting. It wasn't something he usually did but as the coachman, Albert Masters, had taken ill, someone was needed at short notice. And although not a coachman by trade, he did have experience of horse and carts since he was a young lad.

Indeed, Enid couldn't have imagined either Mr Tatton nor Sam stepping into Albert's shoes at short notice like that. Her father was a remarkable man who would give anything a go and he was so pleased to have employment once again. These days he was neither ratty nor unpleasant as he had been at the workhouse and, most importantly of all, he no longer drank any alcohol as he'd started going to temperance meetings at a local hall.

'But why do you think there's still something between them, Sam?' Enid tilted her head to one side as she awaited his answer.

His eyebrows drew together as he replied, 'I've no evidence but Miss Eliza seems happy again. It's almost as though she has some sort of secret the rest of us aren't privy to.'

Enid nodded. 'I do know where you're coming from, as I've heard her singing around the place and, in my experience, when folk do that it's because they're happy within themselves and definitely not pining for someone they're smitten with.'

He shrugged. 'I really don't know what can be done about it though.'

'Mr Darling knows the score now so the ball's in his court. All we can do is be watchful if we notice anything amiss.'

Sam, now cheering up, threw the duster playfully at her and missed as she dodged it and laughed. It was good to see him returning to his old self once again. Miss Eliza had taken Sam's heart and squeezed the lifeblood out of it. It was a cruel stroke, reminding her how a cat toyed with an injured bird or mouse.

As Enid made her way to the kitchen, her thoughts turned to Connie. Her mind had been so full of Miss Eliza of late she'd almost put the girl out of her mind. Almost. She realised she needed to ask Annie to visit The Blue Anchor Inn with her again to see if they could get Connie out of there. It would be far better for her to work here at the house instead of being used by a bunch of men who had little or no care for her.

* * *

As Enid and Annie walked to the pub, linking arms, this time Enid had no fear. The previous time she'd been wary of the low gaslit streets and what might be lurking in the shadows. It wasn't that she wouldn't take care or anything this time, more that she had extreme purpose to get Connie removed to a place of safety. She hadn't liked the look of that Mr Sharpe at all. Going by his garb, he'd looked smart enough, even wealthy, but it was how he earnt his living off the backs of girls and women – some who might even be of a questionable age – that concerned her.

'I don't know how we'll get her out of there though,' said Annie doubtfully. 'You saw what the place was like. Packed to the rafters with leering sailors and all sorts of pond life. I bet there's a watch kept on her, particularly as she's fairly young and good-looking. She has many years left in her whereas Flora and Rosa do not.'

'She'll have even more years if I can persuade her to return to Beechwood House with me, Annie.'

Annie nodded. 'Fair enough. I just think we're going to be met with some strong opposition.'

'But we have to try though. Trying is better than doing nothing,' said Enid, working hard to convince even herself, for the truth was, she had her doubts.

* * *

'May I have a word with you, Mrs Sowerberry?' Edmund Darling steered the woman to one side in the corridor by taking her gently by the elbow. 'I need to speak with Enid.'

The housekeeper raised an inquisitive eyebrow. 'Oh?'

'Yes, it's regarding something we spoke about yesterday. I believe you know all about it?'

She smiled, tentatively. 'Yes, I was there at the time of the altercation and she told me she'd be speaking with you about it as she's concerned for Miss Eliza's welfare.'

He nodded. 'Would you happen to know where I might find her?'

'She's not here, sir.'

'Where is she then?' He looked troubled now.

The woman hesitated before replying. 'From my understanding she's gone to help out a friend. A young woman she met at the Cardiff workhouse who she was hoping might get a position here. I wrote to the workhouse to offer her a job as a maid but it seems she's since left there. Enid found out she's involved in some risky business – or maybe I should say *risqué* business – at The Blue Anchor Inn in Tiger Bay.'

'Oh! I see.' His eyes clouded over. 'And that's where Enid might have headed this evening?'

She nodded. 'Yes, sir.'

'I don't like the sound of that, Mrs Sowerberry. I think I'll go there in my coach to see if I can locate her. It's not the sort of area that a young lady should go alone. Albert's back on his feet now and well enough to take me.'

'She's gone with another friend from the workhouse. A good girl by all accounts who has since left there and lives nearby, so she won't be unaccompanied.'

'Nevertheless, Mrs Sowerberry, I fear for the safety of any young lady setting foot in that area. It's teeming with pimps and prostitutes! I think I'll head there now this very minute.'

Mrs Sowerberry watched her employer storm off angrily, almost as though it were her fault Enid had left the sanctuary of his house. But it wasn't, was it? Enid was no longer a young child, but maybe thinking about it, she ought to have said something to warn her off going there.

'Mrs Sowerberry?'

She turned to see Sam standing behind her.

'Yes, Sam?'

'Is there something wrong?' He frowned.

'No, nothing,' she said with a lump in her throat. 'I think Mr Darling is a little angry with me for not stopping Enid from leaving to go to Tiger Bay this evening. He's going to find her.'

'I don't understand that. She's not a prisoner.'

She smiled at him through glazed eyes. 'No, she's not, fortunately, but her aim was to rescue someone who might be.'

'Pardon?' He was blinking profusely now.

'A friend of hers is in trouble and you know what Enid's like: she has a very large heart.'

She'd been kindness itself to Sam of late even throughout that Miss Eliza business when he'd had a silly crush on the young woman.

The housekeeper noticed a flicker of concern on his face as though he hoped Enid was not getting herself into any trouble. Spotting the master in the hallway as if about to make to leave the house, Sam called after him. 'Mr Darling? Might I accompany you?'

This was a little improper of him, she realised, but if the man was going there he might need help himself. Besides, Sam was also concerned about Enid now.

If Mr Darling was surprised then he wasn't showing it. 'I'm off to the Tiger Bay area. You want to accompany me? But why?'

'Mrs Sowerberry just mentioned you're going to look for Enid. I'm concerned about her myself.'

The master sighed. 'Hurry up and get changed then. You can't go dressed in your footman garb – you'll be a laughing stock in that area,' he said impatiently. 'I'll wait for you in the coach.'

Sam returned wearing a shirt and a long pair of trousers, along with a tweed jacket and cap. He nodded at Mrs Sowerberry as he swept past.

'Take care, Sam,' she said, opening the front door for him. She watched as he seated himself in the coach beside his employer and a few words seemed to be exchanged.

Closing the door, she decided to inform Mr Tatton both Sam and the master had left the house. He'd be most surprised to discover the pair was headed for Tiger Bay.

* * *

The Blue Anchor was busy that night. There seemed to be some sort of a buzz around the place. The clientele was practically spilling out of the door as Enid and Annie tried to get in, elbowing their way past eager men smelling strongly of unwashed bodies, tobacco and alcohol. Once inside, Enid steered Annie over to a corner, where there was a spare table and bench.

That was odd. Why wasn't it occupied? But Enid dismissed the thought.

Both took a seat and looked at one another in amazement.

'I can't make it out,' said Annie, shaking her head. 'Something's going on here, but I've no idea what it is.'

Enid nodded as she watched men scrambling by the bar to get themselves a drink. It was almost a party atmosphere. Then she listened intently to a group of men standing in front of them who were laughing and joking. One of them mentioned some kind of auction.

'Did you hear that?' Enid whispered behind her cupped hand.

Annie nodded. 'Yes, I did. They're auctioning something off. That's what all the fuss is about and it appears to be going on in the next room.'

It was then Enid noticed that tickets were being sold at the bar and men were holding them aloft. So, it wasn't so much the alcohol those men were clamouring for, more like the opportunity to purchase a ticket.

But what for?

A young barmaid served them at the table and they ordered a jug of porter between them, relieved they wouldn't have to queue with the men at the bar, though for the past twenty minutes many of those who had bought tickets had disappeared into the back room.

'Look over there,' said Annie, nodding towards a woman a couple of tables over. 'Isn't that Flora?'

Enid scanned the room until her eyes fixed on the woman. Yes, there was no doubt about it, but she wasn't looking too happy and appeared to be on edge as she sat with a gentleman. Both had tankards in front of them, but Enid could tell Flora was distracted as she kept glancing at the staircase. But why?

* * *

Flora's eyes diverted from the staircase to the table in the corner where she saw a couple of faces she recognised.

Oh no, what where those pair up to now? No doubt they'd come here to look for Connie again and would scupper her plans to help her to escape tonight. It had all been arranged; she'd left the back door unbolted and a change of clothing in the shed in the yard for her. If she didn't get her out tonight, she'd have to go through with that virginity auction that Mr Sharpe had arranged and she didn't want that for Connie. It had happened to her too, many years ago in her own youth. She'd been Sharpe's special girl then, but all that changed when she'd been replaced by another – and another. In fact, so many since that she'd lost count.

If that pair started asking questions about Connie right now, Mr Sharpe was going to suspect something was up. That's why her eyes had been fixed on the stairs, in case he showed and headed for Connie's room to discover she wasn't there.

Flora excused herself from the gentleman beside her and stood. She headed towards the girls' table.

Gritting her teeth, she said, 'Outside now!'

Both young women looked up at her nervously, the whites of their eyes on show. The one called Enid stood, saying nothing, and led her friend by the arm as they walked outside onto the pavement. Flora followed.

'Your timing is flamin' terrible!' she almost shouted, but then, realising where she was, whispered, 'Do your friend a favour and go back home right now!'

'But why?' Enid pulled on the sleeve of her gown.

'Because I've hatched a plan to spring her out of here. They're going to start looking for her soon as she's about to be auctioned off in there.' She glanced nervously behind her.

'Auctioned off?' Enid frowned.

'A virginity auction.'

Enid's hands flew to her face in horror.

'So please for Connie's sake and my sake, get out of here right now.'

The pair looked as if they were about to turn away and do as bid when there was a voice behind them.

Mr Sharpe stood on the doorstep of his own pub. 'What's going on here, Flora?'

* * *

Enid noticed the petrified expression on Flora's face.

Oh no, they'd ruined whatever the woman was up to now. What could they say?

But before she had a chance to reply, Flora turned to face her employer and said, 'Couple of young girls come looking for work...'

'Oh, they have, have they?' He left the doorway to stand between them all on the pavement. 'And what sort of work are you looking for, ladies?' He smirked, appraising them with his eyes.

'B… bar work, sir,' said Enid.

'We haven't got any bar work at the moment but we do have a couple of jobs going as hostesses. You know the sort of thing, entertaining our clientele…' It was almost as though he was mocking them.

'Er no thanks, sir,' said Annie. 'We need to get back home or our father will come looking for us.'

'Oh, sisters, are you?' He seemed interested now. 'I'm sure we can always find work for a pair of good-looking sisters like yourselves…' He looked them up and down, shooting them a salacious smile.

19

Finally, Cornelius Sharpe became distracted by something going on inside the pub, so thankfully, he left them to it, allowing Flora to continue her plea.

'You need to get out of here, now!' She pointed up the street to the girls. 'They've probably just discovered Connie's gone; that's why he's being called inside. Don't worry, she's got money on her to get a cab.'

Enid laid her hand on the woman's arm, which was trembling now. 'I'll never forget what you did for Connie,' she said.

Flora nodded at her and darted back inside the pub.

'Let's hope she's not now in the frame for Connie's disappearance,' Annie said, shaking her head.

'Hopefully, if she's covered her tracks well enough, she won't be.' But, biting her lower lip, Enid wasn't so sure about that.

'Come back to mine for a cuppa before you get a cab back home?' Annie suggested.

Enid nodded. 'I still owe you that cab fare from last time. I've been paid so I can return it to you.'

'Well, I wouldn't have let you flee the country with it.' Annie laughed.

* * *

'Ha, here it is!' said Edmund as The Blue Anchor Inn came into view and their coach drew up outside. There appeared to be a group of people flooding out of its door. 'What's going on here? Heavens to Betsy!'

'I don't know.' Sam raised his eyebrows. 'Whatever it is they're all spilling out onto the streets.' He'd never seen such a crowd.

'Maybe the police have raided it!'

The coach driver dismounted and, opening the door for them to step out, he asked, 'Are you sure you wish to alight right now, sir?'

'Yes, Masters. Just keep the coach near at hand in case we need to return to it right away.'

'Yes, sir!' he said, tipping his hat.

Both men stood outside the pub until Edmund tapped a bloke beside him on the shoulder. 'What's going on here?'

The red-faced man looked at him with glassy eyes and hiccupped. 'Some sort of auction gone wrong. The goods have disappeared.' The man spoke a hybrid of both Welsh and English. 'Seems they had legs and ran away somewhere! Now some sort of fight has broken out.'

'Pardon?'

Sam grabbed the man by the arm and spoke to him in Welsh. The man nodded at him several times then Sam returned to Edmund's side. 'Seems it wasn't the sort of auction we were thinking of, Mr Darling.'

'Oh?' Edmund tilted his head to one side with curiosity.

'It was a virginity auction.'

'I wonder if it was that friend of Enid's who's disappeared. Ask the man if he knows her name.'

Sam submerged himself amongst the throng to find the man and reported back to Mr Darling a couple of minutes later. 'Yes, no doubt about it, it's Enid's friend, Connie. Course, I didn't tell the man that.'

Edmund was about to say something when he spotted a familiar face emerging through the pub's double doors. He narrowed his eyes in a suspicious manner.

'Just hang on here a minute, Sam,' he said, 'in case you spot Enid. There's something I just need to do.'

Feeling flummoxed, Sam stood staring, watching his master head back to the coach where he spoke quietly to the driver. The man handed him something. Surely that wasn't a horse whip? He seemed to be glancing towards the pub's entrance. What was in his mind? Who was he looking at? It soon became evident it was Anthony Clarkson firmly in the master's sights.

Even the coach driver had a look of concern on his face as Mr Darling strode towards the pub.

For every step Edmund Darling took towards the assailant, he did so with extreme purpose.

'Clarkson!' he yelled.

The man turned and held up the palms of his hands.

'W... what's going on?' he asked nervously, the whites of his eyes on show.

'I came here for another purpose but now I've seen you, there's a wrong I must right. You are the filthy bounder who raped a young maid called Enid!'

Sam couldn't believe his ears. Surely that couldn't be right? Enid had been raped by the man?

'Don't be silly.' Clarkson smiled nervously. 'She was a cheap whore, that was all. We all know they're ten a penny. That's why we're both here at The Blue Anchor, aren't we? To pick up some rough stuff!'

'Most certainly not!' Edmund stuck his chin out and pursed his lips as a gesture of disgust. 'I came here to stop that young maid from getting hurt tonight as she's now in my employ. And a very nice young lady she is and all, but that's no thanks to you.'

'Oh?' Clarkson folded his arms with a smug expression on his face.

'Oh, indeed. And I now know what you're like so I don't want to see you near Eliza ever again. If you come within one inch of my sister, then I shall whip you like this!'

There was a resounding cracking sound in the air and heads turned in their direction as Edmund held the whip aloft.

'No!' cried Anthony as he reached out to try to grab the whip, but it was too late – it made contact with his hand. Edmund repeated the manoeuvre, cracking the whip again and again, narrowly missing the man's face.

Finally, Samuel – who had been looking on in astonishment – figured he'd better say something quickly before any real damage was done. 'I think that's enough, Mr Darling. You've made your point.'

Relief washed over Anthony Clarkson's face as he removed a handkerchief from his pocket and dabbed away at his bloodied hand. It might have been worse. Most blows were made to clothed areas, not making contact with bare skin.

'You hear me, Clarkson?' yelled Edmund. 'Next time you won't be so lucky if I catch you sniffing around my sister!'

Sam stood there speechless as he tried to take it all in. Enid raped?

'Come on, we'd better get out of here,' Edmund said, slicing through his thoughts.

'What about Enid though?' Samuel was wide-eyed with worry.

'Go and ask one of the women working here if they've seen two girls enter the pub,' Edmund said, releasing a slow breath.

Samuel nodded and, pushing open the swing doors, he entered the pub tentatively, not intending to get into any fights, but the earlier fracas appeared to have subsided. A tall, willowy woman stood near the bar. The worn expression on her face made her appear as though she'd seen better days.

'Excuse me, madame,' he said politely as she turned in his direction. 'Would you happen to have seen two women come in here this evening?'

The woman threw back her head and laughed. 'This place is full of them, dearie. What sort would you like? Blonde, brunette, red-haired?'

'No, you don't understand. One is a friend of mine. She came here to...' He almost let slip why Enid and her friend had come in the first place. Thinking better of it, he stopped mid-sentence, before saying, 'Oh, never mind.'

Another woman standing behind her turned and looked at him. 'I saw them. They've left now. Gone back home. Don't worry.' Then she smiled at him. Like the other woman, she looked pretty weary and worn too but this one seemed anxious. The whole place appeared to be in confusion, then a tall, well-dressed man appeared beside them and, looking at her, grabbed her by the arm. 'Where's Connie gone, Flora? You were the last to see her.'

'I... er... I left her getting ready in the bedroom. Is she not still there?'

Sam noticed a faint flush spread over her face as her eyes enlarged with fear.

'No, she's damn well not. I want this place searched until you find her. There's a gentleman waiting for her and he won't be best pleased if he doesn't have her tonight after forking out a great deal of money!'

The man watched Flora make her way up the stairs. He was obviously talking about the auction. What a seedy world this was.

Shaking his head, Sam turned away and headed for the door.

Back outside on the pavement, he explained what had happened to Edmund.

'Well, if Enid and her friend are no longer around,' said Edmund thoughtfully, 'I guess we'd better be off then. If that young girl has done a runner, that man in there won't be best pleased.'

Sam found himself agreeing. It was a dangerous place to hang around right now. That fellow would want to take it out on someone and there was no need for them to be in the firing line. But he guessed that poor Flora might take the brunt of it all.

20

It was a good few days later before Mr Darling received a letter from Matron Finchley at the workhouse explaining how Connie had shown up there one night after escaping the clutches of the landlord at The Blue Anchor. She'd enquired if the position of maid was still available for her. As Mr Darling read the letter out to Enid, a big smile crept over her face.

'Oh, sir, please say she can still work here. Please do!'

Mr Darling returned the smile. 'Yes, of course. After viewing that place and that awful man that particular night, I am more than willing to offer her a position here. Oh, and about that other matter regarding Anthony Clarkson...' He paused for a moment as if to gauge her response. '...he won't be causing you any more grief, nor my sister, for that matter.'

'But how can you be so certain, Mr Darling?'

He tapped the side of his nose. 'No questions, please. Let's just say I fought fire with fire and leave it at that. Now then, go and ask Mrs Sowerberry to draft a letter of acceptance for your friend, telling her she may start here in one week's time. She'll have to share a room with you, if that's acceptable?'

'Oh yes, of course it is!' Enid enthused. After having been brought up in a tiny one-bedroomed house in Merthyr where the bedroom was curtained off for privacy, this was luxury itself.

She left the master's study feeling quite pleased with herself – that was until she encountered Sam in the corridor. He'd been acting most strangely with her lately, hardly looking her in the eye nor making any conversation. Had she done something to upset him? She couldn't think of anything so she put it down to him still pining for Miss Eliza. So instead of speaking to him she just smiled and nodded and he did the same in return, mirroring her gesture.

It wasn't until the following day she found the courage to approach him.

'Sam, might I have a word with you for a moment?' she said when they were due a breakfast break. He nodded and she led him outside to the bench in the back garden, the one she thought of as "their bench". It was here they'd had many an interesting conversation.

They both sat in awkward silence for a moment until, wringing her hands, Enid turned her face towards his.

'Have I done anything to upset you lately, Sam?' She could barely look him in the eyes for fear she had.

'No, of course not. What makes you think that?' he replied in a croaky voice.

'You've not spoken to me properly for a few days now and don't even make eye contact with me lately, which makes me feel a bit er... embarrassed to speak with you. It's almost as though there's something between us that wasn't there before.' She raised her chin, her voice trembling as she spoke.

There was a hesitant pause before Sam answered, 'It's not something you've done though, Enid. It's just I didn't know how to broach the subject.'

'Of what?' She blinked for a moment.

'Look,' he said, letting out a stifled breath, 'I accompanied Mr Darling to The Blue Anchor Inn the other night after you'd left here.'

'You did? I had no idea either of you had gone there.'

He nodded. 'Mr Darling was intent in following you there to ensure your safety so I offered to go with him. When we arrived there was some sort of fracas going on. It appeared your friend had gone missing, that girl you were in the workhouse with. Anyhow, Mr Darling spotted Miss Eliza's beau there, that Clarkson fellow. I was puzzled by how angry he was with him. He grabbed the whip from the coach driver and thrashed Clarkson in a most brutal fashion, warning him to keep away from you and his sister…'

Enid's hands flew to her face in horror. Now she looked him squarely in the eyes. 'So he told you what happened to me?'

'Yes. Not intentionally though. He was so fired up with anger, he accused Clarkson of raping you, not realising at the time, I suppose, that I had overheard. He was like a man possessed. I think he'd forgotten all about me being there.'

Enid began to sob as Sam draped a reassuring arm around her as, quite naturally, she laid her head on his shoulder.

'There, there…' he said softly. 'You've been through the mill, duchess, haven't you?'

'W… what m… must you think of me?' she blubbed.

'What do I think of you?' he said, raising her chin with his thumb and forefinger, forcing her to look into his eyes with her own glazed ones. 'Why, I think you're the most beautiful, amazing and kind person, Enid. I really do. It wasn't your fault what happened to you at all. I was so blinded by Miss Eliza that I just didn't see what was in front of me. But I can see now she's not fit to lick your boots, lovely lady.'

She liked Sam an awful lot but now he was turning his attention towards her it seemed strange, particularly as Jimmy was never far away from her thoughts and the fact it was only recently Sam had been absolutely besotted with Miss Eliza. Yet, his caring demeanour warmed her towards him. The way he'd gone to look for her at Tiger Bay like that with barely a thought for his own safety – that had to count for something in her eyes.

They sat in companionable silence for a while, until Sam took her by the hand saying, 'Come on, we'd best go for breakfast.' She nodded and he helped her on to her feet. In truth, she'd felt so secure in Sam's arms she could have remained there all day, but there was work to be done.

* * *

Connie was due to arrive at the house a few days later but there was no sign of her showing up. Had something gone wrong? Enid was so looking forward to being reunited with her friend again and sharing a room with her.

Later that day, Enid voiced her concerns to Mr Darling.

'Please sit down, Enid,' he said softly, and by the look in his eyes, she could tell something was amiss.

Tentatively, Enid took a seat opposite, with his desk between them. 'Is there something wrong, sir?'

'I'm afraid there is,' he said as he nodded, a grave expression on his face. 'I've just received a hand-delivered letter from Matron Finchley to say that Connie won't be starting work here as planned as she has pneumonia.'

'Pneumonia!' Enid blinked in disbelief. This was the last thing she'd been expecting to hear. 'But how can that be?'

'I really don't know. But Mrs Finchley reckons the girl was very run-down when she turned up at the workhouse. So maybe that's why. She's being kept in the infirmary wing of the place until her health improves.'

'So what will this mean? No job for her here any more?'

'No, not at all,' said Mr Darling with a brighter tone to his voice now. 'I've said I'd take her on in my employ and I will, eventually. But first, she needs to get herself well again. Her strength will need building up.'

'I see.'

'There's something else I've discovered...'

'Oh?'

'One of the men who had hurt Connie badly was Anthony Clarkson himself.' Mr Darling's eyes were glinting with anger now. 'To think that man might have got his hands on my sister too! And especially all he did to you, Enid.'

It was bad enough Clarkson had hurt her but to discover that her friend was treated roughly by the same man made Enid realise that he might well go on to harm other young women.

'What can be done?'

'I think we ought to report this matter to the police,' Mr Darling said soberly.

'The police?' Enid gulped. 'I don't want any trouble though.'

She thought she'd seen the last of Anthony Clarkson but now it appeared he was coming back to haunt her.

'There might be other girls and women like you and Connie suffering at that man's hands. He's got to be prevented from harming anyone else. I know I gave him a good whipping and it might well keep him away from this house, but men like him won't stop. They see themselves as entitled somehow.'

Enid agreed. Mr Clarkson had said what she'd been thinking all along. It was good to be considered and believed by someone from his station in life. 'Me and Connie weren't born with silver spoons in our mouths and, to men like him, we're nothing. Just fodder to feed their voracious appetites!' She spat out the words with disgust, surprising herself at the venomous tone of her own voice.

'So, you're willing to speak up?'

Reluctantly, Enid replied, 'Yes,' knowing it was the right thing to do.

'Don't worry, you'll have me for support, Enid.'

Mr Darling shot her a reassuring smile. She realised she was doing this for all the other Enids and Connies out there who had no voice.

* * *

To Enid's surprise, after Mr Darling contacted them, the police took her claim very seriously indeed. Though she wondered whether, if she'd contacted them off her own bat to begin with, they'd have been so agreeable and likely to pursue the man. The old saying "Money talks" obviously proved right here. Mr Darling was of good standing in the community.

It would be a little time before they could speak to Connie though, with her being sick at the workhouse infirmary, but Enid had recounted to the police what had gone on at The Blue Anchor as best as she could, with Annie bearing witness. Something that did concern Enid though was if the case would now affect her employer's friendship with Mr Clarkson, senior. And what about Mrs Clarkson? She'd be absolutely mortified that their son was about to be arrested and taken in for questioning like a common criminal. But then again, Enid told herself, the woman had been keen to turn a blind eye to her son's grave misdemeanour in the first place. She didn't owe either the son nor his mother a damn thing, but she did feel bad for Mr Clarkson, as he'd been kindness itself.

* * *

It was early evening when Enid arrived on the infirmary ward at the workhouse – she'd completed her duties at the house for the day and Mrs Sowerberry had allowed her some time off to visit Connie.

Glancing around warily, she noticed some female inmates lying in their beds as if settled down for the evening, though no one appeared to be asleep, while others sat in a small group on chairs in their workhouse uniforms, chatting quietly. Some looked frail and worn out as though maybe the workhouse regime had got them on to the infirmary ward in the first place, and a couple in those beds appeared as though they might be approaching their final days. The bare boards beneath Enid's feet appeared well scrubbed. Paintings of various scenes around the Cardiff area were displayed on the walls, including the castle and even of the workhouse itself. In the centre of the long nightingale-style ward was a large desk the nurses appeared to be using as some kind of station, which contained a big ledger and an oil lamp. Behind that was a table containing vases of flowers and leafy green plants in pots. A nurse was in the process of removing them from bedside tables to place on it for the night. It was thought that flowers and plants robbed patients of the oxygen they needed at night so this had become a regular practice on the ward.

A row of gaslights were suspended from the ceiling and were now being dimmed. It felt unreal to Enid. It should have felt familiar but it did not. This was the same workhouse she herself had been an inmate of, yet the infirmary ward had a different smell and aura about it. She guessed its odour was disinfectant and the aura was calm and peaceful, as no one was being disciplined by anyone in authority. Here, the only people bustling around were the nurses themselves who worked with a quiet efficiency.

Enid's echoing footsteps stopped at the station and a nurse looked up at her from the ledger she'd been writing in with a fountain pen.

'Yes? Can I help you?' She blinked. The woman wore a navy-blue dress covered with a white linen pinafore and on her head was a white starched cap.

'I'm here to see my friend Connie O'Mara, if I may?'

The nurse shook her head. 'I'm sorry, she shouldn't be having any visitors right now. She's not very well at all.' She pointed to a screened-off area in the corner of the room that Enid hadn't noticed before.

'But she'll want to see me, I'm sure. I'm her best friend. You see, things went wrong for her when I went into service, leaving her here. She left here afterwards, and ended up at that dreadful place down Tiger Bay, then ran away from there too as she was treated so badly.'

The nurse nodded sympathetically. 'Look, I wouldn't normally do this, but you can sit with her for just a few minutes, but then you must leave.'

Enid smiled tentatively, feeling really confused. Just how bad could Connie be?

The nurse rose from her chair, which made a scraping sound on the floorboards, and beckoned Enid to follow her to the corner of the room. For each footfall taken, Enid felt surmounting fear for what she might be about to witness. Then, finally, the nurse drew back the screen.

Enid's heart slumped. Connie looked so small and frail in that bed. Her skin appeared the colour of alabaster and her long hair was fanned out on the pillow, dull and damp. Beads of perspiration had burst out on her forehead and she didn't even seem conscious. Her breathing sounded odd too. As Enid watched the rise and fall of her chest, she heard a rattling sound, which she guessed wasn't a good sign.

The nurse placed a flannel in a bowl of water on the table beside the bed and proceeded to wring it out, and then she placed it on Connie's forehead. 'There, there, dear Connie,' she said softly.

'Is she asleep?' Enid asked.

'Not exactly,' said the nurse. 'She's in such a weakened state that she's been slipping in and out of consciousness with the fever. We've got her on fifteen-minute observations; that's why we're not really allowing visitors, but I'll get you a chair and you can sit with her for a while and hold her hand. You never know, she might be aware you're here.'

Enid nodded gratefully at the young woman who then went in search of a chair, returning instead with a small wooden stool.

'Sorry, this'll have to do you as all the chairs are being taken up by the inmates this evening.'

'That's all right.' She smiled at the woman, grateful she'd been allowed any time with her friend at all.

'Now, I'll return in five minutes to check Connie's observations. I need to take her temperature regularly and check her pulse – it's doctor's orders.'

The nurse left Enid after returning the screen to its original position to shut out the rest of the ward.

Enid sat on the stool not knowing what to do for a moment but then she reached out and took Connie's hand.

'Don't you worry none,' she said softly. 'I've come to see you, Connie. It's Enid. We're going to get you all better and then you can come to Beechwood House with me as planned.'

There was no response from Connie.

A solitary tear coursed down Enid's cheek as she remembered their times together in the workhouse. Connie had been her best friend, the one friend besides Jimmy she'd been able to rely on in this cruel world.

The five minutes passed in a flash and the nurse drew back the screen. 'I'm sorry, you'll have to go now as promised, Miss...'

'Enid, Enid Hardcastle.' She forced a smile in the nurse's direction.

'Well, Enid, you are welcome to come again and sit for a few minutes. Who knows, if Connie realises you are around for her, it might improve her chances of recovery. I just spoke to Doctor Becker and he agrees. So if you turn up and I'm not here, you can tell the staff that Doctor Becker and Sister Harrington have given you permission.'

Enid nodded gratefully. 'Thank you so much for giving me the opportunity. Is there anything I can bring in for her?'

'No, not at the moment. But maybe if her strength builds up you could bring some fruit, oranges or whatever. But right now, no.'

Enid was wondering if Connie would ever recover, the way the nurse said that. Oh, she was pleased to see Connie again, but she didn't want to see her collapsed in a hospital bed looking waif-like and vulnerable. Would her friend ever recover at all?

* * *

Enid had been back and forth to the hospital every day at varying times for the past week or so, and one day, when she stepped on the ward, Sister Harrington was waiting to have a word with her. Her stomach lurched. Oh no, was Connie gone for good? But no, that didn't appear to be the case as Sister's lips curved into a big smile.

'Connie's awake!' she said. 'And guess who she's asking to see?'

'Me?' Enid said in disbelief, holding the palm of her hand to her chest, eyes wide in expectation.

'Yes, you. I've told her how you'd been at her bedside every day. She said what a good friend you'd been to her.'

'Oh, I can't wait to see her again! I wish I'd brought those oranges now!'

Enid couldn't have wished for better news and when she approached Connie's bed after the nurse had removed the screen, the girl was sitting up in bed.

'Oh, Enid,' she said, tears forming in the corners of her eyes, 'I can't believe this happened to me after all I've gone through at the hands of that man.'

Those men, thought Enid, but she didn't voice her thoughts – Connie was probably referring to Sharpe, the landlord.

She took a seat by the bed and reached out for Connie's hand. 'I thought maybe we'd lose you...' Her eyes blurred.

'Never! Not me!' Connie shook her head and smiled.

'But what happened? How come you got pneumonia?'

Connie emitted a soft sigh. 'Doctor Becker thinks it didn't help that the night I escaped and wandered the streets, it was pelting down with rain and I got soaked to the skin. Probably didn't cause it as such but he reckoned I must have been very run-down after all I'd gone through. And I did have a bit of a cough before that.'

'You need to build up your strength, my girl. Are you eating again?'

'They gave me some onion soup last night when I woke and I've had some oatmeal and a piece of toast so far today.'

'You need more than that!'

'Apparently, they have to slowly introduce foods into my diet so I don't get sick. I'm not all that hungry, to be honest with you. One thing I'm worried about though – will Mr Darling now take me on at the house, do you think?'

Enid nodded enthusiastically. 'Of course he will. He's already agreed to it.'

Connie's eyes were shining now. 'And I can't believe that you came every day to see me. You're a real friend to me, so you are.'

Enid gave Connie's hand a reassuring squeeze, realising how close she'd come to losing her friend forever.

21

The day finally came when Connie was well enough to leave the infirmary, but for the present she remained at the workhouse to build up her strength.

Nevertheless, the police thought that the sooner they struck the better. There was no time to waste as they were building a case against Cornelius Sharpe and trying to track down any of the girls he'd had working for him, especially those who did so against their will.

Mr Darling took both Enid and Connie back and forth to his lawyer's office to prepare the case against Anthony Clarkson. Rape had been punishable by death until 1841. Imagine if he'd raped her back then in those days? No matter how she felt about the man, she wouldn't wish him dead, far from it. But he did need to be punished and put in prison for his crime.

William Stead, the newspaper editor of *The Pall Mall Gazette*, had published a series of articles the previous year where he'd exposed the exploitation of young girls. Joshua Formby, the lawyer, had copies of the newspaper and urged Mr Darling and both girls to read them.

'The trouble is,' he began, 'many rape charges never even reach as far as court, as they're often either settled outside of it or the charges get dismissed beforehand. So, we're really up against it here. You'll be expected to tell your stories in front of a male audience. This will include graphic details of both of your encounters with Clarkson. The defence team will do all they can to discredit you and bring you down, both of you. So you shall need to keep your wits about you.'

Enid shot Connie a concerned glance and then she swallowed hard. Was it worth them going through all of this if the cards were stacked against them? When their accusations might be turned upon themselves?

But then Mr Formby carried on saying something that gave Enid hope. 'But, in this case, the police who are getting involved in proceedings are most definitely on your side, ladies!'

Enid brightened up to hear that.

'They are?' said Connie, blinking several times in disbelief.

'Oh, most certainly.' Mr Formby emerged from behind his large oakwood desk and perched on the edge of it. 'You see, they've been trying to shut this establishment down for a while. Mr Sharpe doesn't just own The Blue Anchor Inn but he's also conducting nefarious business from the premises including prostitution, gambling and fencing stolen goods, amongst other activities. He also owns several other properties across Cardiff.' He paused for a moment as he stroked his chin. 'The reason I mentioned William Stead to you is because he's interested in slavery amongst young women and girls. There is some evidence that Mr Sharpe is kidnapping them and paying for them to be transported from the Port of Cardiff to the Continent, namely France and Belgium.'

Enid sat there agog, mouth agape. 'I didn't realise all that was going on.' She turned to Connie whose face immediately flushed pink. 'Did you?'

Slowly, Connie nodded. 'I did have an inkling, to tell you the truth. A couple of young girls stayed at the pub one night. They'd not long arrived from Cork. A couple of days later, there was no sign of them whatsoever. I had no proof, of course, but I did overhear talk in the bar from a couple of sailors about how they regularly took what they described as "fresh meat" to French and Belgian seaports and, to tell you the truth, the very idea disgusted me!'

'Yes,' said Mr Formby, 'girls are sent to licensed brothels in Belgium and France.'

Mr Darling, who had been sitting quietly, deep in thought until now, raised his head and said, 'I had no idea this sort of thing existed in this country. It beggars belief it could even happen to young girls and women here.'

Although Enid realised Mr Darling hadn't exactly led a charmed life, she guessed his upbringing had provided him with a cushioned existence of sorts, but the main thing was he believed them and was willing to help. Miss Eliza was fortunate indeed to have a brother like him, otherwise she might well have ended up marrying that brute Clarkson. And what would life have held for her then? Possibly a houseful of kids while her husband carried on his nefarious activities with ladies of the night. A lucky escape indeed.

* * *

As the court date for the trial of Anthony Clarkson drew near, Enid felt butterflies in the pit of her stomach. As if sensing this, Sam had asked her to go for a walk with him. He took her by the arm as they strolled around the lake at a nearby beauty spot. It was a glorious day with barely a cloud in the sky. People were out togged up in their Sunday best outfits, women in pretty pastel-coloured gowns holding sun parasols over their heads as the ribbons on their bonnets fluttered in the light breeze. Men looked dapper in striped or linen blazers, heads topped with straw boaters. Children trailed along by the side of the lake either following a toy wooden boat or just happy to hop, skip and jump around or run after a large wooden hoop.

Enid felt she ought to have been happy to have an afternoon away from the house. Should have been pleased things here were going to be drawn to a natural conclusion that someone like Anthony Clarkson would receive the punishment meted out to him at long last. And all it would take would be for her and Connie to stand in the dock and answer some questions. To give a good account of themselves.

'Try not to worry too much about things,' Sam said softly, taking her gloved hand.

She turned to face him as her eyes searched his. 'Is it really that obvious?'

'I'm afraid it is. Look, let me buy you a strawberry ice,' he said, pointing to a small wooden cart with the name "Bellini's Ices" embellished on the side of it.

She nodded thankfully. He released her hand to join the queue to purchase the ices for them. Sam was most generous with his time and money.

And then she spotted him, across the other side of the lake. Anthony Clarkson strolling with a young lady. Her mouth suddenly dried and she almost dropped her parasol on the grassy verge. Tears blinded her vision as she struggled to breathe. This couldn't be happening to her. Not now. Not ever again!

As if sensing her distress, Sam came bounding over.

'Whatever's the matter, Enid? You look like you've seen a ghost!'

Wordlessly, she pointed to the couple across the lake. 'It's him. C... Clarkson,' she said, taking a shuddering breath.

Sam squinted and held the palm of his hand to his forehead to shield the penetrating rays of the sun from his eyes. He stared for a moment and then brought his gaze to meet with hers.

'It's not him,' he said with confidence, shaking his head.

She looked again and could see this time it was most definitely not Anthony Clarkson. She lowered her head as if in shame.

'I really thought it was him and that poor woman was in danger.'

'That's totally understandable after what you've been through, Enid. Come on,' he said gently, guiding her by the arm. 'Let's get out of here. You're tensed up over this trial. I know a nice little tea shop across the way.'

She nodded, feeling she could do with a cup of tea to settle her jangling nerves. She'd be glad when all of this was over.

Later at the tea shop, Sam reached out for her hand across the table.

'Enid,' he said softly, 'when all this has come to a conclusion, and hopefully one that metes out justice to all concerned, would you consider, I mean er...'

For the first time she noticed how red his face had become and he extracted a handkerchief from the top pocket of his blazer to mop his brow.

'What is it?' She searched his eyes.

'The truth is I've had feelings for you for some time now. You must be aware of that?'

'I am, yes,' she said, nodding, confused as to where this was going. This didn't feel right at all, not when Jimmy was still on her mind. It felt like a betrayal towards him. She didn't like how this conversation was heading and she wished she could stop it.

'I just wondered if you'd consider marrying me?'

She gulped. Marriage? Courtship was one thing but marriage was a whole new ball game.

'Oh, Sam,' she said barely in a whisper. 'I have strong feelings for you, you know that, but at the moment all that's in my mind is bringing Anthony Clarkson to justice. I can barely think of anything else right now...'

He nodded and then he looked away and caught the waitress's eye, and she came over to take their order, the proposal now relegated to the bottom shelf of Enid's mind.

* * *

A couple of weeks before the trial was due to take place, Enid left the house on her break time. She needed some air and to clear her head. She'd been up early for work but had barely slept all night. All sorts of things were running through her mind about her time at Hillside House, when the rape had occurred and all that had happened after it.

She was about to cross the road to visit the pharmacy. It was a pretty little shop that sold all manner of things beside medication. She needed something for a persistent headache. As she was about to step away from the kerb and cross the road, a strong arm yanked her back onto the pavement. Thinking maybe she'd been about to step into the path of danger as she'd been preoccupied, she was about to thank the person, when she turned to see it was Anthony Clarkson who had grabbed hold of her arm.

Her heart began to pound profusely.

'Let me go!' she protested, struggling to get out of his grasp.

He sneered at her, tightening his grip. 'I'll let you go when I see fit, missy! I'm here to warn you that what you say about me in the courtroom will go against you and your family!'

Her body trembled from top to toe, but this time it wasn't fear like the night of the rape, this time it was anger coursing through her veins. Looking him squarely in the eyes and with her chin held up in defiance, she said, 'There's not a thing you can do about what I intend to say in that court! Hopefully, they'll put you behind bars for a very long time, especially with your involvement with the slave trading that goes on at a certain pub! I hear you and the landlord are in cahoots together!'

Raising his free hand, he swiped her hard across the cheek, the strike causing her to stagger backwards into oncoming traffic. For a moment her field of vision was blinded as she saw pinpoints of coloured light before her eyes. It was a busy road where carriages, cabs and carts travelled all day long. Turning, she rushed through them as a costermonger cart almost clipped her. She ran for her life, weaving in and out of the paths of various vehicles. Anthony Clarkson was intent on doing some damage to her – that much was evident.

Something warm was oozing down her face and she realised her nose was bleeding. Then she heard it. A woman's high-pitched scream as she ran to safety on the other side of the road. Dare she look behind her?

She turned slowly to see Anthony Clarkson lying on the ground as a horse reared up onto its hind legs and whinnied, trampling the lifeless form.

'He's dead!' a man yelled out as she ran into the pharmacy shop.

Then she felt a reassuring arm around her. Dazed from her ordeal, she couldn't comprehend what the woman was saying to her. Tears blurred her vision and she was pressing a handkerchief into her hand. But why?

'Here, to wipe the blood away, dear.'

She appeared to be a customer at the shop.

'I saw what happened there,' said another woman who had just emerged from behind the counter. Enid could hear clearly now. 'That man attacked you. He ran headlong into that traffic chasing you. Come and sit down, dearie, I'll send my husband to fetch a policeman.'

Enid took a seat and a glass of water was placed in her trembling hands. Outside, above the various coloured bottles of lotions and potions that were displayed in the window, she could see Anthony Clarkson's body being moved from the road to the pavement by two men.

Where had he come from though? It was as if he'd been waiting for her with a view to stop her speaking at the court.

What would happen now?

22

As if things weren't bad enough, Enid discovered from Mr Formby that once Cornelius Sharpe realised Flora's involvement in Connie's escape, she'd been badly beaten by him. However, a few broken ribs, blackened eyes and a missing tooth were not about to prevent the woman from testifying.

Enid was still severely traumatised and couldn't seem to shake herself out of the shock of Anthony Clarkson's death. Although it had not been her fault, she'd felt responsible for it no matter what anyone said to her, and she became melancholic as a result. Her appetite was poor and she slept fitfully at night.

The trial had begun and was a big deal, attracting the press from as far afield as London. Sharpe had links there too to several establishments where he'd bartered young women. The whole thing was a seedy affair.

'Enid, you really need to shake yourself out of this, *cariad*,' her mother said one morning as she was helping the children get dressed for school. Normally, Enid would pop to the apartment to help her from time to time, but this morning she was late.

'I know, Mam, it's just that I... I...' To her horror her shoulders began to convulse and huge, racking sobs took over her body. The thought of giving her testimony in front of all those people, it was all getting too much.

'Iris,' Martha called to her younger daughter, 'finish dressing Jonathan, there's a love. Enid needs me right now.'

Iris emerged from one of the bedrooms and looked at her sister warily. It would have been odd for any of them to see Enid break down like this as she tended to keep her emotions to herself, but then Iris looked at their mother and nodded. Taking Jonathan by the hand, she led him to the bedroom to get dressed.

'W... where's Michael and Dad?' Enid asked.

'Now, you don't want to go worrying about either of them. Michael's with your father helping him paint the study room for Mr Darling. He's a thrifty one for saving money, no wonder he's got pots of it!' It was just like her mam to say something like that. She always spoke her mind. 'But...' she carried on, 'he's most generous with us and I think that's down to you, our Enid.' She wrapped a comforting arm around her daughter's shoulder. 'You've been through such a lot this last year or so, and you've grown up into a fine young woman.'

She guided her towards an awaiting chair by the table.

Her mother looked on with sympathy in her eyes. 'Please don't let that man hurt you yet again, Enid,' she said softly. 'He's hurt you enough already as it is. None of this is any of your doing.'

Tears welled in Enid's eyes. And, as they took a cup of tea together, neither said a word to the other but to be close at hand with Mam was all that was needed right now.

* * *

Enid had been working for the best part of the day and she was just finishing off tidying up Mr Darling's study. Her father and brother had made a good job of painting it. The walls had been given a coat of a cream-coloured paint that brightened it up and the skirting boards had been varnished. They'd left some sheeting covering the bookcases behind and some old pots of paint and brushes, so she folded the sheets and ensured their utensils were placed to one side ready for collection, when there was a light knock on the door.

Mrs Sowerberry came in and, looking at her, said, 'Mr Clarkson is here to have a word with you, Enid.'

At the mention of the Clarkson name, Enid's heart began to pound profusely. Of course it wouldn't be Anthony Clarkson, but his father, yet nevertheless, the name conjured up his image. She nodded.

'Better take him into the drawing room as the paint fumes are still quite strong in here,' Mrs Sowerberry said.

'Yes, Mrs Sowerberry.'

She made to pass the woman who laid a reassuring hand on her arm. 'Try not to worry – you've done no wrong.'

Enid smiled at her thinly. How could she not worry though? The man's son was dead and the funeral was later that very week.

Patting down her hair and ensuring her pinafore was securely tied at the back, she walked towards the drawing room to find him in there, standing near the fireplace with his hand on the mantelshelf.

What had he been thinking before she arrived? Had he come to tell her off? For taking his son away from him? But now, here he was looking at her with a great deal of compassion in those eyes of his.

'My dear,' he said, stepping forward and taking her hands in his, 'how are you?'

Quite naturally, but unexpectedly, she stepped into his warm embrace where he held her for the longest time as she wept.

'You've been through such an ordeal, Enid,' he said softly, almost in a whisper as he caressed her cheek.

'But you, Mr Clarkson, your son has been taken away from you,' she said, looking up at him.

He nodded. 'To say I don't feel anything about Anthony's tragic demise would be an understatement. I feel angry and saddened at the same time, if that makes any sense to you at all?'

'Yes, yes it does.' It made perfect sense as that's how she felt herself, angry that she'd even encountered Anthony in the first place and about his treatment of her, yet saddened for his family by his sudden death.

Mrs Sowerberry had dispatched Daisy to fetch a tray of coffee for them both and they were able to chat at length before Mr Darling joined them.

There was no animosity whatsoever on Mr Clarkson's part and he spoke of taking Enid away for a break in the country to West Wales where his sister lived for a few weeks when the trial was over. She was surprised by the suggestion but it did appeal to her. It might be just what she needed.

* * *

Afterwards, when speaking to Sam about it, his face clouded over.

'I think he's got designs on you for himself!' he blurted out quite suddenly as they were seated on their garden bench together.

'Don't be so silly, Sam!' snapped Enid. She could hardly believe her ears. 'He's just a kind, older gentleman, that's all.'

'That's not what I've been told!' His eyes were glittering with anger.

'And just what have you been told?' This wasn't making any sense whatsoever to her.

'That he used to take you out in his carriage and buy you fancy frocks and such. Treating you like a lady!'

Enid remembered how she'd once confided in Daisy and Penny about that – not in a boastful fashion as such, more in a way of underlining just how kind the man had been. It must surely have been one of them who had told Sam – how else might he know? She stood now, wanting to get as far away from him as possible and he followed suit, invading her space as he carried on ranting. 'Why, the way he's been behaving towards you, someone might assume you are his mistress!'

Hearing those words stung and before she knew it, she had raised the palm of her hand and was about to strike him hard across the cheek, causing his mouth to gape open at the shock of it all. But she stopped herself in time, dropping her hand to her side as she recalled how Anthony Clarkson had struck her in the same manner.

This had all come to a head between them both. Initially, she'd longed for him to have designs on her but he'd favoured a daft fantasy about Miss Eliza instead. For a while, he appeared to show her genuine affection but then had rushed things in his pursuance of her with a view to marriage. She had far too much on her mind right now to even consider such a prospect.

'I'm beginning to think the sooner I get away from this place after the trial is over, the better!'

She marched off towards the house with tears streaming down her face. The truth of the matter was that although, with time, Sam might come to realise how foolish his words had been and even regret them, the ugly head of jealousy had arisen there and it wasn't a good look.

Sam was no Jimmy Corcoran and maybe for a while she'd wanted him to be. The truth was, no one could ever replace Jimmy in her heart. He was her one true love.

* * *

The day arrived when Enid and Annie were summoned to give evidence, testifying how they'd witnessed Connie working at The Blue Anchor Inn and that Cornelius Sharpe's manner had been threatening towards her. Also mentioned was that final time they'd visited when he'd shown signs of wishing to procure both of them to work for him.

Relieved it was all over, both girls took a seat in the courtroom as they watched Connie give her evidence. Flora, who now looked a shadow of her former self, gave evidence supporting all that Connie said and how she'd helped her to escape the night Sharpe had put her up for auction.

Over the following days, more young girls came forward to give evidence, some as young as fourteen years old. At that age, those girls should have been having fun, having the best days of their lives, thought Enid, but they, like her, had their virginity stolen from them without their consent. In one sad case a mother had sold her daughter to Sharpe for the price of gin money. That had shocked and sickened Enid.

Members of the constabulary were called in to give their evidence. One sergeant in the area described The Blue Anchor Inn as a "den of iniquity". He went on to explain how Sharpe was a libertine who lacked morals, his only thought being what people could do for him and how best to make money out of them.

By the fifteenth day of the trial, the jury was despatched to make a decision and a sentence of twelve years was awarded to Sharpe with lesser sentences handed out to some of those also involved.

'He should have got more than that!' Enid protested as she and Connie left the courthouse.

Connie nodded. 'Probably, but at least there are twelve years on this earth when he can't get to any young women...'

That was true enough, Enid supposed. And the thing was, by the time of his release he would be quite an elderly man and maybe not such a threat as he'd been in the past. Well, hopefully.

So with a lightness in her step, they set off for Beechwood House where Connie was due to begin work the following morning.

Both girls were excited to share a bedroom that night and they chattered away until the early hours when they finally drifted off to sleep, Enid realising thankfully it wouldn't be like that every night; this was an exception as they were reunited at last.

But when Enid rose from her bed the following day, there was no sign of her friend whatsoever. Was she keen to begin work at the house and had risen earlier? But a strange feeling told Enid that something was very wrong.

Enid quickly washed and dressed as fast as she could, then she ran down the corridor breathlessly, almost colliding with Mrs Sowerberry in her haste, who was just emerging from her bedroom.

'Where are you going in such a hurry, Enid?' the woman said sharply. 'You know you aren't supposed to run in the cor—'

'I'm sorry, Mrs Sowerberry. But have you seen Connie? She's disappeared from our room.'

The woman shook her head. 'No, I haven't.'

'Might she have gone to start work somewhere? Did you ask her to?'

'No. I was going to find her and give her a welcome-to-the-house sort of chat first and show her around, like I did with you. Come on, we'll search for her together and if we don't find her, you can speak to Mr Darling.'

Enid nodded but knew in her heart that Connie had fled for some reason.

They just couldn't find her anywhere. Mr Darling even sent Enid in his coach to the workhouse just in case she had shown up there, but Matron, who was concerned herself, hadn't seen her either.

When she arrived back at the house, Mr Darling reassured Enid that at least the girl couldn't return to The Blue Anchor Inn as it was now boarded up. That did little to reassure Enid though, as her concern was that maybe Connie had been taken in at another pub somewhere and employed once again as a working girl.

'Oh, why didn't I keep an eye on her? I was so absorbed myself in the trial, I just didn't think,' Enid confided in Mr Darling.

'Enid, if Connie has chosen to abscond from here there's nothing you can do. You did your best to help her.'

What he said was true enough, but it did little to console Enid right now.

* * *

Over the coming weeks, there was no sign of Connie and, as planned, the following month Mr Clarkson arrived in his coach to take Enid to West Wales. Connie had been reported to the police as a missing person and some even thought maybe she'd returned to Ireland on a ship bound for Cork.

As Enid left with a trunkful of clothing, Samuel was nowhere to be seen either, and she was thankful for that. Her family were there to wave her off though. Everything that had happened lately had taken its toll on her: the court case in particular, having to hear all those harrowing accounts from young women. She needn't have stayed to listen, of course, but she'd chosen to. Somehow, hearing of others going through the same sort of ordeal gave her the strength to cope.

Donald Clarkson's sister, Matilda Ambridge, was an absolute treasure. A woman of diminutive stature who had been widowed years since. She lived alone in a modest cottage overlooking the sea. Enid was able to relax there for the first time in ages. Early mornings she'd take long walks on the beach and watch the sun rise. Every day it was like watching a new painting from God the Almighty, creator of all.

Matilda loved to embroider and she showed Enid how to do so. Being at the house calmed her mind and soul, whether it was picking flowers in the garden or walking in the nearby woods – it was just so peaceful here. She was company for the woman, she realised that, but Matilda knew when to leave Enid alone in her own company. She was a wise old sage.

When Enid had been there for three weeks, a recognisable coach turned up outside one afternoon and she realised it was Mr Darling's. Enid stood staring at it for the longest time. That definitely wasn't Mr Darling inside, it was a female! Someone wearing a very fancy-looking bonnet.

Who could it be? Miss Eliza?

Then the coachman dismounted and he tipped his hat at her with a big smile on his face. Enid stood there speechless as he walked towards the coach door to open it and assist whoever it was down.

Her heart was racing. She could feel its constant rhythm as it thrummed in her ears.

The lady emerged from inside and lowered her head as Albert took her gloved hand to aid her. The top of her beautiful bonnet was now visible in a plethora of pink and purple satin.

Then she lifted her head and made eye contact for the first time with those beautiful violet eyes! She smiled in Enid's direction.

It was a smile that Enid knew all too well. There was a catch in her throat as she felt about to cry but these tears of emotion were happy ones. She ran towards her and hugged her close.

'Oh, Connie,' she sobbed. 'Thanks for coming back to me. I've really missed you, my dear friend.'

As Albert tactfully left their side to sort out the luggage, taking it around the back of the property, Enid continued, 'But what happened after the case? You disappeared? I thought I'd never see you again!'

'Enid, I'm so pleased to be reunited with you once more. I just found it all so hard to cope with. Hearing all those girls in court giving their evidence like that and then having to give my own.'

'Yes, of course.' Enid understood so well.

'But then again it must have been difficult for you too? You went through the same thing.'

'I did, yes. Though it wasn't as raw and as recent for me as it was for you.'

Connie smiled tentatively. 'I think it all became too much for me because I suddenly realised that if there hadn't been a stop put on Sharpe's antics that I might well have ended up shipped off to another country and kept a prisoner or even worse.'

'So, where did you go in the end?'

'To that nice elderly lady's home, the one who runs the tobacconist shop, the one who came to my aid that night of my escape – Mrs Tibbs. I found myself retracing my steps in that direction when Sharpe had been taken away. Don't think I'd have dared otherwise. I just needed to feel free on those streets. Anyhow, she offered to put me up for a while, which was most kind of her, so it was. I stayed there for a time until I felt able to cope again, and then I returned to the workhouse. When I felt up to it, Matron took me to see Mr Darling to ask if it was too late to take the maid's job.'

'Oh? And?' Enid searched Connie's face for answers.

Nodding, she smiled through her tears. 'He said, "Yes, of course," as he's a very kind man. He had a word with Mr Clarkson and arrangements were made to send me here with you. Oh, Enid, I'm so excited to be able to spend time with you and when we return, we'll be sharing a room together!'

'But does Matilda, Mr Clarkson's sister, know you're coming today?'

Connie nodded eagerly. 'Yes. 'Twas all arranged by letter.'

'Well, the crafty so-and-so!' Enid laughed. 'She never told me!'

'Mr Darling and Mr Clarkson decided it would be a good idea to surprise you! They must have told her to keep it a secret.'

Enid beamed. 'It'll be just like old times...' she said, taking her friend by the arm and escorting her inside the cottage. And as Enid closed the door behind them, she realised it would be the start of a new beginning for them both.

ACKNOWLEDGEMENTS

Thank you to my wonderful editor, Emily Yau, who sees the story hidden amongst the trees and manages to hack away at all that dead wood! Thanks also to the amazing team at Boldwood for your help with this book – you're all amazing!

ABOUT THE AUTHOR

Lynette Rees is the bestselling author of several historical fiction titles and lives in Wales.

Sign up to Lynette Rees' mailing list here for news, competitions and updates on future books.

Visit Lynette's website: www.lynetterees.wordpress.com

Follow Lynette on social media:

- facebook.com/authorlynetterees
- x.com/LynetteRees0
- instagram.com/booksbylynetterees7
- bookbub.com/authors/lynette-rees

ALSO BY LYNETTE REES

The Winter Waif

The Workhouse Girl

Sixpence Stories

Introducing Sixpence Stories!

Discover page-turning historical novels from your favourite authors, meet new friends and be transported back in time.

Join our book club Facebook group

https://bit.ly/SixpenceGroup

Sign up to our newsletter

https://bit.ly/SixpenceNews

Boldwood

Boldwood Books is an award-winning fiction publishing company seeking out the best stories from around the world.

Find out more at www.boldwoodbooks.com

Join our reader community for brilliant books, competitions and offers!

Follow us
@BoldwoodBooks
@TheBoldBookClub

Sign up to our weekly deals newsletter

https://bit.ly/BoldwoodBNewsletter

Milton Keynes UK
Ingram Content Group UK Ltd.
UKHW042126200524
442865UK00002B/5